ASCEND

THE CURE CHRONICLES, BOOK THREE

K. A. RILEY

SUMMARY

Brought down by the trauma of recent events, Ashen Spencer resolves to step up the fight against her enemies in the Directorate. With the help of an unlikely friend, she infiltrates the Palace Grounds to steal a priceless object...only to find something even more valuable.

With new strength and faced with more challenges than ever before, Ash and her companions begin to accept the grim inevitability of the coming war. Their allies in the Consortium must gather to take on the Directorate the only way they can: by revealing the bitter truth about the government that has lied to so many.

But with an enemy who will stop at nothing, is victory even possible?

For my Father, his new knee, and his not quite as new (but very excellent) mind.

PREFACE

The last time I saw the boy I love, he was lying lifeless on the dirt floor of the hellscape known as the Arenum.

I felt for his pulse, his breath, for any remote sign of life.

But there was nothing, except for a quick, almost imperceptible curling of his fingers.

A moment later, he was gone.

A million times since then, I've told myself his death was a trick, an illusion. Finn is—*was*—strong, after all, and he wore a silver uniform like the one I'm wearing now. A uniform that enhanced his strength tenfold.

Maybe, just maybe…he survived.

But the truth is probably far more grim.

Maybe I'm in denial.

Maybe it's torture to think I'm the one who ended his life, who stole him from this world with a blast of violent energy that came from a hidden place deep inside me.

Maybe I can't live with myself, knowing it's my fault.

But until I see a body, until someone presents me undeniable proof that Finn really is gone, I refuse to believe it.

Because if it's true, the last fragile pieces of my soul will shatter, and there will be nothing left of me but dust.

DEAD OR ALIVE

My beautiful Ash,

If you're reading this, it means you won our battle. And that's a good thing.

Never think otherwise.

It means that inside you is a weapon that may help our side win the coming war.

There are more weapons out there, and many of them are secret.

Some, like yours, are special. You are the only one who can wield it. The only one who can control it. It's my gift to you, though by the time you read this, it may feel like a curse.

Please forgive me for not telling you about it before our fight. I hope you can see now that I had no choice.

I'll be with you always, if only to watch over you from the shadows.

I love you,

~F

It was several hours before I came across the note that Finn, in his own inimitable way, had left for me. He'd concealed it in a pocket in my silver uniform—a pocket I only discovered in a moment of quiet desperation, my eyes burning with never-ending tears as I searched for a clue—*any* clue—as to how the most cataclysmic event of my life had managed to take me completely by surprise.

I've read the note dozens of times. Looking, I suppose, for some hint, a coded message telling me he's still alive and out there somewhere. Waiting for me to find him.

I'll be with you always...

That's what people say before they die, isn't it? A sweet assurance that's actually a lie.

The dead don't linger. The dead vanish, and we never see them again. Their faces slowly fade from our memories until we can no longer quite recall what they looked like in life. We're left with nothing but disintegrating strands of the past as we clean up the pieces of our sorrow, pretending we're strong when the sad truth is that we're anything but.

Every loss breaks us just a little more.

My father.

My mother.

And now...

No.

I refuse to think it.

The only reason I'm even able to breathe is my brother, Kel. The light of my life, sent to live in the darkness of the Pit with those known as the Consortium—old allies of my father's. Rebels willing to give their lives to fight the Directorate and all it stands for.

If not for Kel, for the fleeting thoughts of his smile, his voice, his joyful laugh...I don't know how I'd so much as raise myself to my feet. As strong as Finn's silver uniform makes me, right now I'm barely able to summon the strength to do anything more than weep.

Folding the note and tucking it back into my hidden pocket, I let out a breath that sounds more like a quiet sob and curse myself for my weakness.

People die every day. The rational part of my mind knows it.

Still, I tell myself, Finn can't be dead. He just...can't. I'd *feel* it. I'd know it in my soul. It would seem like a vital organ had been unceremoniously torn out. I'd feel his absence as certainly as if someone had removed my heart.

Instead, all I have is this hideous, tremulous uncertainty.

"Ash? Are you okay?"

I'd nearly forgotten I'm not alone.

Rys is standing in the doorway as I sit, my body rigid as steel, on the edge of a bed that isn't mine. It belongs to some former Dreg from Sector Three—a young man who died a few days ago in one of the Directorate's so-called "Trials," which are nothing more than glorified murders.

When he brought me here, Rys assured me the residence would remain mine for as long as I need it.

Ironic that my best friend who became my worst enemy weeks ago has somehow crawled back up to best friend status. He's saved me from death on multiple occasions, watched over me when I was terrified and alone.

Now, he's simply a much-needed presence, though I would never admit as much to him.

Atticus, the mechanical silver owl he created alongside an entire army of exquisitely realistic bird-shaped drones, is perched on my nightstand, watching me intently. Normally, having a set of cameras perpetually aimed at my face would seem invasive. But I don't mind the owl's constant presence. Atticus is the reassurance I desperately need that I still have allies in this screwed-up world.

"Am I okay?" I repeat, lifting my chin to look at Rys. "No. I'm pretty damned far from okay."

He nods, his jaw set in a tight clench. He knows he can't reassure me. Can't tell me Finn is alive, because he doesn't know that any more than I do. Like me, he can only guess, only hope.

But hope isn't enough. Not anymore.

Rys and I haven't talked about the incident in the Arenum since I made my way, shaken and afraid, into this residence. Every second since has been a frenzy of thoughts and emotions, and it's only now that I'm able to sit and breathe, though each inhalation is tight, each exhalation a futile attempt to calm my raging heart.

"That blast, Rys," I say, my voice wavering. "The thing that came from my hands—that blue flash of light—I didn't know I could do something like that—I didn't know *anyone* could."

"Neither did I," he confesses.

I pull my eyes to his. There's sympathy there. Too much of it.

The sort of sympathy one has for someone who's lost everything.

"Could he possibly have survived it?" I barely manage.

Rys chooses his words carefully. "I can't say. But I do know Finn a little. I know how his mind works. He understands the human brain and our capacity to focus energy the same way I understand tech and electronics. He knows how to tap into our most basic strengths and enhance them far beyond what most people ever imagine. And he knows the consequences."

"What are you saying?" I ask, heartened by the fact that at

4

least Rys is talking about him in present tense.

"I'm saying the power you used in the Arenum, the power he gave you—it was...intense. But Finn knew what was coming at him. So he probably prepared for it in advance. He was wearing the silver uniform, which may have helped, at least a little."

"*May* have." I try and fail to force optimism into my voice.

Rys pulls his eyes to the floor, like it pains him to be brutally honest. "Or not."

"Or not," my lips repeat without a sound coming out.

"He gave you a weapon. He wanted you to have it, for better or worse. He...*enhanced* you. Also for better or worse."

He's right. There's a weapon inside me. A strange, twisted gift from the boy I love. But I would so much rather have Finn than any power in the universe.

"He robbed me," I snarl with an angry shake of my head. "He stole himself from me. Weapons are no good to me if I have no strength to use them, no reason, no motivation."

"You will find strength, Ash. You have to, for all the people who are suffering and dying at the hands of the Directorate. I know it's hard right now..."

"No," I snap. "You don't know. You have no idea how hard it is. How exhausted I am, after...everything."

All I want is to escape the fate that's been pursuing me for far too long. I'm more than tired. I'm utterly drained. The rebel who's been gaining strength inside me is weary, and wants only to lay her head on a pillow and mourn the future she's lost, a life she'll never know.

"I want answers," I finally say. "I need them. I need to know what happened to Finn after..." I swallow, bracing myself for the next few words. "After I...did that to him. If he's really dead, I need to find closure or I'll lose my damn mind."

Rys steps over and sits down on the bed next to me and for once, I don't distance myself from him. I don't recoil.

He's earned my trust, if not my affection. He's the closest thing I have in the Arc to family. And while I may never forgive him for the role he played in my mother's death, I will admit, at least to myself, that I need him.

He lets out a sigh, his eyes directed at the floor. "I will say this: I can't imagine Finn meant for you to kill him. I think he wanted you to stun him, to hurt him badly enough to shock the crowd into confusion. He was counting on the mayhem to garner sympathy for you both—or to give you a chance at escape."

"A chance at escape," I reply in a whisper, a thought racing through my mind. "And in the end, I only escaped because of you. Because of…"

I close my eyes and see them: a flock of silver birds of every size and shape, tearing the Directorate's drones apart like they were made of tissue paper. I can hear the screams of the crowd as they cowered in fear. The pounding of my heart as my eyes locked on Finn's lifeless form…

"Did Finn know?" I open my eyes and turn to Rys. "Did he know about your plan to unleash the birds?"

He frowns and shakes his head. "He had some idea, but we didn't have a plan. I couldn't talk to him in the days before the bout; the Duchess had him under lock and key. But I suspect he knew I'd do what I could to help. I only wish I could have helped sooner. Before—"

He stops himself, not daring to say the words "You killed him," because if he did, I would certainly break.

"Does the Directorate know you're the one behind the attack on their drones?" My heart starts racing, panic setting in. "They must know. How could you hide a thing like that? You must be in danger. They'll…"

"Ash," Rys says, reaching a hand out. But he seems to think better of it and pulls it back. "No one knows. I mask everything I do behind layers of misdirects, encryption, you name it. Everything I build is concealed from their eyes and their systems. There's no known record of any of it."

"How is that even possible? How can you be so sure?"

"I told you a long time ago, I'm smarter than those bastards." He leans in close and speaks under his breath, as if someone is listening—though I know perfectly well he's found a way to block them from hearing or seeing us. "I know ways of moving through the Arc that no one else does. I know about Conveyors small enough that no person can fit inside them, passageways large enough for small silver spheres but little else. I know every hidden corner, every drone, every new project the Directorate develops. I see everything in this place, because those fools allow me to. And I have bad news."

"Oh, God. What?"

What could possibly be worse than what's already happened?

"My birds are far from the most advanced tech being developed in this place. You should see some of what they've come up with. It would make your skin crawl."

"Do I even want to ask?"

He winces. "Let's just say I'm hoping you never run into any of the Directorate's 'creations' in a dark alley. You or any other rebels."

"That bad, huh?"

"Worse. Which is why I like to counter their designs with my own."

I almost want to smile. Despite the grimness of what he's telling me, he's so self-assured, so confident. So…Rys.

"Something's confusing me, though," I tell him. "If you see everything in this place...then why haven't you seen Finn? Why don't you know what happened to him after...I mean, if there's a body..."

He bows his head once again and shakes it. But when he pulls his chin up, he's smiling.

"What?" I ask, irritated that he's amused by my sorrow.

"I may be smarter than the Directorate," he tells me. "But there's one person who's more intelligent than I'll ever be."

I'm almost shocked that Rys would admit such a thing.

"You can't possibly be admitting Finn is smarter than you."

"I'm afraid I am," he nods. "He orchestrated something miraculous in the Arenum. He wrote and, with your help, acted out a Romeo and Juliet story for modern times. *The Aristocrat and the Brokenhearted Dreg.*"

"Romeo and Juliet both die in the end," I say. "So you're not exactly giving me hope here."

"Those two were young and stupid," Rys chuckles. "You two may be young, but you're no idiots. Besides, Finn loves you, and he's strong. He's not the kind of guy who just gives up the best thing in his life. He's also not the kind of guy who lets the bad people win."

His use of present tense fills me with a brief, fleeting hope.

Finn has to be alive.

Or else...

No. I can't think it. I can't allow that sort of grim darkness to enter my soul or there will be no turning back.

As we sit in silence, Rys's wrist implant lights up. He swipes a finger along his skin and a message I can't read scrolls rapidly in the air above his forearm.

He pulls his sleeve down, lets out a hard sigh, and turns to me.

"What is it?" I barely dare breathe.

"The Duchess has announced a memorial service for Finn. Tomorrow morning, in the Royal Gardens on Level Two-Ninety. They're shutting down access to anyone who's not an Aristocrat."

"What?" My heart thuds cruelly, my voice cracking as I leap to my feet, pacing frantically through the small room, my hands shaking. "No. That means there's a body. That means..."

He shakes his head. "No casket. No body. It's not a funeral. They're calling it a 'Celebration of a Young Life Cut Short By The Forces of Evil.' It will probably have little or nothing to do with Finn. It's all propaganda to rally the so-called troops against the Arc's lower forms of life."

"Against Dregs, you mean." I stop moving, relieved, but only a little. "People like us. The Enemies of the Powerful."

"Yes. And I think you and I should attend the service."

"Are you nuts? I'd be arrested the second I set foot in that place. They're just waiting for an opportunity to take me down. There will be cameras, drones, everything, just waiting to film my death. And this time, there's no way they'll put me in an arena to fight. They will want a swift end for the traitor from Sector Eight."

Grinning, Rys says, "The memorial is an Aristocrat affair, remember. Everyone will be hidden behind the usual masks, except for the Duchess and the Duke. I'll set you up with a fake identity. Trust me, no one will be able to tell who you are. And who knows? Maybe seeing that Finn isn't there—that they don't know where he is—will put your mind at ease."

"Nothing will put my mind at ease until I have him next to me," I snap. "Preferably walking out of this godforsaken place as it burns to the ground."

2

MEMORIAL

Rʏѕ ʟᴇᴀᴠᴇѕ me alone in the residence only after assuring me he'll return before tomorrow's memorial service.

But the thought of spending the next several hours on my own—in this stagnant, haunted apartment that belonged to a now-dead boy—is too much. I'm certain I'll collapse into a black hole of doubt, guilt, and horror if I spend another minute here wondering whether I'm the murderer everyone thinks I am.

Fortunately, Rys has provided me with everything I could need to work my way around the Arc anonymously: clothing, tech, even a series of different-colored wigs. I could step out in the uniform Finn gave me—the silver cloaking outfit I wore during our so-called battle. But I can't bear to be invisible just now.

I don't want to fade into the shadows just yet.

I choose a disguise in the form of jeans, a pair of black-rimmed glasses, an impressively detailed blond wig, and an enhanced wrist Inhibitor that jumbles the Arc's systems into thinking I'm a lowly resident of Level Eleven. When I'm confident I've covered every base, I make my way out of the residence to the nearest Conveyor.

My destination is the public marketplace on Level Twenty-Three, where I wander aimlessly, eyeing over-ripe fruit and vegetables, doubtless rejected by those on the Aristocratic levels before moving to one of the lower markets. The place is teeming with Wealthies who aren't quite rich enough to occupy the Aristocrats' floors, but who *are* rich enough to have left their homes in the city behind forever to buy their coveted residences in the Arc.

If only you all knew you'd spent your life's savings on lavish prison cells, I think as I watch them. *Do you have any idea what really goes on in this place? Do you care that the Directorate regularly murders people like me?*

I wander the aisles, acutely aware that my appetite has abandoned me and the fruit and vegetables that used to beckon me with their bright colors now look dull and unappealing.

When I pick up a bruised apple from the display in front of me, a series of holographic screens flare to life in the air. Startled into thinking I've somehow summoned them, I drop the apple which rolls wearily along the floor away from me.

My chest tightens, my breath trapped inside.

Other shoppers stop and stare, too, though none of them looks as horrified as I feel when I see what's displayed in stark detail above us.

It's the face of a ghost.

Projections of Finn's handsome features loom larger than life above the other shoppers. No—not just his features. His head and shoulders, rendered in perfect three dimensions, rotating slowly so that everyone gets a look at just how beautiful he is.

Or...*was.*

As a sinking feeling takes over my gut, a horrible, familiar voice barrels its way through the speakers, forcing my mind into grim shadow .

"Finn Davenport. A young life cut short far too soon by a Consortium-loving Dreg."

The voice belongs to Finn's mother. The woman known as the Duchess—an ostentatious, ridiculous title she gave herself as a gift.

To my horror, she keeps talking.

"A murderer whose name is Ashen Spencer."

Invisible claws dig into my heart with each syllable. Her voice is a weapon, her words a dagger slicing at my flesh and mind simultaneously.

"Do not trust Dregs. Do not let them into your homes. If you see any suspicious activity—anyone who doesn't belong on your level...report them immediately. Anyone providing information leading to Ashen Spencer's arrest or death will be rewarded handsomely."

As Finn's perfect features still hover over us, her use of "handsomely" seems deliberate. She knew how beautiful her son was, too.

Yet she sent him into the Arenum to die.

"If you see Ashen Spencer, inform the Directorate at once."

I cower in my spot as a three-dimensional projection of

my own face appears, rotating slowly for every person in the Arc to study in graphic detail.

"She is a rebel. A traitor. The worst of humanity. But some misguided individuals among you regard her as a role-model, which is exactly why she must be stopped at all costs."

The shoppers in the marketplace study the image, but when the occasional set of eyes finds my own, not one person seems to recognize me. Their curiosity is casual at best, and I remind myself that they, like most people in the world, simply want to live their lives. They have no interest in performing some act of twisted vigilante justice.

And most of them probably don't care much about the Duchess's loss.

Even the Wealthies know what a harpy she is.

When I've convinced myself I'm not about to be arrested, I head back to my temporary residence to conceal myself from further potential discovery. I spend the next several hours pacing, chewing my nails...and trying to figure out how I can ever live with myself after what I've done.

⊗

Late the next morning, after a night of restless sleep and more than a few tears, I open the bedroom door to find Rys standing in the hallway with today's outfit in hand: a long black gown with a matching mask, an Inhibitor designed to look like expensive jewelry, and a silver necklace made of flat, round discs attached together by a thin silken strand.

"The mask and Inhibitor will scramble any attempts to uncover your actual identity," Rys says. "Your name, by the way, is Sharina Lawson—she's an Aristocrat who lives on Two-Sixty-Eight."

"Is she real?"

Rys nods. "Very."

"What happens if she shows up at the service?"

"She won't."

His tone is mischievous, his smile confusing.

"How can you be so sure?"

"Because she's a hypochondriac who just received notice that there's been an outbreak of smallpox on Level Two-Eighty, and that the risk of exposure is great."

"Wasn't smallpox eradicated eons ago?"

Rys shrugs. "As far as our friend is concerned, it's made an unfortunate resurgence."

"You're an evil genius."

"I am. Now come on—it's time to get ready."

When I've ducked into the bedroom to change into my inappropriately lavish black gown, a silk shawl draped over my shoulders, I head back out to find Rys wearing a formal black suit.

"You look way too good," he says. "It's almost too bad you'll be covering up your face with the mask."

"Honestly, I'd rather just show up invisible," I tell him self-consciously. I'm not comfortable being admired, especially not today. "I could wear the cloaking uniform instead of this. I could just stay in the background…"

"This is better," Rys says with a wink, and I almost envy his calm, casual nonchalance in the face of what we're about to do.

His well-tailored black suit is paired with a silver-gray tie and shiny shoes. He pulls his mask to his face then tells me to do the same. As he speaks, his voice sounds odd—lower and richer than usual.

"Is that the mask?" I ask. "Doing that to your voice?"

"You're not the only one with an assumed identity. I'm going as Sharina's brother, Pete. Your mask will do the same; it's all part of the disguise."

When I pull the mask on and say "Test," I find that my voice has altered to something higher-pitched than I'm used to.

"Weird," I say. "I sound so...*cute.*"

"Like a little chipmunk. Come on, let's head to this fake funeral, shall we?"

"As long as you keep telling me it's really fake."

"My gut tells me it is. That's not particularly reassuring, I realize, but...

Shaking my head, I squeeze his arm to make him stop talking. "I'll take it."

Sticking close together, we arrive at the Gardens a few minutes later. A series of slow-moving Aristocrats have already begun to process in a long line toward the tall, groomed hedge maze where Rys and I met to talk on one of my early days in the Arc. When we arrive at its center, we find fifty or so chairs set up in a broad circle.

"I guess they've limited the crowd," Rys whispers, leaning in close. "Which only confirms that this is all about the Duchess's motives, and not about Finn."

I'm relieved to hear it, but slightly terrified to think what Mrs. Davenport could have in mind for the next few minutes. My nervous eyes move to the single microphone positioned on a stand at the circle's center.

Not daring to speak further, we take our seats several rows

back, attempting to look inconspicuous among the masses of elegantly dressed Wealthies. Each is in black, their gowns and suits lavish and expensive. It's as if they're taking this opportunity to show off their affluence, even from behind their masks.

Around us, the hiss of whispers meets our ears.

"He was so young..."

"She was heartless..."

"They say she did it with her bare hands..."

"Dregs are all the same, aren't they?"

"I can't imagine the Duchess won't seek the most severe punishment when they catch her, and well she should..."

The words aren't unexpected, but they still sting. I hate these people with every cell in my body, but somehow it pains me to think they actually believe me capable of murdering Finn in cold blood.

I may represent everything they despise, but I'm no murderer.

At least, not yet.

When a woman behind us murmurs, "They say there's no body," I stiffen and reach for Rys's arm.

The man next to her asks, "What do you mean, no body?"

"No corpse, Henry," she says, loudly this time. "Nothing to bury or burn. Isn't that odd?"

"I suppose," he replies. "Maybe it was the girl's doing, hiding the evidence. That boy is definitely dead."

"Why do you say that?"

The man named Henry lowers his voice, but I can still make out his words. "Because that blast—the one that came from the girl—I've seen that sort of thing before, only it was shot from a weapon. *No one* survives it. I tell you, Finn Davenport is dead."

I shoot a glance at Rys, stifling the cry of anguish that wants to emerge from my throat.

So, it's true.

I'm a monster.

Rys leans in close and whispers, "Don't listen to that guy. Finn's no idiot. He wouldn't hand you a power that would automatically turn you into a mass murderer."

"I'm not so sure anymore," I whisper. "If only I could ask him. If..."

Desperate, I look around, scanning the crowd. If he is alive, Finn might have found his way here just as we did.

And if he had, he'd look for me. He'd let me know he's okay.

But the sea of black masks that stares back is confounding. Even beyond their rigid outlines, I fail to spot anyone who looks like he could possibly be Finn. No hint of his hair, his familiar, beautiful frame. No evidence of those glorious eyes, staring out from behind the thick gloss of a mask.

I lean toward Rys to ask a question, but think better of it. Instead, I clasp my hands in my lap, my fingers tightening around one another until each of them is strangled by a tension that makes me want to explode.

After a few more torturous minutes, the Duchess appears from an opening in the hedge and glides to the circle's center, wearing a gown made of a flowing fabric that moves like oil. I'm almost surprised when she doesn't leave a trail of glistening black in her wake.

She's not wearing a mask. *No, of course she isn't. She feels no need to hide who she is, what she is.*

To the Aristocracy, she's an object of beauty, of pity and awe, all at once.

A grieving mother. A powerful figure.

A symbol of the Directorate's hatred for people like me.

She's here looking for sympathy, because sympathy is a weapon she can use against these fools.

"Ladies, Gentlemen, Honored Guests," she says slowly when she's reached the microphone, "thank you all so much for coming."

As she speaks, a large projection of her face flares to life above her. Her eyes are red, as though she's been crying. Though part of me refuses to believe the woman possesses tear ducts, let alone the capacity to feel any emotion other than disdain and hatred.

Looking around, I spot the Duke seated behind the Duchess. His face, too, is mask-less, his cheeks blotchy from apparent tears of his own. Oddly, though, there's no sign of their youngest son, Merit. No ten-year-old boy sitting by his father's side, mourning his older brother.

Why not? Why wouldn't he come to a service for Finn?

"As you all know by now," the Duchess purrs once she's got the crowd's full attention, "we lost my son, Finn, two evenings ago, when he was viciously murdered by a Dreg. The brutal killing was a crime not only against my son, but against us all —the Directorate and the Aristocracy. It was a crime of passion, of rebellion."

No words of remembrance. No tribute to Finn.

Rys was right.

This isn't a memorial service. It's a condemnation of people like us.

If I weren't so possessed by guilt right now, I'd scream.

But before I have the chance, a man in the crowd rises to his feet. Like the rest of us, he's dressed entirely in black. His suit is tailored and expensive-looking, his hair thick and gray, but I can't discern anything more about his appearance.

"Why did you pit your son against a Dreg in the first place?" the man calls out, interrupting the service before it's even begun. "What kind of mother does that to her child? It's one thing to use Champions to fight for our cause, but this is getting out of hand. First, the King sends his only son to fight that girl—now this? Why have you not learned she's stronger than she looks? Ashen Spencer is a menace, and should be dealt with accordingly."

The crowd lets out a series of disjointed gasps, combined with scattered applause. Challenging the Duchess—one of the Directorate's most powerful figures—at her own son's funeral seems foolish, though admittedly courageous.

The Duchess raises a hand to calm the growing chorus of murmurs.

"It's all right," she says, her voice saccharine. "It's a perfectly valid question."

She locks her eyes on the man and says, "My son committed a serious crime. He aided and abetted Ashen Spencer, a known menace, as you called her yourself. And as we all know, the Directorate is fair. It is just. It was necessary to punish Finn, to see him suffer consequences for his...*transgression*. Of course, under normal circumstances, my son would have beaten her handily. But in my defense, I did not expect the Dreg to *cheat* in battle."

Enraged, I tighten in my seat, my hands clenching into stone-hard fists at my sides. Rys reaches out and touches my arm as if to tell me to settle down before I get us both killed.

The man standing in the crowd, seemingly satisfied by the disgusting answer, takes a seat and the Duchess continues. "I called you all here today, not for a traditional memorial service, but to let you—the most valued members of the Aristocracy and the Directorate—know that in the name of my son Finn, I am starting a new military force in the Arc. A militia, if you will, made up of powerful individuals. Their sole job will be to seek out rebels like Ashen Spencer, those who wish to bring down the Directorate, and those who are disloyal to our government."

The crowd erupts into applause, and my stomach curdles. What was meant to be a service in memory of an incredible person has turned into some authoritarian nightmare.

The Duchess is creating a force specifically to hunt me and others like me. From the sounds of it, they'll even hunt down Wealthies who don't approve of the Directorate's methods.

"This isn't going to end well," Rys mutters, leaning toward me as those around us shriek with approving cheers.

"No kidding," I reply, but along with the others, we leap to our feet, applauding raucously.

"We all know," the Duchess continues, "that there have been rumblings in the Arc about rebellion, about quiet pockets of resistance forming on various levels. But I want you to know, in memory of my dear son, that the militia's soldiers are remarkable, and you have nothing to fear. Our warriors will take every rebel down. We will tear down the Arc's walls to get to them, if necessary."

The Duchess holds up a hand in an elegant gesture, and the screen showing her face alters to reveal a symbol—the Directorate's gold rose, rotating in the air. But as we watch, it's joined by a long, sharp dagger. Twisting and contorting itself, the rose's stem wraps itself around the dagger's blade, its thorns shooting out in threat.

"This is the symbol of the Cyphers," the Duchess says. "Our new force. Those who wear it on their chests will keep the Arc safe from the traitor Dregs and anyone foolish enough to join them."

I stare at the symbol—an elegant promise of violence—and wince.

"Together, we will make the Arc a safe and secure paradise for those who belong, and take down all those who don't."

Those who don't belong, I mutter under my breath, *were dragged into this place by people like you. You don't get to invite us in, only to steal away our lives when we choose not to worship you like gods.*

The Duchess gestures with a flick of her fingers and almost immediately two Chaperons—a man and a woman—step toward her from the opening in the hedge. Two men follow close behind, both wearing uniforms decorated with the Cyphers' symbol. One is short and slight, the other tall and muscular.

The Duchess steps over to the Cypher closest to her, the shorter one, whose hair is dark red. Reaching out and touching his arm gently, she says, "Show the people what you're capable of, Vlad."

I half expect the man to pull a concealed weapon from his clothing and shoot someone. But instead, he takes one step toward the female Chaperon, fixing her in his gaze.

The woman stares back. It comes as no surprise that her eyes are expressionless, as are those of all Chaperons. Drugged by the Directorate, they lack emotion or agency. Chaperons are little more than walking corpses serving at their masters' pleasure.

Yet beyond the veil of numbness, I still sense fear in the woman. I can all but smell it on the air.

"Kill her," the Duchess says with a triumphant lifting of her chin.

The Cypher steps closer to the woman, leans forward, and whispers something in her ear.

The drugs in her system prevent her from reacting. She may well feel terror, but her body refuses to flee or to fight. She's trapped inside her own skin, robbed of her humanity, unable to act on instinct.

Whispers churn up around us, the excited chirping of a crowd accustomed to reveling in communal bloodlust. They, too, know what's about to happen. They're *craving* the murder the man is about to commit.

But to everyone's surprise, including my own, the Chaperon reaches out, pulls a knife from a sheath at the Cypher's side, and slits her own throat.

3

SHOCK

"What the…?"

I'm not sure if I whisper the words or scream them. The world is spinning, the crowd around me a cacophony of combined horror and wonder.

We've just witnessed an apparent suicide. And not just *any* suicide.

One by a Chaperon. The least volatile, least emotional beings in the Arc.

The Cypher—or Monster, or whatever we're supposed to call him—turns to face us. Against my will I stare into his eyes, which are a light, cloudy, unnatural shade of gray. Slowly, they morph to brown, as if an impossible switch has been flipped somewhere deep inside the man.

"What *is* he?" I ask Rys under my breath.

He leans in close and whispers, "I've heard rumors about the development of soldiers with specific, refined abilities— something to do with breaking genetic code, which is why they call them Cyphers. It's almost like…"

"Like what?"

"Like what you did in the Arenum. An amplification of extremely concentrated power. The weapon you hurled at Finn...."

Horrified, I turn toward the Cypher and hiss, "You're telling me I'm one of *those* things?"

He shakes his head. "No. These two men have been stripped bare of emotion. They're mindless servants— Compliants, like the Chaperons. You're anything but."

As we fall into silence, the rest of the gathered crowd has questions of their own.

"Did he really just make that woman kill herself?" someone behind us wails.

"Looks that way," his companion replies matter-of-factly.

"He did it with his mind," someone else says. "Didn't he?"

"Doesn't matter. She's a Compliant. It's easy to get them to obey commands."

The Duchess seems to overhear this, because she turns to the man who spoke.

"Would you care to put the Cypher to the test?" she asks.

Nodding, the man rises to his feet and steps forward, crossing his arms haughtily over his chest. "No one is going to convince me to hurt myself," he says. "But go ahead and try."

"Oh, I would never want you to hurt yourself, Timmin," she replies, giving away his identity as if to spite him. "But let's see if he can influence you at all."

She issues a quiet command to the smaller of the two Cyphers, who steps over to the man and whispers a few words to him.

As if in a trance, Timmin steps to the larger of the two men, pulls the knife at the Cypher's waist, and holds it to his broad chest in threat.

"Not wise," the Duchess says with a click of her tongue.

"To threaten such a large fellow. But you don't *actually* want to, do you?"

Timmin shakes his head, his hand trembling, but he seems unable to control himself or to pull back. Instead, he moves closer, pressing the tip of the blade into the Cypher's chest.

"Down," the Duchess says simply.

At first, I think she's talking to Timmin, ordering him to drop the weapon.

But a split-second later, the crowd gasps as the larger Cypher throws the Aristocrat to the ground, a hand around his throat, the dropped blade lying uselessly next to him.

"What have you done to me?" Timmin croaks as the hand slowly strangles him.

"I've simply proven a point," the Duchess says. "Never doubt me again."

She orders the Cypher to release Timmin, who pushes himself up and scurries back to his seat, gasping for breath as his wife puts an arm around him.

The Duchess nods, and the two Cyphers pick up the bloody corpse of the Chaperon and carry it away, leaving her companion and a ghastly splatter of red behind. I study the male Chaperon for a reaction, anything to prove to me he's still human.

His lower lip quivers for a moment as he stares blankly into the distance. But then it goes still, like he's forced it into submission.

"The Cyphers will serve us well," the Duchess announces as she silences the crowd with a wave of her hands. "They are strong, as you can see. But more importantly, they're loyal. So do not fear the so-called rebellion they say is building in the Arc. The rebels have nothing on us. They lack our resources, our scientists. Once we have an entire army at our disposal, there will be no risk to our safety or to that of the Directorate."

Once we have an entire army.

So you don't. Not yet.

You just gave away your greatest vulnerability, Duchess.

With a smug grin, she adds, "The ceremony is now over. I hope you can go in peace, knowing now that you have little to fear. We have already won this war, and the Arc remains as magnificent as ever."

As we rise to our feet, most of the crowd has already forgotten we were supposed to be here to mourn Finn. Instead of solemn remembrance, they're chatting excitedly amongst themselves, scheming from behind their masks, eager to get in on the Directorate's plan to take out anyone who dares to speak out against them.

The service ends not with talk of Finn's brief life, but with a mob eager to murder anyone who doesn't show them utter loyalty.

I turn to Rys, feeling more desperate than ever to end this living nightmare.

"What do we do?"

"We leave, just like everyone else. We walk out of here like nothing out of the ordinary has happened."

"I don't think I can do that."

"You don't have a choice." His voice is gruff as he takes me by the arm. "If they see you're upset, you may as well just paint a target on that mask of yours."

Setting my jaw, I nod and begin to trudge along reluctantly at his side.

"These people are unbelievable," I tell him under my breath as we make our way out of the hedge maze and toward the nearest Conveyor. "Constantly looking for new ways to kill, like it's the next fashion trend. Don't they have any normal hobbies?"

"That *is* their hobby." I can hear the sneer in his voice. "The powerful get bored easily. They're all about committing crimes without actually getting their hands dirty."

"But they have everything they could possibly want. Why—"

"No one has *everything* they want," Rys interrupts. "Not a single person in the world. Not even the King and Queen, bathing in diamonds in their Palace Grounds. These people *live* for excess. More money, more power, more property. There's no satisfying them, so they find new ways to ruin the world, and any challenge to their power is a personal affront. They justify their killings by telling themselves they're more important than anyone else on the planet—that those of us incapable of accumulating wealth aren't worthy of life. More importantly, though, anyone who threatens their way of life needs to be killed."

Biting my lip, I nod. He's right, after all. It's not just wealth that matters to the Aristocracy—it's something far more abstract. It all comes down to the notion of holding onto something that's tenuous, fragile, desirable.

But in the end, the Directorate's hold on the Arc is weak. Their power relies entirely on lies and deceit.

And if the threads of those lies were to snap...

So would everything else.

We just have to figure out how to sever the threads.

"What's our plan?" I ask, trying to distract myself from what just happened, not to mention the fact that I didn't spot Finn at the service, that I still haven't seen a single speck of evidence that he could possibly be alive.

"We head back to the residence," Rys says, looking around

to make sure no one is walking close enough to hear when he adds, "We should check in on the Consortium. With the Duchess building an army of thugs, we need to get our revolution rolling before too many more people are killed."

"Without Finn?" I shake my head. "No way. I can't...I can't..."

"Ash," Rys says between gritted teeth, "*No* isn't an option here. You heard what that bitch said. She wants every rebel dead. We don't have time to sit around hoping Finn will magically appear. I'm sorry, but it's the ugly truth."

I stop in my tracks, tensing, and turn his way. I'm angry, but I'm not sure if it's at him, myself, or the entire world.

"I need to know if he's really gone," I whisper as a couple of Aristocrats pass us by.

"I get it. I do." Rys grabs my arm and forces me to walk again. "But waiting around isn't a strategy. Neither is sitting on our hands. If Finn is alive, something tells me he'll find us when the time is right. But for now, I need you to focus on those who are still living and breathing. They don't know what's coming for them."

I go silent for a few seconds, then finally ask, "What do you want to do, then?"

"Simple. We need to get our hands on the Batts."

"The what?"

"Batts. The things the Consortium calls *Quantum Sources.* The power supply that will get the Pit functioning properly and get the trains running between the Consortium strongholds. If we can do that, maybe we can increase our numbers."

"You're right," I breathe. The seemingly impossible power sources Illian and Kurt told us about had escaped my consciousness, my grief pushing them from my mind.

The Pit, where Kel is currently residing along with a

couple of hundred other people, is engulfed in darkness, but the Quantum Sources could illuminate their world and change their lives. "But Illian told us the Batts are on Level Three-Hundred. That's the Palace Grounds, isn't it? The King's domain."

"It is."

So your plan is for us to somehow steal priceless items that are on the highest, most inaccessible level of the Arc?"

"Yep. That's exactly what my plan is."

"Well then. What are we waiting for?"

4

PLANS

"Before you tell me I've lost my whole damned mind," Rys says, "I need you to hear me out. Which means we need a little privacy."

He leads me past the crowd toward a small, white wooden gate set in a long hedgerow.

I look back to watch people stream into the Conveyor we took to this level. "Shouldn't we have gotten in, too?"

"It wouldn't be prudent. If someone sees that we're heading to the lower levels..."

"They'll know we don't belong with them," I conclude.

"Right. So we're going to take the back route. Let's call it the servants' entrance."

He leads me through the pretty garden gate, which creaks when he pushes it open. Together, we head down a dirt path toward a cozy-looking, moss-coated stone cottage with a thatched roof. For the briefest moment, I feel as if I've simultaneously stepped outside and into a peaceful English countryside. It's almost enough to make me forget the turmoil raging inside me.

Almost.

"Is this place real?" I ask as I study the small building in front of us, stepping forward to run my hand along the stone. "The moss...it wouldn't normally grow indoors. It would need moisture. Regular rain."

"The moss is real," Rys tells me. "But that doesn't mean the house isn't a *little* deceptive." As I watch him use a small silver Disruptor to open the door, I begin to understand.

The building's interior has exactly nothing in common with its antique exterior. The space inside is ultra-modern and white: a large, bright room filled with desks covered in surveillance equipment. Disabled drones, keyboards, and wiring are scattered over most of the surfaces. Screens float in mid-air, showing views from the Royal Gardens of stragglers from the so-called memorial service wandering slowly around the property, sniffing this or that flower, or pointing out aspects of the scenery.

"This cottage is a surveillance hub?" I ask.

"Like so many spaces in the Arc," Rys replies bitterly. "The Directorate has invested billions in this tech. Ironically, they're horrible at using it, which is pretty evident given the Duchess has decided to create a whole army of enhanced humans to sniff out rebels like dogs."

"How can they be bad at using their own tech?"

Rys shrugs. "They never thought they'd have to. The arrogant bastards never expected a rebellion, so they have no idea how to deal with it now that it's at their door."

"I'd say they're dealing with it pretty effectively, if those Cyphers can take us down with nothing more than a whisper."

"There are more of us than of them," Rys replies. "It will take the Directorate some serious time to raise an entire army of those braindead psychos. In the meantime, we have more important matters to attend to—namely the Batts. Without them, we have no hope of amassing what we'll need to take this place down."

He guides me through to the small cottage's back end, where a narrow staircase leads to a small loft. On its wall, in contrast to our pristine white surroundings, is a large oil painting of a lush garden.

"Monet," I say as I look at the work. "I think. There was a garden in France he liked…"

"Giverny," Rys says with a nod. "Priceless."

I gasp as he shoves his palm into the painting's center, pressing so hard that the middle of the canvas collapses in on itself.

"What the hell?"

The question is almost immediately answered when a set of Conveyor doors slides open next to the painting. "I nearly had a heart attack just now, for the record. I know that's not an original Monet, but still…"

"You've got to admit that some things about this place are pretty cool," Rys laughs as I scowl behind my mask. "The illusions, the secret passageways. There's a lot more to the Arc than meets the eye."

"Sure, it's a super-fun place if you're into deceit and psychopaths. I hate everything about this hell-hole. The constant lies, the people. Nothing is real here except for the pain."

Thoughts of Finn are bubbling up inside my mind again. Questions without answers. Sorrow without comfort. Nothing matters to me as much as finding out what happened to him after our fight in the Arenum.

Rys pulls his mask off and runs a hand through his hair. I follow suit, relieved to be able to breathe properly once again.

I inhale, my mind clearing and a new determination taking hold.

Don't mourn Finn. Not until you know for sure what's happened to him. For now, your mission is to help the Consortium to take the Directorate down. It's what he wanted. It's what he may have died for.

"Not all the people in the Arc are unholy terrors," Rys reminds me.

"No," I reply, recalling what he said after Finn's and my battle in the Arenum. *The Arc is a place of illusions and deceit... but not every deception is the work of the Directorate.* "I suppose that's true. But what if Finn is..."

Rys levels me with a stern look. "The road to Hell is paved with hypotheticals, Ashen Spencer," he says. "I need you to believe he's out there. Finn is too smart to get killed by a weapon he created for you."

"My father was killed by his own weapon," I remind him. "And he was the smartest man I've ever known."

Rys lets out a deep sigh. "You're making it very hard to argue with you, and I'm trying to be a friend here."

"But..." I'm about to ask *what if* again, but I force myself to stop. I know perfectly well I'm just preparing myself for a brutal fall. Trying to convince myself I can survive, if Finn really is gone.

I already *know* I can survive, at least on a fundamental level. But who the hell wants to go through life with a hole in their heart the size of a continent?

"If Finn *is* alive," I say slowly, "Don't you think he would have shown up at the service today?"

"I don't know."

"Well, I do. He would have found a way. I know him. But

he wasn't there. I looked at every mask, every head of hair, every set of shoulders."

"Well," Rys says with a shrug that's far more casual than I would like. "Maybe you're right. Maybe he's gone, after all. I can't say. All I know for sure is that Finn wanted us to fight the Directorate and to win. He didn't want us to give up in a sea of self-pitying what-ifs. He didn't want whatever this is... this questioning, this wallowing in misery. He wanted a better world, plain and simple."

"You've started talking about him in past tense," I scold, my heart sinking. "You haven't done that before."

Rys clams up, locking his jaw shut like he's realized he just tacitly confessed something horrible. He nods once, then goes silent.

I can't think of Finn as a *was*, as something that existed only in the past. In my mind he's still my future, as impossible as it seems right now. But Rys is right—whether he's dead or alive, his voice still lingers in my head. Urging me to find strength, to fight for a cause greater than any of us.

"How are we going to get our hands on these Batts of yours?" I ask. "Since we're supposed to be looking to the future, tell me how you plan to get them."

"You'll see soon enough," Rys tells me. "But for now, get ready—we're about to get off this Conveyor. I may have the cameras disabled, but there are still people roaming these halls, and they have eyes."

Just before we step through the sliding doors in full disguise, Rys fidgets with the Inhibitor in his hand, scrambling the cameras in the corridor just long enough for us to get to the door of my temporary residence.

When we've entered the apartment and shut the door

behind us, I breathe a heavy sigh and head into the small bedroom to change into the silver uniform Finn gave me.

As I slip it on, a shuddering array of hideous recollections infects my mind. All of a sudden I don't want it touching my skin—I want to destroy it, to tear it apart piece by piece for what it represents. But I remind myself that this uniform saved me once by concealing me from searching eyes, and I may well need it to do so again.

When I'm dressed, I head back out to the living space where Rys is waiting for me. "Are you ready to head to the King's domain?"

"What—right now? You can't be serious."

I'm exhausted. Spent. I want nothing more than to lie down, weep into my pillow, then let sleep overtake me.

Rys nods. "What better time than now? The Directorate is probably getting ready to command their Cyphers to start killing innocent people. We need to put a stop to the madness as soon as possible."

"So you and I are going—alone—to the King's property, to steal something incredibly valuable that's probably guarded by a hundred members of the Directorate Guard. Just the two of us."

"It's not as nuts as it sounds. I know those grounds pretty well—and how to gain access. What's going to prove difficult is lifting the Batts. Those things weigh a ton."

"We used to fetch giant jugs of water on our own with a rickety old wagon. I'm sure we can move some freaking batteries." As I say the words, a smirk plays its way across my lips with the memory of simpler times, when our greatest worry was making sure we had enough to drink and eat. Those days were a struggle from day to day, but at least there was the occasional flicker of happiness.

Or maybe it was just that in those days, I hadn't yet fallen in love, only to have my heart wrenched from my chest.

"You're right," Rys says with a smile. "We're stronger—and smarter—now. So, let's get those Quantum Sources and get the hell out of this awful place. We have a revolution to lead."

Newly energized, I nod.

But the thought of escape is bittersweet. Getting out of the Arc means accepting Finn's death and leaving him behind for good.

It means acknowledging not only that I'll never see him again, but that I'm the one who robbed the world of his presence.

It's a reality I know I'll have to confront eventually.

But right now, I force myself to focus my energy on helping our allies toward victory.

"Level Three-Hundred," Rys says, "is heavily guarded by a small army of trigger-happy Directorate Guards that the King and Queen love to dress up in fancy medieval-looking gear. But I should be able to get us past them. The bad news is that much of the holographic landscape—the hills, the woods—everything—changes daily in order to confuse would-be intruders. There's no such thing as a map of the Palace Grounds. The only thing that remains constant is the King and Queen's chateau, but I can tell you the Batts aren't in there. All the important tech is kept in hidden buildings around the property. We just need to find the right one."

"Great," I lament. "So we're about to walk into a holo-labyrinth guarded by a band of psychos, and we have zero idea what we're looking for."

"Yup," Rys says with a smile and a wink. "Sounds like fun, doesn't it?"

5

THE TOYMAKER

WITH THE GLEAMING silver dagger Finn gave me at my waist and my uniform's cloaking setting activated, I accompany Rys, who is dressed in his dark gray Directorate uniform, out of the residence.

We arrive a few minutes later at the bustling level known as the Escapa. A getaway for the Arc's many wealthy residents, it's made up of a multitude of districts, each representing some part of a foreign country where tourism flourished in the days before the biological weapon known as the Blight stole so many lives.

We emerge in the Italian district, which smells of freshly-baked pizza, herbs, and a faint hint of dark, rich chocolate. It's enough to make my mouth water—and remind me I haven't eaten much of anything in the last few days.

I shadow Rys as he pushes his way through the crowd. The Arc's tourists part when they see his uniform as if they're convinced accidental contact with the Directorate's rose will burn them alive.

"We should probably keep the chit-chat to a minimum,"

Rys whispers over his shoulder. "Your Inhibitor will prevent the Directorate from listening in, but it won't prevent the crowd from hearing us talk to one another."

"Okay," I whisper back. "Just one question, then. Are you going to tell me what we're doing in the Escapa? This is the last place I expected to come today."

"We're here to pick up a toy."

"A toy?" I hiss, but Rys quiets me with a cautionary wave of his hand.

He's having far too much fun with this extremely dangerous game of his. Admittedly, part of me wants to play, too, to take pleasure in defying the Directorate. Little would give me more pleasure right now than breaking their laws right under their noses, under the menacing surveillance drones that hover and patrol the Escapa like flying sentinels.

But the moment proves impossible to savor. The smells meeting my nose, the sounds, the sights of this place—they all remind me too much of Finn, of the ill-fated date we once shared here. He's all I can think of, and right now I find myself craving his face, his touch, his lips, more than ever. Hunting for toys, regardless of how useful they might be, seems futile in the face of what I've lost.

Besides, what happens when we acquire it? Am I supposed to believe we'll simply hop on some Conveyor, head to Level Three-Hundred and ask the King and Queen to hand over the priceless Quantum Sources?

The more I think about it, the more this plan seems like utter folly.

But I follow silently, marveling at how quickly the Escapa's tourists seem to move out of Rys's way, how eager they are to appease him. I see fear in their eyes as they glance at the rose on his chest.

But there's something else in their eyes, too.

Hatred.

It's the first time I've seen that expression on the faces of anyone in the Arc other than disgruntled Dregs. Maybe the rumors are true—maybe talk of rebellion really *has* made its way to the masses. Maybe these people are beginning to understand what the Directorate has done to them—to all of us.

Hatred is a luxury reserved for those who have abandoned fear.

And many of these people aren't afraid anymore.

Rys finally stops in front of a small shop called *Vittorio's Couture.* In its window is a large display of elegant, hand-stitched dresses for sale, made of printed silks and cottons. All of them are exquisite, and no doubt expensive.

As we step inside, Rys fingers the corner of the silk sleeve of a jacket and mutters, "We're here."

"Where's here?" I whisper. "This is no toymaker's shop."

But before Rys can reply, a man who must be the shop owner approaches us. He's short and dark-haired, and the smile on his face relaxes me a little...though it proves short-lived.

"See anything you like?" he asks in a thick, lilting accent.

"I like everything," Rys tells him. "But it's what I *don't* see that interests me more. I'm wondering if you have any red silk in your possession."

The merchant offers up a solemn nod and says, "Come with me. I have an item in the back I believe you'll enjoy thoroughly."

"Very good."

Holding my breath for fear of being detected, I follow Rys to the back room, where our eyes meet a vast rainbow array of fabrics. The shopkeeper nods silently toward several rolls of red silk stacked in the far corner. "There," he says. "I have saved it just for you. But it's the play-thing under the bolts that you will like even more."

"Thank you, Vittorio," Rys says. "I owe you. Many others do, as well."

"Something tells me you'll pay me back soon enough. When I see the sky over my head once again, I'll call us even."

"What the hell was that about?" I whisper when the man has disappeared into the front of the shop.

"Vittorio is an ally who happens to despise the Directorate. He knows what's at stake here." Rys pulls his chin up as the sound of a patrol drone buzzes somewhere in the distance, pauses, then continues along its way.

"I seem to recall that you like silk, Ash," Rys says, gesturing toward the bolts of red fabric. "Why don't you take a look?"

"I suppose I do like silk," I tell him, irritated and confused. "But what are we doing here, Rys? I feel like we're wasting our time."

"Just trust me, for once."

I step over and pull at the first bolt of fabric. Aside from being a pretty piece of silk, I see nothing special about it. It's only when I lift the entire roll up that I spot a strange black box underneath, gleaming as bright and shiny as some of the Arc's high-gloss floors and walls. It's about the size of the old microwave oven we had in my house in the Mire, except that it's completely featureless.

"What is it?" I ask, hesitant to touch the container for fear of marring it with my fingerprints.

Rys reaches down and pulls away the rest of the silk to reveal that the box is more than it appears. It's sitting on six wheels, for one thing, ringed by thick, ridged tires. As I step forward to examine it, a thin line of white light around its edges flares to life and the box begins to roll toward Rys's feet, stopping before it reaches him.

"I designed the Bug some time ago," he tells me. "And Vittorio built it. In another life, he was a successful engineer."

"What is it?" I ask, still confused.

"It's a more sophisticated version of our rickety old wagon from the Mire. It's for transporting undetected contraband through the Arc. It can't be scanned by any of the Directorate's systems, so they can't possibly see what's inside. The Bug is small enough to fit into the tinier service Conveyors… which means it can travel through the Arc all on its own. It's bulletproof, laser-proof, and can withstand a pretty powerful explosion. And the best part is that it will find its way to almost any destination, regardless of what—or who—tries to stop it. Though I'll admit it's not great at navigating over tree roots, so dense woods aren't exactly ideal. In the Arc, though, it'll work like a charm."

"How does it know where to go?"

"The same way my birds do." Rys rolls up his sleeve to reveal the white panel that doubles as a control system for his army of avian drones. "If we manage to get our hands on the Batts—and that's kind of a big *if*—the Bug will help get them where they need to go—even if you and I were to meet an untimely end."

I smile, hopeful for what feels like the first time in days. "I don't know about you, but I have no intention of meeting an untimely end anytime soon." I don't say what I'm really thinking: *I refuse to die before I find out once and for all what happened to Finn.*

"Good." Rys rubs his hands together and leans forward to

speak to the Bug. "We have a job ahead of us. A dangerous one. You up for it?"

As if in answer, the small vehicle pulls away from its hiding spot and begins to charge its way across the floor, expertly navigating its path between the shelves.

"And you?" Rys asks, turning my way. "Are you ready, Ash?"

"Ready? No. Absolutely not." I pull the silver uniform's mask away from my face and narrow my eyes at him. "But I'm ready to take down the Directorate, once and for all."

6

THE PALACE GROUNDS

PULLING the silver fabric down to cover my face, I become Rys's shadow once again. But instead of returning through the throngs of bobbing tourists in the Italian sector, we weave our way behind the vendors' shops and booths until we reach a part of the Escapa I never saw when I was with Finn, though I immediately recognize what looks like a Paris neighborhood.

Elegant gray buildings with black, sloping roofs and tall windows loom up before us. Cafés occupy every corner, complete with charming outdoor tables and chairs. The scent of fresh croissants, coffee, and cigarettes meets my nose as we move, and I find myself envying the people sitting casually, enjoying a relaxing afternoon of leisure without a care in the world.

We walk in silence until we arrive at a courtyard large enough to display a massive glass pyramid several stories high. Surrounding the courtyard is what looks like an enormous chateau of exquisite stone, a host of beautiful windows and classical details accenting its façade.

"The Louvre," I whisper as I sidle up next to Rys. "I've only ever seen it in pictures. That's what this is—isn't it?"

"Yes," Rys says quietly, pulling his chin up as if studying the structure. "It's a pretty good replica, don't you think?"

"It's *insanely* good. I feel like we're actually in Paris."

I mean it. It feels surreal to stare at the building before us, which must match the one in France perfectly, right down to its sprawling size. The enormity of the Arc has never hit me so hard as it does at this moment, and I find myself awestruck.

"Let's go inside, shall we?" Rys says with a mischievous grin.

"We don't have time for sight-seeing," I hiss under my breath. "And I have no desire to stare at the Mona Lisa. I thought we were after Quantum Sources."

"We are. And I'm well aware we're in a rush. That's why we're here."

Surrendering, I sigh and follow along as Rys guides us down a long ramp leading into the depths below the glass pyramid—the entry to the museum itself.

The guard who looks like she's meant to take Rys' ticket bows her head reverently when she sees the symbol on his uniform and gestures to him to enter.

As I follow closely behind, almost invisible to the naked eye, I find myself wondering once again how my old friend managed to climb so quickly through the Arc's ranks. How he convinced the Directorate and all who serve them that he is worthy of access to the most secure locations in this entire, gigantic complex. It has to be more than just his betrayal of my family. Then again, he's Rys. He's conniving and clever, and has always been a charmer. Even when I've hated him, some part of me couldn't help but like him.

He leads us past a line of tourists waiting for their tour

guide and we continue to walk until we reach a door marked with the Directorate's gold rose and the words, "Directorate Guard Personnel Only."

Rys presses his palm to a white panel on the door's right, and it slides open, eager to please. Trailing invisibly, I stay close as we make our way down a narrow corridor to a waiting Conveyor.

When we're inside with the doors sealed, Rys pulls his face up and speaks, but not to me.

"Rystan Decker initiating weekly testing protocols on the King's Aggressor Drones. Palace Grounds access requested."

When a small, shiny red object detaches from the ceiling and floats down to hover in front of him, I feel myself pressing back against the wall for fear of being seen. But the small ladybug-like flying machine scans Rys' face then lets out a cheerful, "Authorized," before flitting up to its nest as the Conveyor begins to shoot us upward.

I don't dare speak for the entirety of the ride. We're playing with fire right now, and I'm all too aware that one wrong move could result in death for us both.

When the Conveyor halts at Level Three-Hundred, the doors sweep open to reveal a stunning sight: a long expanse of perfectly trimmed grass guiding my eyes up to what looks like an exquisite castle in the distance. Flanking a gravel pathway that leads toward the structure is a series of elegantly sculpted green topiaries pointing in perfect symmetry at the artificial sky.

I inhale the scent of fresh-cut grass, my mind convinced that I'm standing outdoors and not inside an enormous building filled with synthetic versions of nature.

Rys shakes his head just slightly as he steps out of the

Conveyor, sensing that I'm about to say something. "No talking," he mutters out of the corner of his mouth.

I follow as he strides not toward the castle but in the direction of a small stone building about twenty feet away, where two guards stand at attention. Behind us, the Bug motors along like an obedient dog sticking close to Rys's heels.

"Rystan Decker," he tells the guards. "Authorized to complete my weekly check of the Aggressor Drones in the Royal Level's Eastern Sector. I need all personnel in that area evacuated, all drones disabled for inspection."

When he notices the guard eyeing the Bug, Rys turns, leans down and opens its lid to reveal a series of silver tools. "Easier than lugging a tool box around," he says with a smile. "I injured my back a few days ago, so this seemed like a good alternative."

"If you're injured, maybe someone should go with you."

"No need. My back's almost at a hundred percent. I just don't want to aggravate it. You know how it is."

"Very well." A look of extreme boredom has taken up residence on the guard's features. "Take the glider."

The guard nods toward a vehicle that looks like a larger, sleeker version of the old golf carts I used to see people use back in the days when people actually played golf—only instead of wheels, it seems to hover half a foot or so above ground.

Rys hops into the driver's seat and like a whisper on the air, I climb in next to him. The cart takes off down what looks like a narrow asphalt road and we travel in silence for several minutes before we finally arrive at what looks like a security gate. A man waves Rys through, saying, "All drones disabled. You have an hour, Decker. Be sure to check out when you're finished."

"Of course." Rys nods, hitting the gas when the gate opens to allow the glider through.

It's a couple of minutes before he dares to speak again.

"This section of the Arc is the most heavily-guarded there is. The only reason they give me access is that I understand their drones better than they do, and I'm better at fixing them than anyone else. I monitor them every seven days, make sure their systems are up and running and that no one has tampered with them."

I'm about to ask if he ever tampers with them himself when the sight before us grabs my attention.

Rolling green hills draw my gaze into the distance, some of them trimmed with tall, white wooden fences. Contained within the fields are herds of beautiful horses, exquisitely powerful-looking and elegant, their necks arching as if they're showing off.

"Are those…real?" I ask. "Or holograms?"

"Very real," Rys replies. "As is the grass. So strange, isn't it, to think of horses way the hell up here. It feels wrong to keep them inside…though I have to admit, the grounds designers did a great job of making the land as authentic as possible. That grass they're grazing on is top-notch, and the UV rays piped in from the phony sky above us means their environment is highly realistic. It's possible the horses really don't know the difference between this and the great outdoors."

"They're so beautiful," I say. "Why do the King and Queen keep them here?"

"What's a Royal family without horses?" Rys asks with a snicker. "Those bastards are all about status, appearances. Of course, they hunt, too—the King, Queen, and that grotesque son of theirs."

"Hunt what?"

Rys winces. "I'm not sure you want to know, Ash."

"You're not serious," I mutter as a chill makes its way over my skin.

"I think you know the answer to that." Rys lets out a deep breath. "In the early days of the Arc, whenever the Dregs misbehaved, they brought them up here and released them. The King and Queen—and a few invited guests like our friend, the Duchess—would mount the horses and pursue them. Oh, they gave them a head start of a few minutes, but..."

"But..."

"I've seen some of the footage from those days from the surveillance feeds on the grounds. The Aristocrats used guns sometimes, but also crossbows, spears, lances, you name it. It was all very...inhuman."

"Why am I not surprised?" I ask. "Those gorgeous animals being used to chase down innocent people. Teenagers, even. There's literally no bar too low."

When we finally arrive at an elegant set of matching stables, Rys pulls the glider over to the side and cuts the engine.

Beyond the stables, a thick forest leads my eyes into the distance. Thousands of trees that are likely nothing more than an invention of the Arc's clever holographic designers.

"You can come out of stealth now," Rys tells me. "Remember, all cameras and drones are disabled, so no one will see you. Plus, you're kind of freaking me out, Invisible Woman."

"I'll give you my face, but that's it. I'm too nervous to show myself."

"Whatever makes you happy."

I peel back the fabric to reveal my features, grateful when I reach down and feel Finn's dagger still at my waist.

A swell of nausea hits when I remember it's not my only

weapon. There's also the one deep inside my flesh and bone—the weapon called the Surge. As I recollect the last and only time I used it, I feel a strange tingling in my fingers, my palms, as if my body is itching to unleash it once again. A desire overtakes me to find out just how powerful I could be if I learned to control it, and I wonder with a frisson of terror how much damage I could do against a group of the King's soldiers.

But I shut down the thought, telling myself I don't want to know. What happened in the Arenum was a horror I don't care to revisit.

"My research tells me," Rys says, "the Batts—the Quantum Sources—are kept in the woods not far from the stables. The only problem is that I have no idea where."

"Well, that's super-helpful. How the hell are we going to find them? These woods look like they go on for miles."

"We'll start in there," Rys says, nodding toward the stable.

"You think the Batts could be in one of the stalls?"

"No. But there's something inside that will help us find them. *Two* somethings, actually."

I stare at him, convinced he's joking. But apparently I'm wrong.

"Can't we just take the Glider?"

"The Glider only runs on magnetized roads. If we tried to drive it over the grass it would crash to the ground after after a millisecond."

"Funny that you should mention crashing to the ground, because I haven't been on a horse since I was five. And that was a tiny freaking Shetland pony. The King's horses are enormous."

"They're just big Shetland ponies," he shrugs. "They're no different."

49

"Except the ground is a lot farther away when you're on their backs. Which means the sudden stop hurts a lot more."

Rys crosses his arms and lowers his chin. "Ashen Spencer, I'm surprised at you. I've never known you to shy away from a challenge."

"I'd be less likely to shy away if I weren't worried about a broken arm, neck, or back. Something tells me the Arc's hospitals wouldn't exactly go out of their way to help a Dreg murderer in need of a body cast."

"If you shatter a bone, I'll splint it myself. Promise."

"I'd rather die."

"You're not going to die, you wuss. Come on."

When we've stepped into the stable, Rys turns and opens a side compartment in the Bug to extract what looks like a small metal orb. I only realize when he cups it in his palms and strokes his fingertip along a fine line down its center what it actually is:

A silver egg.

The orb cracks open and inside is what looks like a perfect little sparrow, who immediately flies up into the support beams under the stable's roof.

"Klondike will be our eyes out there," Rys says, nodding toward the broad, open doorway. "He'll scan for any sign of a storage unit. We don't have a lot of time. In less than an hour, every camera and drone in this place will be reactivated, and we'll be screwed."

I look up to see the sparrow twitching, his head moving in every direction as he bounces on his feet, surveilling his immediate surroundings.

We quickly locate the stable's tack room and carry out two polished saddles. Rys selects two horses—one a dark brown gelding with a black mane and tail, one a deep chestnut mare —and opens their stalls.

"That one's a bay," I say, gesturing to the brown and black one, whose shoulder is higher than the top of my head. "I remember that from my brief horse-crazy phase when I was a kid."

"Impressive," Rys replies. "Here's hoping you remember how to ride."

"Like I said, I never *knew* how to ride. Other than get on and hope for the best."

"Hoping for the best is all we can do, Ash."

Rys slips the saddle on and tightens the girth, and within a few minutes, we've sorted out how to get their bridles on, though I'm anything but confident in our plan.

We guide our mounts outside and Rys helps me onto the chestnut before hoisting himself onto the bay's impossibly high back.

Reaching down to stroke my horse's neck as she twitches under me, I silently plead with her not to throw me.

"We were too poor to afford lessons when I was a kid," I tell Rys, "and I never did learn much, other than that you're supposed to keep your heels down when you're riding. Oh, and don't pull on the bit any more than necessary. I'm pretty sure there's a lot more to it than that, though."

"Controlling a fifteen-hundred-pound animal? How hard can it possibly be?"

"We're about to find out."

I wait for Rys to lead the way then let the chestnut follow, my hands gripping the front of the saddle for dear life.

We head down a narrow path into the woods with Klondike flying overhead. Rys rolls up his sleeve, consulting his arm band now and then to see if the sparrow has spotted anything that may prove useful in our search.

The ride is mercifully smooth. The chestnut moves evenly and calmly under me as my eyes scan the woods, my mind trying to determine if what I'm seeing around us are actual trees or mere projections. Given the grim silence and lack of scents meeting my nose, I determine that nothing but the grass can possibly be real. If these were actual woods, surely the King would have imported some kind of wildlife—squirrels, birds, rabbits—but there's nothing here but static decor.

After a time, Rys holds up a hand and tells me we're stopping. "Klondike has spotted something—a silver shed at three o'clock. We'll have to head off-trail to get to it."

He leads the way and I follow silently, looking around warily, fully expecting a crossbow bolt or worse to come flying at my head.

We arrive at our destination after five or so minutes. It looks like a typical garden shed, except for the fact that it's constructed of strong-looking, shiny steel. Unlike the trees, its façade is unmistakably real.

"How are we going to get inside?" I ask.

When he pulls up, Rys leaps off his horse and strides forward to study the door. "A simple lock," he says. "I'm surprised, honestly, considering what might be in there. But I should be able to get in easily enough."

He pulls a device from his pack and inserts it into the lock, twisting it until it clicks open.

I dismount, allowing the chestnut to graze as I join Rys inside the shed, which turns out to be entirely empty.

Its walls are bare, its floor smooth concrete. There's not so much as a hook on any of the walls. No cobwebs, even.

Just...nothing.

"We'll have to keep looking," I sigh. "There must be other buildings around here."

"This doesn't make sense," Rys says absently as we walk out.

"What doesn't?" I ask.

"An empty shed," he says, turning to stare at its façade. "Why bother putting this here, without tools, or feed, or anything else inside?"

"A misdirect, I guess? In case anyone comes snooping around. You said yourself the lock was a simple mechanism. There's no way the King's people would store Quantum Sources in a place that was so easy to get into."

Rys shakes his head. "No. But…"

"But what?"

"This shed exists for a reason. It has to be more than it appears."

"You think it's another illusion?"

"The lock and door are real," he says, stepping inside again. As I follow, he adds, "I felt them with my own hands. But…"

I watch him stalk forward until he reaches the back wall.

"I hear something," he tells me. "A buzz. Low frequency. Almost like…"

"Like what?" I ask, but even as the words come out, Rys steps forward again…right through the wall, the Bug following at his heel.

In the distance, his echoing voice cries out, "Ash! You have to see this!"

7

HIDDEN

THE SIGHT that awaits us on the other side of the holographic wall is a shock to my system.

I have no idea how, but Rys and I are standing inside a massive, cavernous warehouse filled with storage crates of all shapes and sizes.

Klondike, seemingly eager to explore, disappears into the rafters to begin his reconnaissance mission.

"This doesn't make sense," I say, gasping at the enormity of the place. "How did we not see it from outside? I'm shocked our horses didn't plow right into it."

"The horses know their way around—they would have avoided the outer walls, even if they were hidden from us. From where we were, all we saw were the projections of trees set in place to shield this place from view. It's clever, really. Like you said, the little shed is nothing more than an optical illusion."

With those words, my mind goes to Finn. I'm still holding out hope that his death was as clever a ruse as this warehouse's concealed location. A trick of the light, a well-executed misdirect.

Anything but reality.

But I shake the thought off, forcing myself to focus on the present. Finn wanted us to find the Quantum Sources. He wanted us to succeed, even if it cost him his life.

We must succeed.

With the small glass screen in hand so he can monitor Klondike's progress, Rys leads us at a brisk walk through the warehouse, which is brightly illuminated by rows of halogen lights far overhead.

"There's really no one here?" I ask, puzzled once again. "I have to say, this all seems a little too easy. I would have expected some sophisticated internal security system."

"I guess the Directorate is arrogant enough to think their little illusion will keep would-be thieves away."

"True," I concur. "Still, we should get what we're looking for and get out as fast as possible."

I follow him down what seems like a never-ending aisle all the way to the far end of the warehouse. The multitude of shelves overwhelms me, each covered in containers that hold anything from weapons to grain to machinery.

"What exactly does one of these Batts look like?"

"They're not very big," Rys tells me. "The type we're looking for is about the size of a stick of butter."

"But I thought they were heavy," I protest, remembering what Finn said when he described them to me.

"That's the tricky part—they are. Extremely. Deceptively. It's one reason I wanted the Bug with us," he says, nodding down to the black box that's still accompanying us every-where we go. "It can hold several hundred pounds without its suspension collapsing under the weight."

After a few minutes, we come to a corner of the warehouse

that glows brighter than the rest. I look up at the ceiling, trying to figure out why. But the simple halogen bulbs are the same type as elsewhere.

It takes me a few seconds to realize the air itself is glowing, as if enhanced by some invisible, powerful force. A throb works its way through my head, a dull, slow-burning ache overtaking my insides.

"I'm beginning to understand why the King wouldn't want the Batts in his home," Rys moans, pressing his fingers to his temple.

"The *Batts* are doing that to us?"

He nods. "But don't worry—they're not dangerous. Just very powerful."

"Oh, good. I'm glad to know I'm not about to melt into toxic human soup."

"Here," he says, chuckling as he gestures toward a shelf made of thick, reinforced steel. On its surface are what look like a hundred or so tidily layered black bricks.

I reach out for one, but Rys cocks his head skeptically. "Good luck lifting it," he snickers.

"You're forgetting," I reply, wrapping my hands around it and pulling it off the shelf with ease, "I'm wearing Finn's uniform. *Heavy* doesn't mean much to me."

Rys raises an eyebrow and smiles. "All right, I'll admit that's pretty impressive."

Holding the Batt in one hand, I watch as Rys lifts off the top section of the Bug to reveal a hidden compartment. "In there," he says, and I set the Batt gently down before turning to reach for another one.

Rys tries to follow suit. He grunts, shifts one of the Batts about half an inch on its shelf, then turns to me with an exaggerated frown. "I guess I forgot to do my pushups this morning."

"Yeah. I'm sure that's all it was," I scoff.

When I've slipped three more Batts into the Bug, Rys says, "We should get going. Our time is running out."

Klondike joins us as we make our way quickly back to the other end of the warehouse. We slip through the holo-wall into the small shed, but Rys stops me before we're outside.

"Klondike—scan the area for threats," he commands, and the sparrow takes off like a dart into the artificial treetops.

"All clear?" I whisper after a few seconds.

"So far, yeah," Rys tells me, rubbing his eye.

"You seem agitated," I say when I detect a note of worry in his voice. "That's not like you."

"We've been out here a long time. We need to get back."

We slip out of the shed and grab hold of the horses' reins, readying ourselves to mount again when above us, Klondike begins chirping wildly.

"Oh, God," Rys spits.

"What is it?"

"A member of the King's Guard," he replies, pointing toward the path ahead. I can just barely make out movement among the trees in the distance. "On horseback—which means it's one of the Knighthood."

"Knighthood?"

"You'll see."

Instinctively, I pull my uniform's shielding mask back down to cover my face, hideously aware that Rys will now have to explain what he's doing at the shed with not one, but two of the King's horses.

"Should we mount up and try to get away?" I ask in a whisper, my voice shaking.

"No," he says. "These men are expert riders. He'd catch us in seconds. Let me handle this."

"Rys..."

"Don't say another word, Ash."

He barks an abrupt command at the Bug, which begins wheeling away rapidly in the direction of the Conveyor where we first entered the Palace Grounds. Its thick, grooved rubber tires allow it to easily navigate the terrain, but I have my doubts as to whether it will reach its destination before being confiscated and eventually torn to pieces by members of the Guard.

When I hear the quickening thud of heavy hooves on the ground, I spin around to see a massive horse charging in our direction. As it moves, the trees between its rider and us flicker, falter, and finally disappear, as though the horse's hooves are smashing each holographic projection to pieces.

Slowly but surely, the rider breaks down every barrier between us until all that remains is a sea of green grass and a wide, open space—a blank canvas on which a pretty lie was painted for a time.

Behind us is the shed, still surrounded by holo-trees, the warehouse still invisible to the naked eye.

The rider is dressed in armor—not modern tactical gear, flak jacket and the like, but full-on medieval-style silver armor, complete with a royal crest on his chest. It looks ridiculous, unwieldy, and incredibly heavy.

It also looks impenetrable.

But it's not the outfit that frightens me, or even the weapon sheathed at the man's side.

It's the creature padding along in front of him.

8

KNIGHT

WHAT LOOKS LIKE A LARGE, metallic silver panther accompanies the man like a threatening shadow, stopping when the horse stops, its body low to the ground and poised to strike.

It looks alert, feral, and as real as any beast I've ever seen, though it appears to be made of the same sort of metal as Rys' birds.

Its ears flat back on its head, the cat snarls to reveal a gleaming array of razor-sharp fangs, and I remind myself that even Finn's miraculous uniform won't protect me from a set of vicious teeth embedded in a steel jaw.

"I am a knight of the King's Guard, " the armored man calls out in a fake-sounding English accent. "Who goes there?"

When he utters the final three words, I come perilously close to letting out a laugh.

The King and Queen and their freaking pomp and circumstance. Always trying to seem more important than they are, as though they actually rule a kingdom instead of a gigantic metal prison filled with their brainwashed minions.

"I'm here to assess the drones," Rys tells the knight, stepping forward. "I'm just finishing up. What seems to be the problem?"

The "knight" raises his silver mask and narrows his eyes at Rys before turning to Klondike, who's perched on the pommel of the chestnut mare's saddle.

"Where did that bird come from?" he asks.

"How should I know?" Rys retorts. "It's a bird."

"There are no birds in the Palace Grounds. The King despises them."

Rys shrugs. "Sorry, but I can't help you."

The knight dismounts. My hand goes invisibly to my dagger's hilt and I wonder with a quick hit of bloodlust how difficult it would be to pierce his armor. The man moves toward Rys, striding along the grass more easily than I would have expected given the apparent weight of his uniform.

The metallic cat slips along at his side, letting out a low growl as it gets close. "Are you aware of the incident that occurred in the Arenum a few nights ago?" the knight asks.

Rys shakes his head, and if I didn't know better, I'd guess he was terrified. He clears his throat before saying, "I'm too busy with my work in the tech wing to follow the goings-on in that place."

"An army of birds attacked the King's drones. Decimated them. I don't suppose you — a guy who apparently knows a *lot* about drones and who happens to be hanging out with a little silver bird—have heard anything about that."

"I haven't," Rys replies, his tone even. "Like I said, I wasn't there."

The knight smiles. "Right. It's just a coincidence that this little sparrow is here with you, then?"

"I told you, I don't know where it came from."

"Uh-huh."

The man reaches for the weapon at his side which, to my horror, turns out to be a sleek-looking handgun. He points it first at Rys, then at Klondike. When he pulls the trigger, the bird shatters into a thousand pieces.

It's all I can do not to let out a wail of sorrow. Klondike was a mere robot—a metal object, and nothing more. Yet I'd grown attached to him in our short time together. There was something entirely innocent about him, something pure and sweet.

And now, like so many other beautiful things in this world, he's gone.

I force myself into grim silence, my eyes locked on the knight.

"I'm not even going to ask why you have two horses with you," the Guardsman says as he re-holsters his weapon. "You're in violation of all kinds of rules, and I'm sure the King will be only too happy when I tell him I'm taking you to the Hold." He raises his wrist to his face, an electric-blue display glowing along his silver armor.

If he manages to convey a warning message, we're as good as dead.

Before the man has a chance to speak, I peel the fabric from my face, disable my silver uniform's cloaking ability, and step forward.

"Stop!" I shout.

The knight turns my way, his eyes wide.

Rage forces my voice into a barely controlled quiver. "I can't let you tell anyone we're here."

His eyes narrow as he says, "You're the fugitive who killed the Duchess' son."

I wince at the words.

Killed.

He speaks the word with such certainty that my heart tumbles, shattered, into an abyss.

"I'm the fugitive who will kill *you*," I tell him, forcing steadiness into my voice.

"Good luck with that," he snickers.

"The crest on his chest," Rys murmurs out of the side of his mouth.

My eyes veer to the man's armor, to the crest emblazoned with the Directorate's rose, grasped firmly in the talons of an eagle.

"What about it?" I whisper.

"His armor is holographic. Hit the crest with your blade and it'll cause a short. The armor will disappear, along, I hope, with his communications."

"Are you sure?"

Rys lowers his chin and eyes me as if to say, "Am I ever wrong about anything?"

Hesitating only for a moment, I snatch the dagger sheathed at my waist and hurl it at the man's chest. When it hits squarely in the center of the King's crest, the armor flickers once, twice, then disintegrates. All that's left is the dark uniform of a Directorate Guardsman.

The man slumps to the ground, the dagger still jutting out from between his ribs. His horse turns and gallops away, too sensible to stick around any longer.

I don't have time to register what I've just done before the metallic cat lunges at me, leaping into the air as if in reaction to his master's death.

With no time to think, I thrust my palms outward, a shrill cry of terror escaping my throat.

A shock of blue light explodes in the air between us, sending the cat flying backwards as if hit by an invisible tsunami of the purest, most intense power. He explodes in mid-air, shattering into a hundred jagged metal pieces before raining down onto the ground below in a pile of half-melted steel.

I sway on my feet, dizzy, nauseated, and spent, robbed of my capacity to think.

A hideous memory shoots through my mind of the last time I sent a blast of energy through the air. What I did to Finn, to me, to our futures.

"You all right?" Rys asks.

I nod. "I'll be okay," I tell him, my breath tight. The words feel like a lie, but I desperately need them to be true. "We have to get out of here before anyone else comes."

"Which should happen any second now," Rys replies, pointing toward the knight's left arm.

As I scramble to pull the knife from the man's chest, I glance over to see the display on his armor is glowing red along his forearm:

Intruders in Eastern Sector

"We were a little too late in disabling his comms system," Rys moans.

Mere seconds later, the thundering sound of hoofbeats on the ground meets our ears. We spin around to see a mass of trees fading from sight as dozens of members of the King's Guard charge toward us, weapons drawn.

Our horses—the chestnut and the bay—have fled, no doubt seeking shelter in their comfortable stable.

They're so much smarter than we are.

"Do you have another blast in you?" Rys asks, his voice desperate. "We could really use your gift right about now."

Pressing my hands to my chest and willing the power to return, I close my eyes.

Please, I whisper, pleading with my mind to engage. *Please.*

But all I can see is Finn's face. All I can think about is his body flying backwards and the sickening sound that met my ears when he collided with the ground. The horrible pallor in his skin as I ran to him in the Arenum as the crowd called out for more violence.

Forcing the image away, I thrust my hands at the air, my open palms toward the encroaching army...

But nothing happens.

"I can't," I cry. "Oh, God, Rys. Why did we do this? Why did we come up here? They'll..."

"They'll lock me in the Hold, then kill me. I know the drill." His eyes locked on the horsemen, Rys takes my hand and squeezes. "It's okay, Ash. If I die here, it's okay."

"You can't die," I half-sob. "I won't let you."

"I don't think they're going to give you a choice," he says, nodding toward the charging knights. "But you need to disappear. You can get away, even if I can't. The Batts—you need to—"

"Stop talking," I command with a shake of my head. "I'm not leaving you now."

"You don't have a choice." His jaw set in a grimace, Rys steps forward, his hands in the air in surrender to the encroaching forces. "Ash," he shouts, "Go!"

The horses are less than a hundred feet away now. A few of the King's Guardsmen in the front line have their guns drawn, and others are carrying what look like lances or epees.

"No," I repeat. "I won't."

Stepping forward to join him, I reach for Rys's arm and squeeze as I clutch my dagger in my other hand and wait.

"We could hide in the warehouse. Maybe..."

Rys shakes his head. "No point. We'd be sitting ducks in there."

"Then I guess this is the end."

We stand strong, two old friends who have been through hell, been torn apart and somehow brought back together, waiting for death to take us both in a wave of galloping killers.

I picture us both getting trampled into the grass, our bloody, mangled corpses unrecognizable in the aftermath.

It's inevitable now—the horses are moving too swiftly, their unrelenting pace terrifying to behold.

There's nothing left to do but watch...and wait.

The horses are thirty feet from us when the first of them comes to a sudden, unnatural stop, its head twisting around at a sickening angle. It crashes to the ground, its rider under its belly.

A second horse follows suit, then another, and another. A fourth stops abruptly and the knight on its back flies forward out of his saddle. It's only when the rider slams to the ground, his body broken, that I begin to piece together what's happening.

"Something is stopping them," I say, my legs shaking beneath me. "Something solid. But I can't see it."

"A shimmer-wall," Rys gasps. "It's an electrical barrier— extremely hard to create. Someone is preventing the knights from getting to us."

"Shimmer wall..." I repeat, staring. I can see now that between us and our fallen enemies, the air sparkles here and there as if accented by droplets of dew. But each time I try to focus on one, it disappears. *The wall is a mere shadow, just as I am when my cloaking uniform is activated.*

My voice cracks when I murmur, "You're telling me you didn't do this?"

"I don't have that kind of tech in my possession. It's all but impossible—I've never seen a shimmer-wall in real life. I've only heard theories. The power needed to create one is..."

He spins around, frantically searching for our protector. I do the same, but at first, I see nothing but the small silver shed, the faintest outline of the warehouse's still-masked outer walls, and the vast lawn of grass stretching out where the holographic forest used to stand.

But as if on cue, after a few seconds a lone figure emerges from behind the shed. Dressed in the same suit of silver armor as our would-be assailants, he steps toward us, a weapon in hand.

I pull my blade and prepare to hurl it, my chest heaving with confusion, fear, and rage.

I don't know if the man we're looking at is an enemy or our savior. But if he's the former, I'm determined to kill him. After all, I have blood on my hands now. There's no going back.

But the knight holds up his hands in a gesture of surrender, dropping the gun to the ground. He cocks his head to the right as if he's assessing Rys and me.

"The shimmer-wall won't hold long," Rys warns me. "We have to get out of here. So if you're going to kill him, I'd suggest doing it now."

But for some reason, I drop my hands my sides and stare at the knight, puzzled. *Why did he drop his weapon? Why doesn't he attack us?*

"You're a member of the King's Guard, aren't you?" I ask,

stepping toward him. "I'll bet you were once like me. A Dreg, someone born in unfortunate circumstances. You're torn inside, aren't you? About what to do here. Whether to kill us—two Dregs, like you. You're the one who put up the wall, because you know it's wrong to murder us where we stand."

A muffled voice comes at me from somewhere beyond the holo-armor.

"I was never a Dreg."

I can't tell if his tone is snide and judgmental or if it's a simple observation. All I know is that he's not behaving as I'd expect a member of the King's Guard to behave.

"Never a Dreg," I reply. "Okay, then. Well, whoever you are, there are two of us and one of you. Do you know who I am?"

He nods. "Ashen Spencer," he says, his tone ominous. "Killer of Aristocrats, traitor to the Directorate. You're the most wanted fugitive in the Arc."

I want to offer a retort, a defense, but I have nothing.

He's right.

As of only a few minutes ago, I am most certainly a killer.

"So you know I'm perfectly willing to take your life," I threaten. "I'm not afraid of you. And believe me, I have nothing left to lose." I hold up the blade Finn gifted me—the beautiful silver bit of perfection that looks like it could slice through a diamond without a moment's pause.

"You can't kill what's already dead," the man says with a chuckle. "So I'd put that away if I were you."

I glance sideways at Rys, who looks as confused as I am.

"Are you telling us you're undead?" I ask, losing patience. "Because I'm pretty sure the King hasn't got zombies in his service."

K. A. RILEY

"I'm telling you the world *thinks* I'm dead," the knight replies. "But the world, as we know, is foolish and ignorant."

With those words, the knight's holographic helmet fizzles away to reveal a head of dark, curly hair and eyes that could easily melt my soul.

9

GHOST

EVERYTHING HAPPENS IN SLOW MOTION.

I look back toward the few knights in silver who are still standing, still trying to force their way through the invisible barrier in the distance.

My eyes move to Rys, who looks as stunned as I feel.

He, too, sees the ghost with the exquisite eyes.

The last time I looked into those eyes, I thought I was about to die.

I have no idea what's happening—whether I'm dreaming or awake. I don't even know where I am right now. The world is a blur, my eyes brimming with tears, my heart on the verge of explosion.

Finally, I force myself to focus on the man in the holo-armor standing before us. A young man, his features so beautiful, so familiar...

Dropping my blade, I fall to my knees, shaking.

It seems I've wandered into the strangest, most wonderful dream of my life.

This isn't real...

It can't be.

"Finn," I breathe. "Is it…"

"It is." He glances over at the Guardsmen angrily pounding on the shimmer-wall. "You two have to come with me. Rys is right—the barrier won't hold much longer. There will be lots of time for conversation, but only if we can get out of here alive."

He turns to lead the way, deactivating his holo-armor to reveal a silver uniform that matches my own.

I don't want to wait. I'm desperate to ask him every question in the world.

How did you get here?

Where have you been?

Why didn't you tell me you were alive?

…and why didn't you kiss me just now?

But even through my tears, I can't quite bring myself to demand answers. My relief is too great. I feel light for the first time in days, like there's a future now, a chance for us all now that Finn's here to fight alongside us.

I feel my strength returning to me bit by bit, his presence granting me new life.

"I've been to this level many times," he tells us over his shoulder as he moves swiftly ahead of Rys and me. "My parents used to come up here all the time to meet with the King and Queen. I know every nook and cranny of the Palace Grounds—even the sectors that are masked by the constantly shifting holograms. There are a lot of escape routes, but only if you know where to look."

As we put distance between ourselves and the knights, he guides us under a long, arching arbor covered in green vines. I reach out to touch them, to see if they're real—to prove to myself that I'm not dreaming.

Wordlessly, we follow Finn even as the sound of angry shouts crescendoes behind us.

"The wall is down," Finn informs us, his voice eerily calm. "They're coming this way now."

"You've been hiding this whole time," I finally say as I follow breathlessly, reality sinking in with each step. "You've been in the Arc all along..."

"Hiding? Yes, I suppose I have. But it's not for lack of desire to see you. I—"

"Guys!" Rys barks. "Focus. Please." He looks over his shoulder, his skin pale, his face shiny with perspiration. "They're going to be on us in seconds."

I glance back to see several of the horsemen charging our way once again, though their mounts are skittish and in disarray, seemingly terrified that another unseen wall may rise up to break their necks.

Calmly, Finn turns to look ahead, pointing toward a row of perfectly coiffed hedges. "This way," he says, guiding us to a spot where a tall shrub seems to split apart just slightly. He slips into the opening and we follow, pushing our way through the greenery.

On the other side, we find a white-washed wooden wall lined with a series of doors that look like something out of a drug-induced dream. Each is a different shape, size, color. Red, blue, pink, purple, yellow, green.

"Another hologram?" I ask, frustrated.

"No. This has been here since I was a child," Finn explains. "When I was younger, we called them the Magic Doors."

"Do you know which to take?"

"Depends. Where did you send the Quantum Sources?"

"Service tunnel on the Sector Eight rail line," Rys says.

With a nod, Finn guides us to a teal door whose handle is

shaped like a silver dolphin. He pulls it open, but instead of walking through, he spins around to face us.

"What are you doing, man?" Rys snaps. "Just go!"

"In a second. They're close. If I don't stop them, they'll catch up. We can't risk them following."

I can feel the rhythmic beating of the horses' hooves in my feet, and instinct tells me to grab Finn and pull him through the door. But instead, I choose to trust him and watch as he works another miracle.

Holding a small silver gadget in his hand, he closes his eyes, his body tightening, the tendons on his neck jutting out prominently as though it's taking all his strength to press the button on the gadget's surface.

After a few seconds he's crafted another wall, another blockade to save us from death.

When he's finished, he lets out a heavy breath, turns to the door, and says, "Let's go."

Rys and I slip through before Finn follows us into a sleek white Conveyor and calls up a menu on his wrist implant, selecting our destination.

I scan the Conveyor, expecting the walls to start flashing red at any second. Surely the alarm will sound and the entire Arc will soon know what's happened.

"Don't worry, I've disrupted the system," Finn says. "Just enough to get us to our destination. We'll soon reach the Quantum Sources you two so cleverly swiped."

"You've been anticipating all this," Rys replies, a reluctant note of admiration in his voice. "You knew our plan..."

"I knew you two would go find the Batts, yeah," Finn replies. "And I wanted to help, for obvious reasons."

He glances at me, and I'm acutely aware that he hasn't yet touched me, held me, kissed me. It's almost like he's reluctant to prove to me that he's real. I'm terrified that if I reach out to slip my fingers along his flesh, my hand will go right through him.

My chest tight, I ask, "How did you know we'd be in the Palace Grounds?"

"For one thing, I followed you after the so-called memorial service," he says with a sardonic chuckle. "I overheard your conversation. You two need to learn to be more careful. You never know who could be listening."

His calm demeanor and the casualness of his tone set a slow-growing anger simmering inside me. I step over to him, press my hands to his chest, and force him to look into my eyes. "You were cloaked behind us and didn't say anything?"

"It wouldn't have been prudent."

"You let me think you were dead!" I snap. "You have no idea what that did to me, Finn. How it tortured me."

"I didn't want to be a distraction," he says, his tone oddly matter-of-fact and devoid of apology.

This isn't the Finn I know and love. This isn't the Finn who tells me with nothing more than a reassuring look that fate will find a way to be kind to us both, and that I have nothing to worry about.

"It didn't occur to you that constantly thinking I'd murdered you was a distraction?" I ask, my voice quivering with a combination of rage and self-pity. "That living with what I'd done was like being stabbed in the heart every waking moment?"

Finn takes a deep breath and fixes his eyes on my own. "You really thought I was dead?"

"Of course I did!"

My anger increases when a smile spreads itself across his lips.

This time, instead of simply pressing my hands to his chest, I push him so hard he stumbles backward into the Conveyor's wall. "I'm so pissed off at you right now. You have no idea."

"I'm sorry," he replies with a chuckle. "I really am. It's just —if you thought I was dead, that means the illusion worked better than I could ever have thought. It means we're one step closer."

"To what?"

As the Conveyor slides to a halt, Finn says, "Victory."

When the doors open, we slip out into a passageway so dark I can barely make out my hand in front of my face. "The Service Conveyor is up ahead," Rys says. "We'll find the Batts there."

He pulls a device from his uniform's pocket and lights our way through a nearly impassable tunnel filled with crumbling concrete and twisted rebar. This passage evidently isn't used frequently—which hopefully means no one will expect to find us here.

"What do we do when we reach the Batts?" I ask, shoving my anger aside just long enough to focus on the task at hand. "I mean, Finn and I can only carry them so far, and I can't imagine the Bug can follow us through the woods. It's a long hike back to the Pit."

"I have something in mind," Rys says, "to take us as far as we can go via the old highway. The rest we'll have to do on foot. In the meantime, I'll send word to the Pit via Atticus that we're on our way."

When we come to a fork in the tunnel, Rys signals us to be silent before turning right. We pad along quietly behind him until we're certain no one is lying in wait for us. After a hundred feet or so, we come to a small door that slides open on our approach to reveal the Bug.

"We need to move fast," Rys says as our rolling black companion begins to move along at his feet. "The King will be aware soon of what's happened. He'll lose his mind and there will be no escape."

We jog after him until we reach another Conveyor, which Rys programs to bring us to Sub-Level Four.

"This is the level where they store the vehicles the Chaperons and others use," he tells us. "So all we have to do is take one for ourselves."

"Sounds so easy," I reply. "Why do I get the feeling it won't be?"

"It'll be easy if you both cover your faces, go into stealth mode, and keep your mouths shut. I can't disable the cameras down here—they're on a system I don't have access to, and the garage's security is multi-layered. Meanwhile, I'm going to put on my best *I belong here* face and hope no one notices what I'm doing."

Finn begins to pull the fabric over his face, but hesitates, turning to me. He puts a finger under my chin and lifts my face to his. "I'm really proud of you," he says softly. "And I promise, I won't fake my own death again. At least, not without telling you first. I never meant to hurt you, Ash. I only wanted to save your life."

"I'm still mad at you."

"Are you?" he asks, leaning in to press a soft kiss to my lips. "How about now?"

"Slightly less," I reply with the faintest hint of a smile. "If you want to make it up to me, you'd better be prepared to tell me everything. The King has freaking cat-bots and the Duchess—well, you were at the memorial service. You saw what she has in her possession. Those Cyphers are killing machines."

"Yes. I saw. But I want you to know they were never..." Finn says, his gaze and voice suddenly distant. "The Cyphers' tech is stolen. They shouldn't exist."

I press a palm to his cheek, trying to pull his eyes back to mine. "What are you saying?"

"I'll explain everything I possibly can," he promises in a soft, sweet voice that half melts me where I stand, and I'm relieved and grateful when he focuses on my eyes once again. "But some things have changed, Ash, in ways I can't control."

Rys clears his throat, and I can tell without looking that he's ready to punch us both in the face. "Come on, Romeo and Drooliet. Mask up and let's go. We don't have time for this."

When Finn and I are masked and cloaked, I ask Rys, "Where are we going, then?"

"Follow me," he says, guiding us along by the dim light of his handheld device.

We eventually come to a steel door that Rys opens with a press of his palm to a security panel. We're greeted by the cleanest, whitest parking garage I've ever seen, filled with shiny vehicles like the one that picked me up at my home in the Mire on the first day I came to the Arc.

Rys guides us through to the far end of the garage, the Bug following obediently.

The car he brings us to is larger than the others. Silver and sleek, its wheels are streamlined, smooth, and devoid of detail, its windows tinted dark.

Rys presses a hand to the driver's side door, which lights up with a blue input panel. When he strokes his fingertip over a series of shapes, the door slides open upwards, as do the other three doors and the trunk. Finn and I deposit the Batts and slip into the back seat together as the Bug disappears into the shadows at the far end of the garage.

Rys leaps into the driver's seat and the doors descend, sealing us inside.

I examine the vehicle's interior, stunned at the opulent details: a small bar, complete with crystal glasses. Several holo-screens displaying picturesque views outside the Arc. Off to one side is a small set of drawers, and when I pull one open, I'm met with a series of silk ties and elegant masks like the ones the Aristocrats wear to social functions.

One of the ties is emblazoned with the Directorate's gold rose held in the talons of an eagle, rendered in exquisite detail.

"Rys," I say, my throat parched, "whose vehicle is this?"

"Wouldn't you like to know?" he chuckles.

He starts up the engine, which is virtually silent, and we begin to glide as if floating on the air.

To my surprise, we don't cruise up an exit ramp. Instead, Rys steers us toward a plain white wall at the far end of the garage, accelerating as he goes.

"Uh...Rys?" I stammer nervously as we speed toward an inevitably fatal collision.

"It's okay," he assures me. "A little trust?"

I sit back and swallow hard. He's right. I owe him a *little* trust...

Still, I reach out and grab Finn's hand, holding on hard as I stare death in the face for what feels like the tenth time today. Finn squeezes back, but somehow he feels too calm, too complacent, as if he knows something I don't.

Just as my mouth shoots open to utter a cry of terror, the white wall slides open and we go tearing up a steep, cylindrical tunnel just barely wide enough to accommodate a vehicle of this size.

As if he's done it a million times, Rys steers the car expertly along the narrow passageway, its lights dim orange and disorienting.

We glide along for what seems like an eternity before Rys finally says, "Brace yourselves. The really dangerous part is coming up. But by my calculations, it'll be tons of fun."

I pull the cloaking fabric away from my face for a moment, turn to Finn and smile, easing back in my seat.

Once again, we're taking our lives into our own hands. But by some miracle, I feel...happy.

ON THE OUTSIDE

BLINDING AND SHARP, the sun's piercing rays shoot through the windshield like daggers as we leave the tunnel's darkness. Still, Rys seems calm and collected when he hits the accelerator.

When my eyes finally adjust, all I can see ahead is a broad, open highway that was once populated by thousands of tourist-filled cars. A sea of trees and mountains surrounds us, but I'm all too aware of the open sky overhead, of how visible we must be to every camera on this side of the Arc. We're a fast-moving silver bullet shooting away from a fortified dungeon the likes of which the world has rarely seen.

"We're too vulnerable," I mutter, twisting to look behind us as we distance ourselves from the monstrous structure known as the Arc. Thanks to some clever visual tricks by its designers, it appears to float weightless several stories above the ground—an illusion intended to make it appear impenetrable from the outside.

"I wish we had a stealth vehicle," I lament.

"Me too," Rys replies. "But at least this one's bullet-proof. And *kind of* explosion-proof."

"What?" I pull my hand away from Finn's and lean forward, pulling the silver fabric from my face. "You're joking."

"I'm not."

"Rystan," Finn growls, clearly as nervous as I am. "Exactly whose car is this?"

At first, Rys doesn't answer. I peer at the rearview mirror to assess his smiling eyes. If it weren't for the fact that he's driving at what must be close to two hundred miles an hour, I'd seriously consider punching him.

"Rys!" I shout. "This isn't funny! Tell us!"

"Fine. It *may* belong to the King. It's not his prized possession or anything, but...look, he has dozens of cars. He won't miss it."

"Please, for the love of God, tell me you're not serious right now."

"I...can't."

"Even if every camera on the western side of the Arc wasn't watching us right now—didn't it occur to you that the Directorate would notice someone *stole the King's freaking car?* You don't think a convoy of drones will come after us any second now?"

Infuriatingly, Rys shrugs. "I'm counting on it."

"That's it!" I bark. "Pull over. Hide the car in the trees, I don't care. We'll hike the rest of the way."

"Nope," Rys says. "You know as well as I do they'd track us down and kill us in the woods before we get anywhere near the Pit. Some of us can't vanish into thin air like fancy-pants magicians, you know."

I twist around in my seat to look through the back window.

"What's your plan if drones chase us down in this stupid car?" I ask.

"I don't exactly have a plan for that," Rys confesses. "Look, I can't be a genius *all* the time."

"Well, you'd better think fast," Finn says, gesturing behind us. He's out of stealth mode now, his face exposed to reveal an expression of rage. "Because they're coming."

I turn around again to see that he's right. At least five large, armed drones are soaring in a V-formation from the direction of the Arc's upper stories.

I glance over at Finn, who looks far calmer than I feel, considering we could be on the verge of losing one another again.

Feeling suddenly desperate, I close my eyes and beg some unknown entity for mercy.

Please...don't take him away from me again. Not yet.

As the drones descend to close in on us, their gruesome buzzing—like that of a swarm of giant insects—grows so loud I'm convinced the leather seats are vibrating under us.

"Here it comes," Rys says, his giddy enjoyment palpable on the air. "Like clockwork."

"Here *what* comes?"

My question is immediately answered when a robotic voice booms out from somewhere above us.

"Driver, stop the vehicle. It is the property of the King, and has been taken without authorization. Failure to comply will result in incarceration and eventual death."

"Well, the good news is that Ash and I have been through

both of those already," Finn says. "I don't suppose you plan to obey their orders, Rys?"

Rys shakes his head.

"Pull over immediately!" the drone-voice calls out, louder now. "You have exactly thirty seconds before the Type-Alpha Drones open fire."

Rys lets out a sigh and shakes his head. "They're so predictable, aren't they?"

"Why aren't you taking this seriously?" I snarl.

"Because I know how drones work."

"Drones kill people, Rys."

"Not very often. See, the thing is, the Directorate's drones are programmed to assume people will comply. When people don't obey their commands, they get confused. More often than not, they malfunction and freak out."

"That voice doesn't *sound* confused. It sounds like we have thirty seconds before we're blown all to hell. Actually, more like ten now."

Instead of replying, Rys just continues to drive, stone-faced and fearless.

No, not fearless.

Reckless.

I'm shaking now, trying not to count the seconds down until the assault begins. But I know it's coming, and I know he's not planning to do a damned thing to stop it.

When the first shot hits, it feels and sounds like an explosion against the vehicle's silver exterior.

"Oops, I guess I was wrong. They're using blast shells," Rys says with a shrug. "They blow apart on impact. A direct hit from one of those turns a person into hamburger meat."

I let out a shriek when the second slams against the back window, mere inches from my head.

"Rys!" I cry. "Do something!"

"Like I said, it's okay. This car belongs to the most paranoid psychopath in the Arc," he responds with a chuckle. "Nothing can take it down. But if it makes you feel better, I can make the drones disappear. It's a favorite magic trick of mine."

"Whatever you're going to do," Finn growls, "I'd suggest you do it now. Stop playing these stupid games."

"Playing games?" Rys spits, glaring over his shoulder. "You want to talk about games, Davenport? How about what you did to Ash in the Arenum? How about breaking her heart? How was that for a fun little game?"

Finn goes silent then, and I can feel the heavy wall of angry tension forming between the two of them, hanging toxic in the air around us.

"I'm not sure this is the time for this particular conversation!" I shout as more blast shells slam against the car. "Get rid of the drones, Rys, or nothing else will matter."

"Fine." He pushes his left sleeve up and, after tapping a number of symbols on the white panel wrapped around his forearm, he sits back in his seat and hums a tune to himself as several more drones join the first five and an all-out assault begins, pelting the car in an unrelenting stream of small but terrifying explosions.

I slam my hands over my ears, crying out as the deafening noise doubles me over.

"The thing is," Rys yells when the round of blasts dies down, "the Directorate loves to automate everything. They love drones, because drones can, in a pinch, kill for them. But it never occurred to them to worry that maybe someone would figure out how to kill the drones."

I spin around in my seat, realizing the sound of exploding

ammunition hasn't started up again. Instead, I'm hearing another sound—one far more distant.

The cry of a bird of prey.

In the sky above the drones is a golden eagle, its wings spread. In its talons are what look like small metal orbs, which it hurls at one drone then another, exploding on contact. Each time the eagle unleashes one, another appears in its place, replicating as fast as the eagle can hurl them.

"The eagle used to symbolize freedom," Rys says. "I thought it was fitting for a bomber-drone. His name is Sam, by the way."

"The Directorate never anticipated this," I laugh as I watch shrapnel-like shards of metal tumble like rain to the ground behind us.

"No one ever does."

When all the Directorate's drones have been dispatched, the eagle banks away, soaring off over the woods. Rys accelerates and drives another several minutes before finally slowing and steering the car into a deep ditch at the side of the road.

"It's time," he says. "We need to abandon the vehicle— they'll send more drones soon enough, and this time, they'll be smarter about it. We're going to have to hike the rest of the way."

When we climb out, I look up warily, but all I see is empty blue sky.

"Is it safe?"

"Yes. For now."

I glance over at Finn, who's gone silent.

You're still here. Still real.

Rys is right.

Finn did break my heart. For a time, he destroyed me. But emotions, like people, exist within a hierarchy. Some are more powerful than others, and as it turns out, joy is stronger than sorrow. Bliss outweighs pain—and the human mind, as I know all too well, has an incredible capacity for forgetting how acute our pain can be.

It's how we survive. It's how we manage to walk away from trauma yet go on living. Without relief, we would wallow in misery all day, every day.

And Finn's presence here is the greatest relief imaginable.

He and I will talk. He'll explain himself.

And there's no doubt in my mind that I'll forgive him. Because he's given me the greatest gift in the world:

He's brought himself back to life, and for now, it's enough.

THE OAK

WITH THE BATTS weighing us down, we begin our long hike through the woods.

Though I'm eager to see Kel again, I'm almost grateful for the time spent pushing our way through the wilderness, for the distance we're putting between us and the sleek silver car that will surely act as a beacon for anyone hunting for the three fugitives who escaped the Arc.

No, not three.

***Two** fugitives.*

As far as the Directorate knows, Finn is still dead. He's still a ghost to the Duchess and to all the others. And he'll remain a ghost until the time comes to reveal the truth.

We hike in silence, all too aware of how easy it would be to alert any watchers in the woods of our presence. I watch Finn as he strides ahead of me, powerful, confident, and focused. I admire his determination to get to our destination, but as time passes, I begin to wonder why he hasn't so much as acknowledged me since we began our hike. Why each time he turns to look back, he seems to stare straight through me. It's like the most intimate, familiar part of him has been numbed or, worse, stolen entirely away.

I want to ask if he's all right, but I'm too cowardly. Too afraid that he really has altered in some insidious way, and that the Finn I've known all this time is somehow gone.

Did I do this to you in the Arenum? Did I somehow break our bond?

But instead of asking the questions out loud, I simply say, "Your parents."

He stops, turns my way, and focuses his eyes on me.

"What about them?" he asks. His expression is still cold, emotionless, as though every spark of life has deserted his eyes.

"Are you going to tell them you're alive?"

His brows knit together as if I've said something both idiotic and cruel. "Why would I? They forced me to fight you in hopes that I'd kill you—or get killed myself. Either way, what they did is unconscionable. I don't care if I never speak to either of them again."

"What about Merit?"

Finn's younger brother is Kel's age. He's sweet and innocent, not to mention that he worships Finn. I can only imagine what he's going through right now, thinking his older brother is gone forever.

"I'll find a way to tell Merit, of course. But as for my parents, they don't deserve the pleasure it would bring them. I want them to suffer a little longer. They can wallow in it, for all I care."

"That's...harsh."

Though I have to admit that the thought of their suffering brings me a little bliss.

"Not after what they did—to you, to me, to so many

others." He shoots a look at Rys, who is hiking some distance ahead, before adding, "You blame him for your mother's death. But you know whose fault it really is."

I clench my jaw for a moment before relaxing it again. He's right. I've always blamed Rys for what happened. But the only sin he actually committed was telling the Directorate about a painting in my mother's bedroom. Although it was a betrayal, I will admit—albeit reluctantly—that he had no way of knowing it would lead to so much sorrow and pain.

After all, Rys didn't wrestle my mother to the ground or murder her in front of her only son.

"He didn't pull any triggers," Finn continues. "He didn't have the intent to kill. The Directorate is another story, though. We both know my mother's mind. We know how cruel she is. I've given up hoping she'll change, that somehow, love will turn her into a better person. She's a monster with no capacity for love, and it's high time I admitted that to myself."

"You sound like you despise her."

"She deserves nothing more…and nothing less."

Without another word, he turns and continues the hike, his knuckles white as he grasps the Batts in both hands. I've never seen him like this. Never thought he had it in him to feel such hatred for anyone, least of all his parents.

Still, some part of me is proud of him for it. Proud that he's finally putting distance between himself and the devil that is the Duchess, not to mention the spineless coward that is the Duke.

I only wish we could have found our way to Merit and somehow brought him with us.

Taking him from his parents—a crime the Directorate

inflicts on so many—would have been the ultimate act of revenge.

We've nearly arrived at the entrance to the Pit when a familiar *Hoooo* works its way to our ears from somewhere in the branches overhead.

I glance up to see Atticus's glowing eyes peering down at me. If he had lips instead of a beak, I'd swear he was grinning with some sort of intense pleasure.

"Nice to see you, too," I tell him before calling out to Rys. "Has he told the Pitters we're coming?"

He nods. "They know."

Sure enough, as we step close to the oak tree's trunk, the bark splits open to reveal a narrow doorway. Out from the darkness beyond, a small figure emerges and charges at me, clamping his arms around my waist.

"Ash!" Kel cries. "I thought you'd never come!"

I set down the Batts that I'm carrying and hug my brother back as Illian—the Pit's leader—emerges to greet us.

"Atticus has informed us that all is clear," he says, "or we might not have dared to come out. But we should get inside quickly—"

He stops when his eyes land on the dark objects on the ground, then move to Finn, who is still holding the other Batts.

"Are those..." he begins, and it's hard to tell if he's on the verge of tears or laughter. "But of course they are. You've really done it. You've brought Quantum Sources to us. I have no idea how you managed it, but please know you have my gratitude, and that of every resident of the Pit. What you've done will change our lives."

"Happy to help," Rys says with a grin. "Illian, right?"

"You two haven't met in person," I say, astonished to realize it. "This is…my friend Rystan. Rys, Illian."

"You're the one who created Atticus," Illian says, reaching a hand out to shake Rys's. "I know all about you. A miracle worker, from the sounds of it. I'm eager to hear all that you've worked on in the Arc—though I suspect you won't be headed back there anytime soon."

"No. Probably not," Rys chuckles. "I've sort of shot myself in the foot this time, and I can't say I'm sorry for it."

"Well, you're most welcome here for as long as you'd like to stay. Come in, come in, you three—and Atticus, if he likes. We'll have our people working on getting the power restored straight away. Though I'm surprised to see you carrying the Quantum Sources in your *hands*. I didn't think it could be done."

"It wasn't easy," I say, throwing a look toward Finn, whose face is pale, his forehead beaded with traces of perspiration. But something tells me it's not from the exertion of transporting the Batts. "But we managed."

Illian eyes Finn for a moment, and I can tell he's concerned, though he says nothing about it. Instead, he scratches his chin and smiles. "You young people never cease to amaze me. Perhaps one day you can explain how these things are possible—the silver suits, the owl, all of it. It gives me hope that we could actually win this futile war against the Directorate. But for now, I just want you inside where it's safe."

I pick up the Batts, assuring Kel I'm right behind him as he guides us through the doorway and down the narrow winding staircase into the underground network of tunnels and chambers known as the Pit.

Downstairs in the Central Chamber, we find Illian's partner, Kurt, who offers to fetch steel carts to gather the Quantum Sources.

Despite its darkness, the chamber feels warm and welcoming, as always. A cozy hovel, it's a shelter from the perpetually tumultuous storm that is the outside world.

"One Quantum Source should be enough to power the entire Pit," Illian tells us. "Though I'm a little worried that those with the Gloaming won't know what's hit them. We'll have to warn them of the potential shock to their eyes."

"Gloaming?" Rys asks.

"The word we use for those who've lived in darkness for years. Their eyes aren't what they once were. They're remarkable people, each and every one. Masha—the little girl who spends much of her time sprinting through the tunnels in the darkness—can work her way around the Pit without a second thought. She's far better than the rest of us at navigating the tunnel system down here. It's as if she's developed a whole new sense—something far more advanced than vision or hearing."

Illian stops speaking and glances at Finn, who's sitting silently on one of the armchairs by the fireplace. "Mr. Davenport," he says. "I must admit, I didn't expect to see you again so soon. I feel like there's a story in all this, but I'm almost afraid to ask."

"There were some...developments while we were in the Arc," Finn says quietly. "Things happened that made it necessary for me to leave my family and my home for good."

He looks at me, then Kel, and I can tell he's torn. The same question snakes its way through my mind: *Should we tell the whole story and risk horrifying my brother when he learns how close I came to death, or keep our mouths shut?*

"It's all right," I tell Finn. "Kel should know what happened —why it took so long for me to get back here, and why you and Rys are with us. He has a right to the truth."

"I thought you'd be back days ago," my brother moans in plaintive agreement. "What happened?"

"Finn will tell you."

After all, it is his mother who orchestrated our fate. Better that the words should come from him than me.

"The Directorate...more specifically, my mother, learned Ash and I were working together," Finn says. "And in typical fashion, they decided to punish us by making us fight to the death."

"To the death," Illian repeats. "The Directorate does enjoy their drama."

"What?" Kel shoots out, amazed and terrified. "You were supposed to kill each other? Cool!"

"You did not just say 'Cool' to the idea that Finn and I should both be dead right now, did you?" I ask with a laugh, charmed by his perpetual innocence. He's lost both his parents, yet a fight to the death, to him, is still sort of...*fun.*

Despite the morbidity of it, I'm grateful to know he's kept his sense of wonder.

"And yet here you both are," Illian adds.

As he's speaking, Kurt steps back into the room.

"What did I miss?" he asks.

"Simply Mr. Davenport telling us how he and Miss Spencer killed one another."

"I killed *him*, actually," I correct, looking sideways at Finn with a wince. "But in my defense, it was the last thing I wanted to do."

"She didn't kill me." Finn smiles, the softening of his features easing my mind. "But I'm very sorry to say I let her believe she had. It was cruel of me, and heartless."

With that, he throws me a quick look as if to say, "See? I still have empathy after all."

"Why would you do such a thing?" Illian asks, his tone defensive and protective at once.

"I felt the need to protect Ash—and, admittedly, to wreak a little havoc. I needed the Directorate to think I was gone, to think they had one less enemy to worry about. But most of all, and maybe most selfishly of all, I wanted my mother to know how it felt to watch someone she loved die. She's inflicted the same pain on so many people over the years, it was time she got a taste of it."

The room falls into a heavy silence, like the weight of what Finn's just admitted hits us all.

To anyone who knows the Duchess, it's not surprising to hear that anyone—even her own son—should want to hurt her.

To those who don't know her, like Illian, it's probably shocking.

Kurt, on the other hand, is all too aware of the Duchess's nature. A former member of the Directorate Guard, he's seen the psychopaths who run the Arc up close.

"I'm sorry for what your mother is, Finn," he says. "I'm afraid I've seen her leadership skills. I hope you can forgive me when I say I'm not sure she has a heart, so I'm not entirely sure it can be broken."

Finn narrows his eyes for a moment in reflexive defense before letting out a chuckle. "Fair enough. Now, we're not here to talk about my messed-up family, are we?"

As he says the words, the room's walls flare to incredible

life, light hitting Finn's features from every angle. The walls themselves begin to glow bright despite layers of dust and grime that have built up over time.

"They've succeeded," Illian says, reaching for Kurt's hand. "We have power!"

Seeing the room like this—the space around us bright, warm and even more welcoming than it was before—I understand for the first time how the Pit must have looked in its early days. Its ceilings are high, criss-crossed by long wooden beams. All along one wall on the far side of the room, a series of screens flares to life, projecting vivid scenes of mountains and forests like huge canvases on display.

Intrigued, I ask, "Those are your camera feeds from the outside?"

"Yes. Distant ones, from vantage points we haven't been able to access in years. It will take us some time to work our way through all of them. But the most important thing to look into right now is the train to Santa Fe."

"We'll check on its status," Kurt agrees. "But I'm expecting full functionality. The system is intact—it just needs to be activated. Who wants to come have a look?"

I'm about to tell him I'd love to join him when Illian says, "Kurt, take Finn and Rys with you."

"Not me?" I ask, eyeing Kel, who's grown bored with our adult conversation and, along with another young boy, is pointing and staring in wonder at the outdoor scenes projected onto the walls.

"If it's all the same," Illian replies, "I think you and I should take a walk. There's something I'd like to talk to you about in private."

NEWS

WHILE THE OTHERS are off checking on the train that will lead the Consortium members to possible freedom—and could lead others to us—Illian walks me down one of the Pit's quieter hallways. Its walls are newly lit with pretty little round sconces that reveal in stark detail how long it's been since the place last received a thorough cleaning.

Still, there's something beautiful about the years of hand-prints on the walls, the trampled earth beneath our feet as Pitters made their way tentatively through the darkness.

"I would have thought you'd want to be with Kurt for this," I tell Illian, my eyebrows raised. "To see the train in motion for the first time in years."

He smiles. "Normally, I would, but I suppose I'm a little superstitious—I'm convinced that my presence would curse it, somehow. We need that train to run, so superstition wins."

"You run this place like a well-oiled machine. I'm sure the train will be no exception."

"Thank you for your confidence in me." His expression

turns grim when he adds, "But the truth is, Ashen, there's something else I wanted to talk to you about—something other than Quantum Sources or trains."

"Oh? Is it Kel?" With a sinking feeling, I realize I've saddled the Pitters with a babysitting job they never asked for. Another mouth to feed, another child to entertain. They've been so generous, but no doubt Illian feels a need to chastise me for taking them for granted. "He's probably been a handful while I was gone. He's a good kid, I promise. I didn't mean to leave him for so long—"

Illian chuckles and shakes his head. "Of course it's not Kel. He's wonderful. A light in this until recently very dark place. No, it's something we spotted via the solar-powered cameras close to the Pit. A Wanderer, as it were, out in the woods." He stops walking and turns to face me.

"A Wanderer?" I ask, a chill in my bones. "Who?"

"That's what I need you to tell me. I have my suspicions, but I'd be willing to bet you can confirm whether I'm right or wrong. Would you mind taking a look? It feels…important."

"Of course I wouldn't mind."

As apprehensive as I am, I'm far too curious to resist. This Wanderer—is it someone from the Arc? An escapee? Who?

Illian brings me to a small room with a long, curved desk covered in a series of screens showing various views of the woods.

He sits down and navigates his way through the feeds until he finds one particular camera angle, then rewinds until I spot a figure dressed in dark clothing making his—or her—way across the screen.

He rewinds again, stops, and presses play. When I lean in to stare at the mysterious figure, at first all I see is a nebulous shape among a sea of trees.

But when the figure pulls his chin up and stares directly at the camera, I gasp and press my palms to the desk.

That's when Illian hits pause.

"You know him," he says. "Don't you?"

I nod. "That's Peric. He's Veer's adopted son from the Bastille."

Veer, the leader of the town formerly known as Breckenridge, is most infamous for having crafted an alliance with the Directorate. For years, she has sacrificed her own people's children in order to keep the town's adults from harm. It's a scheme both diabolical and oddly benevolent...in a completely twisted way.

"The boy isn't *from* the Bastille," Illian corrects. "He was brought there by Veer, remember."

I nod. "He told me she raised him when his parents were killed. Took me in, looked after him. But..."

"But what?"

"The night I escaped the Bastille--when Veer was set to turn me over to the Duchess—Peric looked surprised to realize she could be so cruel. He tried to stop her, but he failed. That was the last time I saw him."

"You think that's why he's in the woods? As punishment for his support of you?"

I stare at the screen. Peric appears to be dressed in a long, dark coat, and carrying a backpack. He has no weapon and from the looks of it, he's definitely not clothed for a surveillance mission.

"He's been banished," I say. "She's kicked him out." I mean it as a question, but it comes out as absolute certainty.

So, this is what Veer did to her so-called "son."

"Where is he now?" I ask.

"Last we saw, he wasn't too far northeast of here, taking

shelter in a small cavern. Hiding, I suppose, from the Directorate's drones. He's clever—he seems to know what to look for, how to feed himself. But he won't survive long if cold weather hits—or if the Directorate finds him."

I nod. "He knows better than anyone how to listen for the drones. But if he stays out there too long, you're right—he'll be killed. No one can avoid the drones forever, not without a proper hiding place, or cloaking gear. I need to find him."

"Yes. I think that would be wise."

Illian sounds a million miles away, so I turn to study him. His gaze is distant, his mind lingering in some far-off place.

"When I mentioned Peric once to you a long time ago, you acted like you knew him," I say quietly.

That seems to snap him back into focus. "Yes. I believe I told you I knew his parents. Very well, in fact. They fought alongside me when the Bastille was taken. When the fighting became brutal, they lost track of Peric in the fray. They thought..." He clears his throat, pauses for a few seconds, then proceeds. "They thought they'd lost him in an explosion. It shattered them, truth be told. They went—reluctantly—with some of the others to Santa Fe, to try and pick up the pieces of their lives without their son. That was back when the train still ran. I haven't heard from them in years, of course. But as far as I know, they're still alive."

My chest tightens. "You never told me his parents were still out there somewhere," I chastise. "I could have told Peric. I could have let him know Veer had lied to him about the Consortium murdering them—that he'd been living in the Bastille under totally false pretenses. All this time, he's thought of the Consortium as the enemy—he hates you for what he thinks you did."

"It wouldn't have been right for me to tell you Peric's

parents were alive and give anyone false hope. For all we know, there *is* no Santa Fe. Not anymore. It's one reason we need to make our way there, to see what progress—or not— has been made."

I bite my lip. "Well, I need to tell him there's a chance they're still out there. If he knows the truth, he'll probably be willing to join us. He's strong. Disciplined. Loyal to a fault. And, strange though it may sound, I trust him."

"You trust a young man raised inside the Bastille by Veer?" Illian's voice is filled with an understandable skepticism. "You do realize he could have been sent out into the woods as a lure, a pawn in one of Veer's twisted games. Heading out to look for him is potentially as dangerous as stepping on a land mine."

I shake my head. "If he were anyone else, I'd agree. But I told you, I saw his face the night I fled the Bastille. He *wanted* to protect me. And now, he's suffering for his sins. I'm sure of it."

Thoughts swim in my mind of Finn and Rys, of what they would think if I wandered out into the woods to find a young man who by all accounts is the enemy—and brought him back to the Pit with me.

But he's *not* an enemy. And we need all the friends we can possibly get.

"We'll send Atticus first," Illian finally says. "He'll confirm Peric's specific location so you don't endanger yourself more than is absolutely necessary. But I insist that you wait until morning before you go hunting for him. You must be exhausted. Besides, the Directorate will have a full force of drones out hunting you tonight. Safest to let Peric wait it out in his shelter."

"I'd like to find him now, but I have to admit, you're right about the exhaustion. I'll go first thing in the morning, then."

"Good. When the time comes, promise me you'll take at least one other person with you."

"Fine. I'll take Finn."

He nods. "I figured you'd say that. We'll have Rystan keep an eye on Atticus, then." He pauses again, then says, "Speaking of Rystan—he's dressed in the uniform of a Directorate member."

"I know."

"Should I be concerned?"

I shake my head. "He and I grew up together. There was a time when he was ambitious. He wanted to rise in the Directorate's ranks...and he did, quickly. But they'd kill him if he went back to the Arc. By now they know he saved my life in there, and that he was the key to stealing the Quantum Sources. Hell, they probably know about his birds, too. He's public enemy number two, after me."

"Well, then. As I said, he is most welcome here, but we should probably give him something less threatening to wear. In the meantime, it sounds like he will be a great help when it comes to getting our train up and running. Now, before I head back to find Kurt, there's someone in the Pit who's eager to see you. She's been worried."

"Kyra," I say with a smile. My friend and classmate from the Arc—a Dreg who suffered alongside me during Piotr's horrid Training Sessions and who's been looking after Kel since I left the Pit days ago. "I'd love to see her, too."

Illian guides me out of the room and down a series of hallways. "She seemed somewhat despondent when you didn't make it back from the Arc straight away. I believe the sight of you will raise her spirits greatly."

With a warm smile, he gestures to me to knock when we arrive at room 143.

A moment later, Kyra opens the door, beaming when she sees me. It's a relief to see her smile so brightly. There was a time when I thought it would never happen again.

"Ash, Ash, Ash," she repeats, almost singing my name as she hugs me tight. "I thought you were dead."

"So did I," I laugh, pulling back. "It seems I can't step foot in the Arc without someone trying to kill me."

"Yet here you are."

"Here I am."

"I'll leave you two," Illian says, giving us a strange, shallow bow before heading back down the hall.

"Tell me everything," Kyra says, taking my hands and leading me into the room. "Starting with why the damned lights in this place are suddenly working!"

We sit on her bed and I begin with the last time I saw her, as we said goodbye in the Arc. The tale takes an hour or more to tell, but she rarely interrupts and simply listens, intent and curious.

When I'm done, she lets out a slow breath.

"I thought you were going to tell me Finn was gone forever," she finally confesses. "I can't imagine..."

"Neither can I, even though I lived with the thought that he was dead—and that I'd done it. I'm just glad I don't have to anymore. But..."

"What is it?" She takes my hand again and squeezes, trying to coax the words from my lips.

"He's changed, Kyra. He's acting so weird—so far away. I feel like I've found him only to lose a little bit of him every second we spend together. It's like all his brightness and joy are gone. I don't know if I did this to him when I..." I shake my head, my lip quivering with the memory of our brief battle in the Arenum.

"Whatever it is, there's no way it's you're fault," Kyra replies, her tone overflowing with kindness. "He's probably just damaged like the rest of us. The betrayal his mother committed—not just in trying to have you killed, but using him like that, as a pawn in her sick game—it must be shattering for him to know he means nothing to her."

I let out a sigh. She's right, after all. Whether I like it or not, Finn's coldness is perfectly natural, given all that's happened. "You're right. His heart, I think, is broken."

He's just putting up walls to protect it while it mends.

"But he's here now, and so are you," Kyra says. "And Rys. And we're going to fight, aren't we? We're going to take on the Directorate, all of us together." Her face is lit up like the room surrounding us, and I can't help but smile to feel her excitement.

Hope has to be the most beautiful human expression there is.

"Yes, we're going to fight," I tell her. "And I don't quite know how yet...but we're going to win. In the meantime, I need to ask a favor of you—a big one."

"Anything, of course."

"If the train is functional, we'll be heading to Santa Fe in the next day or two, and we can't bring Kel. I don't know what we'll find, but if the Directorate has sunk their teeth into that city, it could be grim. Would you look after my brother for me?"

Kyra puts her arms around me again. "I'll do everything I can to protect him. You know I will."

"If anything happens to me," I say quietly, slowly, "please take care of him, would you?"

She pulls back and looks me in the eye when she nods and says, "As long as I have breath in my body, I'll see to it that Kel stays safe."

PRIVACY

WHEN KYRA and I are finished with our visit, I go to find the others in the Pit's Central Chamber. Finn, Rys, Illian and Kurt are all sitting by the large fireplace, which is glowing with a series of licking holographic flames. The freshly-scrubbed walls glow a cool, soothing shade of blue, and Pitters who haven't seen light in months—or even years—wander in and out of the room, expressions of pure joy on their pale faces as they chatter among themselves.

"So?" I ask as I stride toward the fireplace. "What's the verdict?'

"Success," Illian announces with a satisfied grin. "It seems the train will run. It needs a little maintenance, but should be good to go in a day or two. Which means we'll finally learn if the Santa Fe contingent still exists."

"You can't radio them or something, now that you have power?"

"We've tried, to no avail. Maybe their comms are cut off, or…" He lowers his head for only a moment before concluding, "Whatever the case, I'm eager to get there and see if there are survivors. There was a time when we had good friends in Santa Fe."

"Here's hoping."

I glance over at Finn, who looks a million miles away. Stepping over to him, I put a hand on his shoulder, which draws his eyes to my own. "Could I talk to you for a minute? In private?"

"Sure," he says, pushing himself to his feet.

While the others stay behind and chat, I escort Finn to room eighty-three, the bedroom we shared for a brief time. It's warmer now, brightly lit by a series of overhead bulbs. A roaring holo-fire flares against the far wall, dancing reflectively in Finn's irises as he looks around.

I seat myself on the bed, expecting him to do the same, but instead he stands stiffly several feet from me, his eyes moving to the floor.

"There was a time when you would have leapt onto this bed with me in a matter of seconds," I tell him with a grin, trying in vain to mask the hurt in my voice. "You would have kissed me the second we were alone."

"If you think I don't want to be on that bed—that I don't want to kiss you right now—you're tragically mistaken," he says, his voice strained, his gaze still locked on the floor.

"Finn, look at me."

He forces his eyes to fix on my own, but I can tell he's miles away.

"What's going on in there?" I ask, my voice a timid croak. "I can't read you. I can't...*feel* you. It's like something has changed inside you, but I can't figure out what. Have I done something to offend you?"

Other than almost kill you, that is.

I can see his mind at work beyond his eyes when he says,

"Of course you haven't. I can't even *imagine* you offending me."

"Then why did you hide from me in the Arc? You could have come and found me—why did you wait so long to seek me out?"

His eyes turn strangely glassy, staring through me at some invisible, distant entity when he says, "I had my reasons."

Irritated by his vagueness, my voice rises from timid to angry. "Do you have any idea what you did to me? Do you have any idea how much it tortured my mind, my soul to think you were dead?"

I've asked the question before, but I failed to demand a straight answer. I refuse to make that same mistake again.

"I have some idea how tortured you felt," he replies, his voice soft, pained. His eyes finally seem to focus, the distance between us narrowing as he comes back to me piece by fractured piece. "It was excruciating for me, too. But not in the way you think."

"If it was so excruciating, you could have come and found me, Finn. Hell, you could have told me what you were planning before the fight so I didn't have to go through the torments of the damned. I was destroyed, thinking I'd lost you for good."

He looks torn apart too, like some forbidden truth is colliding with his heart. "I wanted to, Ash—I wanted to find you after what happened in the Arenum. To talk to you, to reassure you. I wanted to tell you I was still here—still the same person you'd always known, but..."

"But what?" I snap.

"But it would have been a lie."

"What do you mean, a lie? You're standing here now, Finn. A few feet from me. Where's the lie?"

He sighs and steps forward, reluctantly seating himself next to me. "Do you remember the state I was in before our fight?"

I nod. "You were out of it, drugged. Your mother had done it to you."

"Yes and no." Shaking his head, he half-whispers, "It wasn't just the drugs that put me into that state. It was something else, too."

I tense, preparing myself for some grimly mysterious revelation. "You can tell me. I survived your death; I'm sure I can survive whatever you're about to throw my way."

He inhales deep, his shoulders rising then falling. "You were at the memorial service. You saw them."

It's all I can do not to let out an exasperated sigh. "You're going to have to stop talking in riddles. Saw what?"

"The two men my mother brought in. The ones she called Cyphers."

He looks into my eyes once again and I could swear his eyes flash in the light like those of a cat. But when I focus on his irises, I see nothing out of the ordinary.

"What about the Cyphers?" I breathe, apprehensive.

"I was the one who created them."

"You?" I breathe. "You did...*that*?"

He shakes his head hard. "I never intended for anyone to create an army of monsters. I only ever wanted to enhance people—to improve upon what we already were. My research has always been about strength and power. About how to harness energy, how to amplify neuro-impulses inject the potency of a powerful weapon into a human being. I wanted to take what already exists inside us to another level." He reaches for my hand, and I give it to him, too confused to resist. "It all goes back to the days when I began developing the tech I showed you in my room that first day you were in our residence. Do you remember?"

I nod. I haven't forgotten the sleeve Finn told me to slip on —the one that gave my arm and hand seemingly impossible strength. The sleeve that led to the development of the uniform I'm wearing now.

"Some of my designs are external, like these uniforms. They connect to our minds and enhance our physical strength in ways no one used to think possible. But for months, I've worked on other projects, too. Internal enhancements so small the naked eye can't see them. Tech that alters us on a cellular level. I designed a form of nanotechnology that could be implanted in humans—tiny chips replicating our cells that change us in ways unimaginable only a few years ago. This nanotech can be implanted in a human being with little more than a tiny needle."

I find myself holding my breath at his words, recalling the small patch equipped with an almost invisible pin that Finn left for me before our fight. His instructions told me to press it into my skin, and I assumed at the time that it was some kind of anesthetic to alleviate the pain I might suffer when he landed the killing blow.

Instead, I was imbued with an extraordinary power.

"The Surge," I say softly. "The power you gave me—you're saying…"

He nods. "Some time ago, the Directorate was working on a weapon that shot an explosion of pure energy at its target. I began to wonder what would happen if we implanted a human with that same potential." Slipping his fingers under my chin, he smiles wistfully. "I've always known your strength. I've known from the start how much power is inside you, waiting to be unleashed. And I knew all too well that if the implanted nanotech worked, you could easily kill me."

"But I never wanted that. I didn't want to hurt you. And I never asked to be turned into some kind of killing machine, Finn."

"I know. And it was wrong of me to give you the injection without telling you the truth about what it was. I only wanted to give you a chance at survival. I knew they'd come for you eventually, whether I lived or died, and I couldn't bear the thought of..."

He stops talking and for a moment, chews on his lip. "I'm sorry for what I did to you...and to myself."

I swallow, my heart racing. *So, I wasn't the only one you implanted.*

"What exactly did you do to yourself, Finn?"

He raises a hand slowly toward the far wall, his fingers spread. In front of the flickering holo-fire, I see the air sparkle as if a sheet of the thinnest glass has appeared before us, dividing the room from floor to ceiling into two sections.

"The shimmer-wall," I gasp. "I thought you used an electronic device to do that in the Palace Grounds. I just assumed...Rys said..."

But as I speak, I realize Rys never said anything, other than that he didn't think a shimmer-wall was even a possibility.

"I didn't need a device," Finn says. "The gadget you saw in my hand was nothing. A trinket. The power came from me—from my mind, my body—from the technology inside me."

Lowering his hand, Finn grinds his jaw before speaking again.

"Before our fight, I injected myself with what's called an Aegis Implant—a highly sophisticated series of artificially intelligent cells. In theory, the implant gives one the capacity to create a powerful shield, seemingly from nothing." He closes his hand into a fist then reopens it, twisting his fingers in the air.

I watch as more shimmering points of light form in a curving shape more delicate, even, than the clear wall he created moments ago. They envelop his hand like a glove of the finest mica, barely visible but strangely powerful. "When you were about to attack me, I used the Aegis to shield my body so that when the Surge came, I would be protected. The blast hit me and knocked me down—but it didn't hurt me."

My brow wrinkles with confusion, relieved as I am to know I didn't hurt him. "I don't see how any of this is a bad thing, Finn. You survived, and you saved Rys and me in the Palace Grounds. We would have been trampled or worse if it weren't for you. You've done something amazing here."

He chuckles, lowering his chin to his chest. "It *should* be good, I suppose. I should count myself fortunate, shouldn't I?"

"What's wrong?" I ask, reaching for him, desperate for the feel of his skin. But when I touch him, my fingertips recoil at the sensation of a hard, impenetrable shell surrounding his flesh.

He's so close, and yet I can't actually feel him.

"The Aegis Implant proved unstable," he says. "It...plays with my mind. I look at you and I want to touch you, to kiss you. I want things to be the way they were before all this happened. But there are these moments when I feel like my mind is being taken over by some external force, where I can't control what I'm seeing or thinking. For the first day or so after our so-called battle in the Arenum, I was consumed by hallucinations, visions that terrified me to my core. It frightens me even now to be close to you, because what's inside me isn't *me*. I feel this insane mix of anger and hostility, a simmering rage that I can't seem to control. Every waking moment is a struggle to keep my thoughts my own, to fight back whatever it is that's ravaging my mind."

"Okay, so we just remove the nanotech," I tell him, mustering something like a hopeful smile. "It's simple. Our fight is over now, so we take it out. It's cool that you can build walls and everything, but we can just—"

Once again, though, he shakes his head, this time more forcefully. "It's not something you can just remove, Ash. It's not like the wrist implant the Directorate gave you when you first came to the Arc. The cells are everywhere inside me, melded with my own cells and growing like a metastasizing illness. They're *part* of me, like my bones and my blood. The implanted nanotech will only grow stronger, and when it does, I don't know what will happen to me."

I pull back, horrified. "What are you telling me? That you're just...not Finn anymore? That you'll never be the same?" I hesitate for a moment before asking, "Will it happen to me, too?"

"No. Not to you. The implant I gave you was flawless. Perfectly designed specifically for you." He pushes himself to his feet and steps over to the shimmer-wall. For a moment, he caresses it with his fingertips as he's so often touched me.

Then, ramming a fist against the invisible barrier, he turns back to face me. "As for me...I have periods of clarity, where I know exactly who I am and how I feel, when I know how much I love you. In other moments, it's like I'm overtaken by something alien...an entity invading my mind, almost like it's trying to communicate with me. I don't know who I'll be from one second to the next, and like I said, it's a constant struggle just to keep my head on straight."

Trembling, I rise to my feet and step over to him. "Do you feel like yourself right now, in this moment?"

"Honestly?" With a weak smile, he cups my cheek in his hand and runs his thumb gently over my lower lip. The hard, protective aegis that surrounded his skin is gone now, and all I feel is *him*. "I feel like I'm outside of myself, witnessing this moment as it passes. I feel like I don't deserve you, but I know I love you. I'm aware of it—I feel it acutely." He kisses me gently and a familiar, lost swarm of butterflies flits through my insides in an all too brief moment of sheer bliss.

"I love you, too." Tears well in my eyes to feel the heat from his skin even as the shimmer-wall shatters behind him, sending a million points of flickering light into the atmosphere. "We can deal with this together, Finn. Whatever this is. We can fight it together."

"I have no way of knowing what will happen in the days ahead. I don't know if I have the strength to fight this—to remain who I am while this thing inside me grows and changes. And I'm not sure I can ask you to wait and see what happens. It wouldn't be fair to you."

"Fair?" I half-sob, taking a step back. "You're talking like it's some kind of punishment, being with you now. You have no idea what it means to me that you're alive—to have even the smallest piece of you, after thinking I'd lost you. You're... Finn. You're *everything* to me. And if all I can have is a moment here and there, it's a million times better than thinking you might be gone forever."

"I did something to you that's unforgivable," he says, pain winding its way through his voice. "By giving you the power —the Surge. I see that now, and truly, I'm sorry. You were perfect before, Ashen Spencer. For me to try and change you in any way...it was the most foolish thing I've ever done."

"You kept us both alive. I don't understand how, not really. But all I care about is that somehow, we're both here now. So I need you stay with me, okay? Fight whatever it is that's happening to you. You're stronger than anyone I know. You can do this."

His eyes red with tears, he kisses me again and this time, I feel it—the abandon, the weightlessness, the thrilling perfection of his touch. For the first time since he reappeared in my life, I feel like I have him back completely, our bodies pressing close, our polluted blood coursing in unison through our veins.

Reaching down, he lifts me and carries me back to the bed, where he lays me down gently. He climbs over me, his powerful arms imprisoning me like the braided bars of a wonderful cage from which I never wish to escape.

I look up into his eyes, searching for the boy I know, and I find him there, clear as a perfect sky.

"Will you stay with me tonight?" I ask.

"I'm not sure what version of me you'll find next to you. If you decide you'd like me to leave…"

Shaking my head, I say, "Never," as I grab him by the collar and pull him close to kiss him again. "Stay. We'll get some rest. We'll talk. And in the morning, if you're up for it…there's something I need you to help me with."

"Anything for you," he says, his lips trailing along my neck, sending shivers along my skin.

"Good. Because you might not like this task very much…"

Finn pulls away and looks down at me, his eyes suddenly glassy and dull.

"Finn?" I murmur, suddenly apprehensive.

"It's Peric," he says quietly, a strange confidence shading the three syllables.

"How…" I ask as he climbs off me and out of the bed, a hand running through his thick hair. "Why did you say his name just now?"

"Am I wrong?"

"I…no. Peric is in the woods somewhere and I told Illian I'd go find him. But how could you possibly have known that?"

He chews his lip for a moment before shaking his head. "Doesn't matter. What matters is that you're planning to risk your life to find the son of a woman who wanted to throw you to the wolves."

"There's more than one woman out there who wants to throw me to the wolves," I remind him with a scowl. "If I judged everyone by their parents, you and I wouldn't be having this conversation right now."

He opens his mouth to reply, but ends up shaking his head and chuckling. "Too true. Touché."

"I'm sorry," I say, reaching for him, but he pulls back. "I'm just trying to say I'm not about to judge Peric for something that's out of his control."

"I get it."

"Then why…" I stop talking and set my jaw. "Finn—come back to me." I rise to my feet and take both his hands in mine. Slowly I pull one to my lips, then the other. The tension seems to leave his body as I stare into his eyes and move my hands to his chest. "You have nothing to worry about, you know. You don't need to protect me from Peric or from anyone else."

"I know. It's just that he…"

"Just what?"

Grinding his jaw, he simply says, "Doesn't matter." He strokes a finger down my neck and presses his forehead to mine. "Nothing matters right now but you and me."

"Come on, then. Let's get some rest. I'd say we both deserve it."

After shutting the lights off, I guide him back to the bed and lie down next to him, my head on his chest. Holding onto him tightly for fear of losing him again, I listen to his slow, rhythmic breaths as I sink into his arms and let sleep overtake me.

NIGHTMARE

I WAKE to a sharp cry from somewhere deep in Finn's chest.

"Are you okay?" I whisper hoarsely, my heart racing as I press a hand to his cheek. In the dim glow of the still crackling holo-fire, I can see that his eyes are open.

But he doesn't seem to hear me.

"I won't let them take you," he growls in a voice not entirely his own.

"Let who take me? What are you talking about?"

"No," he moans, his hands rolling into fists. His body tenses, back arched, the veins in his neck throbbing. "No!"

Frightened, I slide out of the bed and back away, reaching for the light switch. The room surges to life around us, but it's not enough to lure Finn out of his semi-conscious state.

I speak in a slow, measured tone, hoping to calm him. "Finn...who are you talking about?"

"He's just a boy," he murmurs before shouting, "You can't take him!"

"He...? Are you talking about Merit? I'm sure no one has taken your brother. It's all right. He's fine."

"We have to stop them!"

Hurling himself out of the bed, Finn lunges at me. With a fierce growl, he grabs me by the neck, his powerful hands tightening in a terrifying, asphyxiating grip.

"You can't take him!" he cries. "I'll kill you first!"

"Finn!" I croak, grabbing hold of his wrists and trying in vain to pull his hands from my neck.

But he only tightens his grasp even as my legs begin to weaken under me. It's only when I finally begin to slump to the ground that he lets go, the word *No* echoing over and over again from between his lips.

Dragging myself backward along the floor, I gasp for air, putting as much distance as I can between us. My back hits the far wall as Finn sits down on the bed and lets out a long sigh of relief, burying his face in his hands.

"It's all right," he says, more to himself than to me. "It will be fine now. The threat is gone."

I still can't tell if he's awake or asleep. But I'm certain that he has no idea what he's just done to me.

My heart pounds as I stare at him, confused, frightened, gutted, all at once.

After what feels like minutes of eerie silence, he finally pulls his face up. His eyes, newly bright and full of life, lock on mine.

"Ash," he says with a chuckle. "What are you doing on the floor?"

My hand goes to my neck. "You really don't know, do you?" I whisper, each word painful to utter.

"Know...what?"

I shake my head, tears streaming down my face. When he steps over and reaches for me, I recoil. Slowly, carefully, he crouches in front of me and manages to pull my hand away from my neck.

"What..."

As if he's been assaulted by some great force he leaps backwards, pressing himself against the edge of the bed, a look of sheer horror in his eyes.

"I did that to you...didn't I?"

"Y—you thought I was someone else. You were having a bad dream or something. It's okay—I just need to catch my breath, that's all."

But he shakes his head. "I...I can't believe I hurt you. I'm so sorry, Ash...Oh, God."

"It's okay. Really."

"No, it's not. It's so far from okay. I can't..."

He stares at me for a moment before leaping up and rushing to the door, before disappearing into the hallway.

I wonder with a dull, painful throb in my chest if anything will ever be okay again.

The rest of the night passes in the quiet desolation of darkness. I don't manage to sleep. My eyes are trained on the ceiling overhead, my mind racing a million miles a minute. All I can think about is Finn—how he must feel, knowing what he did.

It wasn't him. The voice I heard, the look in his eyes—it was someone else. Someone inside him, trying to communicate, to warn him about something.

It wasn't his fault.

I need to find him. Talk to him. We can fix this.

By the time morning comes, I'm determined to seek him

out and assure him that accidents happen, and we can move past last night's incident.

But when I knock on his door, there's no answer. I head to the Central Chamber to ask Illian and Kurt if they've seen him, but they only shake their heads apologetically.

It's only when Rys comes to me at nine that I receive the first clue as to Finn's whereabouts. "I have something to show you," he says, handing me the small screen he uses to track Atticus through the woods.

At first, I expect him to reveal Peric's location. But the figure I see striding through the forest is unmistakably Finn in his silver uniform. He moves fast toward the waterfall and in the woods where Illian first came upon us. When he arrives, he seats himself to face the shimmering pool where he and I once swam.

"I have to go find him," I tell Rys, holding up the glass screen. "Can I hold onto this?"

"I can do you one better," he tells me. "Come with me."

Confused, I follow him to his quarters, where he pulls what looks like a small leather wallet out of the drawer in his nightstand.

"I managed to bring a couple of things with me from the Arc," he tells me. "Some of my favorite toys." Opening the case, he extracts a small plastic container and hands it to me. "I've been working on this for some time. Only tried them for the first time the other day, actually."

"What's in here?"

"Just open it."

I do as he says, removing the case's lid only to see what look like two separate compartments, each filled with clear liquid.

"Have you ever worn contact lenses?" he asks.

"No. I mean, I tried some on for a costume when I was younger, but that was it."

"Good, so you're okay with touching your eye, which is more than I can say for myself. I'm too squeamish to wear them."

I stare at one of the little pools of liquid, only to see that there's a small contact lens inside, criss-crossed with a set of the thinnest gray lines. "What are these for? I already have good eyesight."

"Trust me, these will only enhance your vision."

I pull a lens out of the case and step over to a mirror on the wall, where I manage to slip it into my eye.

"How does it feel?"

"All right, I suppose. But everything looks the same."

"Put the second one in."

When I've done as he says, I cross my arms, impatient to get to Finn.

"Now, say 'Connect to Atticus.'"

I watch my reflection as I follow his instructions. My reflection disappears and my mind is overtaken by another sight entirely—one of treetops moving rapidly beneath me. In a disorienting surge, I feel myself soaring over the woods among the mountains.

Dizzy, I reach out for support. Rys grabs my arm, steadying me.

"Say 'Disconnect from Atticus,'" he instructs.

"What *was* that?" I ask when my normal vision returns and I feel my feet once again firmly planted on the floor.

"Atticus," he tells me. "You were seeing through his eyes. The lenses you're wearing allow you to see via any of my birds, so long as you know their name. They're self-cleaning and made of incredibly fine material that breathes and won't tear—and you can leave them in your eyes as long as you like. You can even sleep with them in."

"They're incredible," I tell him. "I'd have to get used to them. But…"

"I can see I'm boring you," he concludes as I shuffle impatiently on my feet.

"I'm sorry—I just have to get to Finn before he disappears for good."

"Do you want me to come with you?"

"It's fine." I say with a shake of my head. "I think I need to talk to him alone, if that's okay."

"Fair enough," Rys sighs. "Good luck, Ash. I really hope you find him."

"So do I. You don't know how much."

When I'm ready, I head up to the woods in my silver uniform, the cloaking setting activated, dagger at my side.

Occasionally, I check to see if Atticus has spotted any change in Finn's location. But from my vantage point high in the trees, I can see that he hasn't moved from his spot, eyes fixed on the small pool.

I half-jog as I make my way through the woods to my destination, and when I arrive, I pull myself out of cloaking mode and call out, "You left me once. Please don't do it again."

Finn turns my way, his eyes red and exhausted, his face pale. I can tell without asking that like me, he suffered through a sleepless night.

"Ash," he says. "You came."

I rush over and throw my arms around him, and he hesitates for a few seconds before pulling me close.

"I don't deserve this," he says softly, pressing a palm to my cheek. "I don't deserve any part of you, not after what I did."

"It wasn't you," I tell him. "Last night...that wasn't you. It didn't even *sound* like you."

"No, it wasn't me. That's the problem—I don't know who or what it was, or what's happening to me...and it's my own fault. I did this to myself. I thought I could help. I thought..."

He shakes his head as if there's no satisfactory way to finish the sentence.

"You *have* helped. You saved Rys and me, remember?"

"It doesn't matter. I nearly killed you last night. Those marks on your neck..."

"Are gone now." With a cautious laugh, I add, "And yes, I'd prefer that you not do that again, truth be told. But I'm not afraid of you, Finn."

He braces against the words. "Maybe you should be," he scolds. "I'm afraid of *myself*. I'm broken, Ash. I'm supposed to protect you, and I..." He stops speaking and bites his lip, shaking his head as if it's too painful to go on.

"Your dream—or vision—was it Merit that you saw?"

He bows his head. "I don't know for sure. Maybe."

"It sounded like someone was taking him."

Finn raises his chin, wincing. "I really don't know. It's a blur. All I know is that there was a boy—and I was furious. I wanted to kill whoever had their hands on him." He turns to me. "But instead, I almost killed you."

"It was an accident. It won't happen again."

"You can't possibly know that."

"Finn, you're one of the kindest people I've ever met. And you're still you, regardless of what you may tell yourself. I know you would never hurt me on purpose."

"A knife lying on a table is harmless, but in the wrong hands, it becomes a deadly weapon. Something came over me when I was sleeping—it comes over me sometimes when I'm awake, too. Flashes of a reality I haven't lived. My dreams have become intense visions of what looks like the future. But sometimes they come during during my waking moments, too. I lose myself—I lose the present."

Something occurs to me then, and my heart starts pounding. "Last night, when I mentioned I wanted you to do something with me, you knew I was going to ask about Peric."

He nods. "I saw him," he says. "In the moment. In the woods—hiding in a shelter. Even though I've never met him, I knew exactly who he was. And I could feel a danger in him."

"A danger? Peric isn't dangerous. I saw him through Atticus—he isn't even armed."

Finn shakes his head. "I don't mean right now, and I don't mean he'll ever hurt you or me."

"So what are you talking about?"

He shakes his head. "I can't say—not because I don't want to, but because I don't know. The information comes in flashes, like I said. Rapidly moving images. I've seen fire, death, people running for their lives—but it's all a blur I don't know *where*, Ash. I don't know when, or why."

"Which means you could be wrong. I mean, has any of it actually happened? I mean, in real life?"

"Once. It was something I saw before the memorial service. You and Rys with the Quantum Sources. I saw you clear as day—it's the reason I knew exactly where to go in the Palace Grounds to find you both. But it was strange; it should have been a happy vision. Instead, it felt like a warning."

"Well, there *was* a huge herd of fake knights trying to trample us to death," I tell him. "That seems like enough reason for a warning."

"I suppose that's true."

"Look—if your mind is sending you these alerts, it's probably happening for a reason. And who knows? Maybe you'll find a way to make sense of them. But for now, I need you to help me find Peric. Are you up for it?"

"I'm up for anything, as long as you promise me something."

"What's that?"

"That if I attack you again, you'll use the Surge to stop me. You won't hesitate. You'll just do it."

I cock my head at him. "Finn…"

His voice is tense, his teeth gritted when he says, "Just promise."

"Okay. I promise if I think you're about to murder me, I'll use the Surge. But you won't, so it doesn't matter."

He smirks. "How do you have so much faith in me?"

"Simple. Because you love me, and I love you. Whatever this thing inside you is—whatever it's doing to you—you're stronger than it is."

Finn pulls his eyes away and winces. "I hope you're right about that last part. As for the first part, I *know* you're right."

I kiss him on the cheek and take his hand.

"Come with me, then. Peric's in these woods somewhere, and whether you think he's dangerous or not, he's the one in danger right now." When Finn looks like he's about to protest, I add, "He tried to help me, and now he's being punished for it. You of all people should understand the injustice in that."

"Fine." To my surprise, Finn smiles, his warmth reassuring. "If you think it's a good idea, let's go find the jackass."

I shoot him a *Be nice* look before scanning the trees for Atticus. When I spot him, he flaps down to a nearby boulder and lands, his eyes locked on mine.

"You know where we're going, don't you?" I ask him with a stroke of my fingers to his silver feathers.

With a low hoot, he takes off once again, guiding us north into the dense forest.

Finn is quiet as our hike begins, but the tension between us has dissipated, the clean mountain air filtering the toxins between us away. After a few minutes he stops, takes my hand, and pulls me close enough to feel his breath stroking my skin. His lips smile against mine for a moment before he kisses me needfully, his hands slipping possessively down my back.

In that moment, time rewinds. Last night's anguish ceases to hang heavy in our minds, and we're just two teenagers without a care in the world, kissing under the shade of a beautiful tree.

When we pull apart, I focus on his eyes, seeking out the boy I love. I'm happy to find him staring back at me, still smiling in spite of all that's happened.

"What was that for?" I ask, my head reeling. "Not that I'm complaining or anything."

"Let's just say the fresh air has cleared my head a little, and I had a sudden desire to remind myself how much I like kissing you."

Part of me wants to stay here in the woods with him, to savor the feel of his body against mine, the taste of his skin, the sense of wonder he instils in me with each touch of his fingers.

But a dull, worried throb in my chest reminds me there's a war coming our way, and if we don't do what we need to, we will soon find ourselves on the losing side.

I kiss Finn's cheek. "We should go—much as I'd like to stay here and see how many more kisses you have in you before you get tired of me."

"I'll never get tired of you, Ash. No matter what."

Our hands clasped, we keep walking until we're close to the rocky overhang where Peric is supposedly hiding out. When Atticus lands in a tree and lets out a quiet call, I murmur "Connect to Atticus," and tighten my hold on Finn's hand.

Spotting Peric crouched in his hideout, I disconnect, look Finn in the eye, and press a finger to my lips. "Let me go talk to him alone for a minute."

Finn tenses. "He could hurt you, Ash."

"Peric wouldn't hurt me. Not in a million years."

At least, I don't think he would.

15

FOUND

I HAVEN'T TOLD Finn about how Peric tried to kiss me once, or about his strange, affectionate touch at the Bastille's town dance. But when I back away from him, there's a quiet understanding in his eyes, like he knows, somehow, and forgives me for allowing myself to have been so close to anyone.

"If he *does* try to hurt you," he says, "I won't be kind to him."

I blow him a quick kiss and turn toward the cave, stepping lightly as I approach. It's mid-afternoon by now, and all I can think is that it's odd for Peric to have remained hidden under the heavy ceiling of stone for so long. I haven't heard a single drone since Finn and I began our hike.

Why wouldn't Peric head out to forage, to hunt? He must be starving by now.

But when my eyes land on him, I understand.

Peric is sitting on the cold floor of the small cave, a dark coat drawn around his shoulders. One arm is crossed over his chest, the other holding his elbow as if supporting it.

From the looks of it, his wrist is swollen from an injury.

He pulls his face up as I approach. His cheeks are pale, beads of sweat glistening on his forehead.

"Ashen Spencer," he says weakly, a wince of pain distorting his admittedly handsome features. "We meet again."

I rush over to crouch by his side. "What happened to you?"

"Took a little spill. Well, no, that's not entirely accurate. When my mother—Veer, I mean—had me kicked out of the Bastille, I got into a bit of a fight with a couple of her goons. They shoved me around a little, but I got the better of them."

"This looks like more than just a shove, Peric. I think you've got a broken wrist. At the very least, it's badly sprained."

"You're probably right. I was trying to sound manly and tough." He holds up his left arm and adds, "I think you might be right."

"We need to get you help. I'm getting you out of here."

"Oh, good. Are we going to the nearest hospital? I think there's one just up the road." His sarcasm cuts through the air like a knife.

"Not exactly." I hesitate for a second before adding, "Do you remember the Consortium stronghold that Veer wanted so desperately to find?"

"The one she searched for for years? Yeah, I seem to recall a thing or two about it. Too bad it doesn't exist, huh?"

I shake my head. "It *does* exist. And I'm going to take you there."

Peric chuckles. "Great. You're going to take me to see the people who killed my parents. This will go well. If I'm lucky, maybe I'll end the day with another broken limb."

He's joking, but I can hear the unmistakable hatred in his voice for the people he perceives as killers.

I'm not convinced that telling him the truth will solve anything, but it's worth a shot.

"Peric," I begin. "The Consortium didn't kill your parents."

He glares at me. "Of course they did. Why would you even say a thing like that? Have they tried to brainwash you into being a loyal little sheep or something?"

"No. I say it because the leader of the stronghold knows who you are. He knows your parents. They're alive, and I think I know where they might be."

He pulls back, a look of confusion in his eyes. After assessing me for a few seconds, he says, "You're actually serious, aren't you?"

"I am."

I fill him in on what Illian told me about the battle and Peric's parents being convinced he was dead. "They thought you were dead. It was Veer who took you from them. She stole you, Peric. She stole your life from you, too."

"With all due respect, Ash, why should I believe anything a Consortium leader says? It sounds like a pretty convenient way to absolve himself."

"You don't have to believe him, or me. All I know is I trust Illian, and he told me your parents went to Santa Fe to escape their pain. There's a train from the stronghold, and we're planning to make the journey. You can come, if you want. But you need to believe me when I say the Consortium isn't out to get you. They're good people. Allies."

He hesitates again, then finally nods. "Fine. But if your buddies try anything, I'll...punch them with my non-broken arm. Or something."

"Fair enough."

He flinches as he pushes himself to his feet with his right hand.

"How long have you been out here?" I ask. "Outside the Bastille?"

"Since not too many days after a certain rebel with a cause called Ashen Spencer waltzed in and 'liberated' our Consortium prisoner then ran away. But more specifically, since I yelled at Veer for what she did to you."

"So it's my fault this happened to you. Of course it is. I'm cursed to ruin everything I touch."

"It's not entirely your fault. I got into an argument with Veer. *Another* argument, I mean. She was convinced the Directorate would blame her for losing you—for all of it. Anyhow, long story short, she doesn't trust me anymore, nor should she. I took your side, I was disloyal to her. In my defense, though, she was being a huge asshole about the whole thing."

"I suppose the Directorate probably *is* pretty cheesed off at her," I reply. "But if it makes Veer feel any better, they did get their hands on me and nearly ended my life."

"They *what?*"

"Long story. Come on." I nod toward the woods, urging him to follow me.

As we begin walking, Finn steps out from the cover of trees, bracing when he lays eyes on Peric. The briefest flash of rage crosses his features, but it quickly fades, replaced by a strained smile.

" Finn," I say, "Peric. Peric, Finn."

Peric eyes him warily before saying, "So, you're the famous Finn. I'd shake your hand, but...I don't really want to."

"Famous?" Finn asks, raising an eyebrow at me.

"I may have spoken about you to a few people in the Bastille. It was probably a bad idea, but I missed you, so…"

"She's very loyal to you, you know," Peric says, and I glare at him, fearful that he's going to say something stupid.

"She's very loyal to everyone she cares about," Finn retorts.

"Tell me about it. I tried to kiss her once, but she would have none of it."

And...there it is.

"Really?" Finn asks, eyeing me with an amused smirk. "I never heard about that...incident."

"Because nothing happened," I snap.

"She's right. Nothing happened. Though if I'd had my way..."

"Peric!" I growl. "Don't make me change my mind and leave you out here to rot."

He raises his hands in surrender, letting out a moan as if he'd forgotten about his injury.

"Come on, you idiot. Let's get back to the Pit and get you patched up. Then you can be as much of an ass as you want."

As we start walking, Finn turns to him, his eyes narrowing when he says, "I should probably warn you...If you try and kiss Ash again, I'll turn your face into a Picasso painting."

As we near the familiar oak tree that conceals the Pit's entrance, Illian and Kurt emerge to greet us.

When Kurt holds up a hand, I quietly signal Peric to stop walking.

"Hello, young man," Illian says, stepping toward us. "I don't suppose you remember me, do you?"

Peric narrows his eyes, a fierce glare boring into Illian's chest as he spots the Consortium's symbol. "I've done my best over the years to erase memories of the Consortium members' faces. You're not my favorite people in the world. But then, you probably know that already."

"You seem to forget your parents are Consortium members."

"My parents died. Veer told me so years ago. And until I see proof to the contrary, I'm afraid I'll continue to believe it."

"Veer is a liar and a manipulator. You of all people must know as much, having spent years of your life by her side."

I see Peric tensing. Illian's presence seems to ignite a quiet furor inside him, and I can't help wondering why the Pit's leader seems so intent on pushing Peric's buttons.

"She looked after me," Peric snaps. "She was almost always kind."

"Kind? Veer?" Illian laughs. "You and I must know two very different women. The Veer I knew would have thrown her own mother in front of a moving train before committing even the smallest act of generosity."

Stepping over, Kurt pulls me close and whispers, "Illian is doing this on purpose. Testing Peric's threshold for rage and possibly violence. He wants to make sure he won't lose it if he's invited into the Pit."

The tactic makes sense, though part of me wishes he wouldn't push the buttons of someone so vulnerable. Peric probably hasn't eaten properly in days; he's bound to be short-tempered and cranky.

But Peric seems to understand the stakes, because he takes a deep breath and says, "You know what? You're right. Veer has lied to us all. So I'll take you at your word, but not because I trust *you*. It's only because I trust Ash."

"Fair enough." Illian and Kurt exchange a quick nod before Illian inputs the code and opens the entrance to the Pit.

"I must have walked past this tree a thousand times over the years," Peric says with a sardonic snicker. "It never occurred to me that I was staring at the stronghold's secret entrance. Veer would lose her mind if she found out it was this close to the Bastille all along."

"Well," Illian says, "unless you plan on telling her, chances are she'll never find out."

"The likelihood of me ever speaking to Veer again is close to zero," Peric tells him. "So no worries there."

When we're inside, Illian and Kurt escort Peric to the infirmary while I take Finn aside with a hand to his arm.

"See? Not all your visions are dire. Peric hasn't endangered anyone."

"Not yet," he replies glumly.

We head to the mess hall, where we find Rys eating lunch and join him. When I've seated myself, I remove the contact lenses he lent me, slip them into their case and hand them back. "These were useful," I tell him. "Thanks for the loan."

"You can keep them if you like," he replies. "For future use."

I shake my head. "I don't think I can handle seeing the world through a bird's eyes. It's terrifying enough through my own."

With a chuckle, Rys says, "I'm amazed you managed to persuade Peric to come here with you. But then, he always did have a thing for you. Even from a distance, I could see that the guy was enamored."

"He's still enamored, clearly," Finn replies. "It's a bit annoying."

"Doesn't matter," I tell them both with a shrug. "It's not like anything was ever going to happen between us." I go silent for a few seconds before adding, "For the record, he did help me when we were in the Bastille. At least, he tried. He's in the infirmary right now because he defended me to Veer."

"Well, then," Finn says, "I suppose I should suck it up and

call him a friend. Besides, I can't exactly blame him for being smitten."

To my shock and horror, Rys interjects, "Hell, I've had a crush on Ash since we were little kids."

I shoot him a look, nearly choking on the peas I just scooped into my mouth.

"You're lying," I finally sputter.

"I'm not." Rys lets out an uncomfortable chuckle, raises his eyebrows apologetically at Finn, and says, "I was always destined to be her friend. Then her enemy. And now I'm aiming for friend again. But you're the only guy she wants, Davenport. You lucky bastard."

"Can we change the subject, please?" I plead. "We've got more important things to think about. Like the Consortium. The coming war. Santa Fe."

"Santa Fe," Rys repeats with a nod. "What do you think we'll find there?"

"Allies, with any luck," I sigh, "though we could find ourselves face to face with our enemy. For all we know, the Directorate has taken over the city and killed anyone who could possibly have helped us."

Rys raises his glass and says, "Then here's hoping we'll find some new friends. Hell, maybe some other poor slob will fall in love with Ash. The more the merrier."

If looks could kill, Rys would be lying on the floor in a pool of his own blood right now.

16

TROUBLE

JUST AS WE FINISH EATING, Illian enters the mess hall and approaches our table. Wordlessly, he looks me in the eye.

"What is it?" I ask. "Has something happened to Peric?"

He shakes his head. "He's fine. I mean, he's angry and untrusting, but he's been patched up, given some painkillers, and he'll be fine. But he would like to speak to you."

"All of us?"

"No. Just you, Ashen."

I glance over at Finn, who looks somewhere halfway between amused and irritated, though I don't get the impression it's me who's annoyed him.

"What should I do?" I ask no one in particular.

"You should talk to him," Illian tells me. "Peric is as close as we'll come to an ally from the Bastille. We need to know what he's seen and heard—it will affect our plans for the future. If Veer is still conspiring with the Directorate..."

"Right, yes. Of course," I say, pushing myself to my feet. "I'll speak to him."

I look at Finn once again, curious to see if he'll protest, but he averts his eyes as if to absolve himself of any involvement.

Without another word, I accompany Illian to the room where Peric is staying. It's small and simple, with a bed, a nightstand, and a dresser. He's showered and received a change of clothing, and now looks much more like one of the Pit's regulars than himself, dressed in gray cotton pants and a t-shirt.

"You all right?" I ask him when Illian's left us alone.

He holds up his bandaged wrist and says, "Just a bad sprain." With a smirk, he adds, "As for all right, I'm not sure what that means anymore." Pulling his chin down, he fixes his eyes on me. "My life was pretty good, you know. Before that day we found you in the woods. I should've known."

"Should've known what?"

"That my mother—Veer, I mean—was up to something that morning. The way she sounded so desperate when she sent us out there that early morning. 'There's a prize in the woods,' she told us. 'Something that will turn the tides for us.'" Peric laughs. "When we found you, I hated you. My mother talked about you like you were a treasure. A gift from the gods. You were more important than any of us could ever be —even Cyntra."

"Cyntra," I repeat. I've largely forced thoughts of my former friend from my mind, like she was a gnat begging to be swatted away. But I wonder now what she's thinking and feeling—what Veer is thinking. I stole their valuable Consortium prisoner from them. Hell, I stole *myself*. I robbed the Bastille of assets that could gain them favor with the Directorate.

Though they still have one precious commodity in their possession:

Women capable of giving birth.

For years, the Bastille has supplied the Directorate with toddlers and young women. Gifts for the wealthiest of the Aristocrats. A bribe to entice the powerful not to destroy the Bastille.

The only question is whether those women and children are still enough to appease the Directorate after Veer's recent failures.

"Who would have thought you would become my closest ally after all was said and done?" Peric muses, shoving a hand through his hair. "Ashen Spencer, the girl I hated more than life itself. And then…"

He fixes his gaze on me in a way that renders me slightly uncomfortable. It's too familiar, somehow. Too possessive.

To make things worse, he rises to his feet and steps closer. "That guy. Finn. What is he to you, really?"

Annoyed by the forward nature of the question, I sneer. "He's everything to me."

"He's damaged. You know that, right? I see it in his eyes. He's broken inside."

"We're all broken," I snap defensively. "You, me, Finn, Rys. We've all lost family and friends."

"What has he lost? He's an Aristocrat, right? Tell me, what does he lack in his life that would make him leave the comfort of the Arc and come all this way?"

"For one thing, his mother used him as a pawn. More than once."

"His mother?"

With a nod, I tell him, "You've seen her, on the screen in the Bastille."

"The Duchess." As his lips form the words, they twist into a smile. "Oh, man, that explains a lot. I'd somehow forgotten you're in love with the Duchess's kid. How...*Shakespearean* of you."

"I don't judge people by their parents," I snap. "If I did, you and I would never have become friends."

As soon as I say the words, I regret it. Veer isn't Peric's biological mother. She's barely his *adoptive* mother, from the sounds of it. She's just an authority figure who has tried to twist and mold Peric into another loyal little soldier in her small army.

"I talked to Illian," Peric says, changing the subject. "I'm going with you to Santa Fe, to find my actual parents. If they're still alive, I mean."

He throws himself onto the bed and twists onto his side, turning to look up at me, his face on his hand. "You should come, too. Leave that Finn behind. You, me, Illian and Kurt. We can call it a reconnaissance mission. I'll search for my parents. And you can be my...protector."

He says the last word with a wicked flash of his eyes that's enough to make me want to slap him across the face.

"I have every intention of going to Santa Fe. With Finn. And Rys. And Atticus. I'll help you find your parents, if they're there. But I'm not your damned protector. I never was."

"We both know that's not true," he says, sitting up, his voice softening a little. "You saved my life once. Possibly twice, if you count today."

"I did what anyone would have done," I reply coldly.

A flash of anger crosses Peric's face, and I get the sense I've hurt his pride. "I was never anything to you, was I? I was just someone useful. Someone who might have given you information that you needed. I was the almost-son of Veer, and nothing more."

"You were on the side of the people who were supposed to

be shielding me from the Directorate. You were also a guy who looked like he wanted to kill me in my sleep." My voice softens a little when I add, "And then...you became my friend."

"Friend," he spits like the word is toxic.

"The sooner you realize friendship is valuable, the better. If I'm only useful to you if I offer more than that, then I'm afraid we'll have to stop pretending we can so much as speak to each other. I'm not your plaything, Peric."

"Oh, you're valuable as a friend. I've never seen anyone so adept at surviving situations that should result in death as you are. You're like a freaking cat about to meet its ninth life. The only question is what will happen after that one is spent. Though I'll give you credit—this seems like a good place to put your mortality to the test."

"We're safe here—all of us. Illian is a good man, you know. He and Kurt both. They're kind and thoughtful, and deeply concerned with what's best for all their people. That could include the Bastille, if Veer would come around and join forces with them."

"It would take a serious disaster to persuade Veer to come around. With her last breath, she'll try to persuade the Directorate to strike a new deal with her. She values power too much, and independence. Answering to Illian and Kurt would break her brain. Not that it matters—the Directorate doesn't trust her anymore, thanks to you."

The words are an accusation, but Peric doesn't utter them with his usual bitterness.

"No one should *ever* have trusted Veer," I tell him. "Anyone who's strictly concerned with their own status—anyone willing to sell off girls and children for their own gain—is not to be trusted."

"I couldn't agree more."

"We need to get on that train as soon as it's ready. I'm going to talk to Illian."

I begin to turn toward the door, but think better of it. "I'll tell him we want to leave right away. In the meantime, I want you to be nice, not just to me, but to Finn."

"I'm always nice."

At that, I laugh. "I seem to recall Veer telling you you're a pain in the ass. In this one circumstance, I'm inclined to agree with her."

Peric grins. "Fine. But you have to admit I'm a *cute* pain in the ass."

I narrow my eyes at him, open the door, and walk out before I'm tempted to punch him in the face.

17

THE ROAD TO SANTA FE

I HEAD to the Pit's surveillance wing, where I find Kurt and Illian staring silently at a large floating screen showing an enormous structure made of silver steel, towering over the remnants of a broken city like a cold, quiet sentinel.

The scene looks like it was filmed in some version of hell.

The building looks familiar, as if I saw it once in a dream. At first, I can't quite place it.

"The largest arcology in the country," Illian tells me over his shoulder. "The one known as the Behemoth, in Manhattan. They say it's run by the nastiest members of the Directorate and an Aristocracy that thrives on violence in ways we've never imagined. They rule not only with an iron fist, but nooses, guillotines and worse. Public hangings are a regular occurrence there—and not just in the arcology. They display dead bodies in the streets below, in case any Dregs are considering rebelling."

My throat goes dry at the thought of it. A wing of the Directorate so brazen, so fearless that they don't even try to hide what they are.

"Do you have any contact with people on the inside?"

"Very little," Kurt replies. "We used to have contact with a Dreg from what used to be called Brooklyn, but we haven't heard from him since before our power went down. We're hoping we can re-establish contact now that our comms are up and running."

"Meanwhile, there's something else you should see, Ashen," Illian says, switching the screen to another scene entirely. This one is quieter, calmer, that of a pretty city set in the desert.

"That's Santa Fe, isn't it?" I ask. "It looks…"

"Intact. Yes, it was. At least, as of several years ago, when this footage was taken via Consortium cameras there. That's the good news. The feeds have since been disconnected—which means we have no way of knowing what's happened since, but we're hopeful that it hasn't been destroyed."

"What's the bad news?"

"Look closer."

I lean forward, examining the city as the camera feeds shift from one to another, from street to street.

"What do you notice?" Illian asks.

"It's…quiet. Like, *silent*. I don't see a single person."

"Exactly."

"You…think there might not be any survivors?" My mind is suddenly on Peric, on the hope I gave him that his parents may yet be alive.

"I can't say," Illian replies. "There's only one way to find out for sure, and you know perfectly well what it is."

"We get on that train."

"So let's go," Kurt says with a nod. "There's nothing to stop us leaving in a few minutes. If the tunnel between here and Santa Fe has held, it shouldn't take more than six hours to get there. We'll leave late tonight, and can only hope to be there by dawn."

"Really?" I ask, hopeful for the first time since this conversation began.

"Really. We'll bring a few of our people for reinforcements. You may bring anyone you like, of course—though I advise you leave Kel behind, given that we don't know what we may find."

"Of course. I just need to say goodbye to Kel and check on Kyra."

Finn and I head toward the residences where Kel and Kyra are staying and find them together in a large common room, surrounded by Pitters. Among them, I recognize a pale woman named Petra and her daughter, a girl with cloudy eyes called Masha.

In the brightness of the new lighting, I can see her face clearly for the first time. Her dull skin and eyes seem to have brightened slightly with the advent of light, and her mother, too, looks brighter, somehow, as if the blood has begun to migrate back to the surface of her skin.

I can tell neither of them can make me out clearly, but both seem to sense our approach, because they throw warm smiles our way as we approach.

"Ashen Spencer," Petra says, extending her arms as if embracing the air around her. "Thank you for what you've done. I see light for the first time in a long time, and it's beautiful."

"You're welcome," I tell her. "We were happy to help."

Kel, who's sitting at a nearby table, runs over and throws his arms around my waist.

"Hey, Little Man," I say with a laugh. "You good?"

"Kyra and I have been playing card games," he says. "Now that we can see, there's tons to do down here!"

"There's tons to do for those of us who can't see, too," Masha says with a laugh. She steps over and shoulders Kel.

"Like what?" he asks.

"I can show you, if you'd like."

He nods, then with a sheepish look on his face, apologizes for the silent gesture. "I mean yes."

"Come with me, then," she tells him, taking him by the hand.

"Can I, Ash?" he asks me with a smile.

"Of course," I tell him. "I'm sure Masha will give you some excellent lessons on the Pit while you're at it. But first, I have something to tell you." A surge of guilt rises up in my throat as I add, "I'm leaving tonight, with a few of the others. I may be gone for a few days."

"Gone where?"

"We're heading to a place called Santa Fe."

"Can we come?" he asks, and I can tell he's hurt that I haven't invited him. "Masha and me?"

I shake my head. "It could be dangerous, and all I want in the world is to protect you both. But I promise we'll be as quick as we can. We're going to try and find some people."

"Good people?"

"Yes. I'm pretty tired of finding bad ones, aren't you?"

"Totally."

"Now, go play. I'll see you when I'm back, okay?"

Kel nods vigorously before running off with Masha.

Laughing, Kyra pushes herself to her feet. "I'm going to go after them to make sure they don't wreak havoc," she tells me. "The other day, they found another exit from the Pit—one through a hatch hidden miles away, in the woods. I found them, thank God, but..."

"Thanks, Kyra," I tell her. Impulsiveness tells me to ask her if she'd like to come to Santa Fe, but I think better of it. She seems so happy here, so at peace. Santa Fe could be grim, and the last thing I want to do is stir memories inside Kyra of the ugliness inflicted on so many by the Directorate. "I can't tell you how much I appreciate everything you're doing for Kel."

"I should be thanking him," she tells me with a smile. "He keeps me sane."

I watch as she heads down the same corridor where Kel and Masha disappeared a minute ago, grateful for her vigilance.

"Well, my little brother won't miss me, at least," I chuckle, but Finn shakes his head.

"Of course he will. He needs you. I think you need him, too."

I stare at him for a moment before saying, "You must miss Merit."

"Like crazy," he says with an almost imperceptible wince. He grinds his jaw for a few seconds then adds, "Promise me something."

"Anything."

"When we take the Arc—when we've finally ended this conflict with the Directorate, anyone still standing needs to find a way to get Merit to safety. He's a good kid. He's smart. He doesn't deserve to die for who his parents are."

"Agreed," I tell him. "I'll do my best to make sure he's safe. But I'm not a general leading an army, Finn. I'm not the commander here. You and I are just foot soldiers."

"Something tells me the rebels on the inside will listen to

you, though. You have a reputation. You've escape the Arc more than once now, and you've earned their respect."

"They think I'm a murderer," I say with a scowl.

"Right now they do," he replies. "But they won't always. Not once you reveal the truth to them."

"Me?" I laugh. "I'm not sure how you think that'll happen, or why you have so much faith. You're the one who should be leading, anyhow. You're far more of a natural than I am."

He shakes his head. "I'll always be stained. The son of the Duchess. The son of an authoritarian nightmare. Illian and Kurt may tolerate me, but they'll never fully trust me. I don't have your blood."

"My blood?"

"Oliver Spencer's blood," he corrects, and I'm not sure if I detect a note of bitterness in his voice. Though I can't quite blame him. It was pure luck that made me the daughter of a man revered by the Consortium.

Then again, it was luck that made me a Dreg and thrust me into a life of loss and struggling.

Luck, it turns out, isn't always a blessing.

"Finn, whoever your parents are, you deserve to live just as much as I do—as much as *anyone* does. And so does Merit. All I want—all I've ever wanted—is to create a better world. But look, we haven't even gone to Santa Fe yet. We have no idea what we'll find there, or who. Let's not talk too heavily about taking the Arc down before we've figured out how we can possibly succeed."

Finn nods his agreement. "To Santa Fe, then. Let's go find out what's waiting for us out there."

THE TRAIN

As the clock nears midnight, we prepare to leave.

At Illian's request, Finn and I transport the two remaining Batts into one of the train's storage compartments in a small but impressively strong metal cart. "A gift for our friends—if indeed we find any at our destination," Illian tells us.

I want to ask if he really thinks we can spare them, but it feels vaguely disrespectful to question his decision-making capabilities, so I keep my mouth shut.

The train, as it turns out, is odd, charming, and a little alarming, all at once. It's not sleek and clean like the ones that shoot at high speed from the Mire's various Sectors into the Hub under the Arc. Instead, it's made up of a series of recycled subway cars, sections of old freight trains, and one or two cars clearly taken from old high-speed passenger rail trains. Each has been redesigned to run on the tunnel's single rail, but I can tell just by looking at the mish-mash of disparate parts that it won't be the smoothest—or fastest—ride in the world.

The good news is that it's ten cars long, and spacious enough to transport several hundred people.

In total, there are only six passengers: Illian, Kurt, Rys, Peric, Finn, and me.

Darryn and Mura, two of Illian's most trusted allies, are in charge of controlling the train and keeping an eye out for potential danger.

One of the freight cars contains an entire communications system that Kurt, Rys and Illian have up and running by the time we arrive. Atticus is perched on an upholstered seat to one side of the comms car, his head turning this way and that as he scans the interior.

"What have we found out?" I ask as I climb inside.

"Not much," Rys tells me. "There's no feed coming in from anywhere near Santa Fe, which could mean any number of things. Most likely all the cameras have been destroyed. The question is when, and who did it—though the second answer is probably obvious."

"So you're saying we could easily be heading into a trap."

"Not *so* easily. The Directorate doesn't know about the Consortium's trains. In all likelihood they killed the camera feeds years ago and haven't given the region a thought since. They probably won't be looking for us."

"*Probably?*" Finn retorts. "The Directorate could have killed every man, woman and child in Santa Fe, for all you know, and it's also possible they've destroyed half the track between here and there."

"Not likely. There's a concealed blast door at the end of the track—one that hides the existence of this rail system. Unless the Directorate found it and somehow opened it from the outside, there's no chance they've damaged the track. Still..."

He turns to Rys, who's staring at a screen next to the one Illian's been looking at. "Can Atticus see in the dark?"

"Of course. He's an owl."

"He's a *drone*."

"He's a drone who can see in the dark, thank you very much."

"Right, then. In that case, he needs to fly ahead of the train to make sure we're not putting ourselves in unnecessary danger. Is that possible?"

"Shouldn't be a problem."

"Good. Thank you. Your owl may be the key to our survival for the next several hours."

When we're finally ready to go, Rys sends Atticus flying ahead, telling us he's programmed him to let us know if the track is damaged or if he sees any other cause for alarm.

"I'll keep an eye out, too," he tells Illian and Kurt. "But I also want to know what we're up against. Which means I need you two to tell me about anything I should be looking for."

The two men exchange a glance then give their agreement.

Meanwhile, Finn and I head to one of the passenger cars, where we find Peric skulking in a corner, his eyes staring through a window at the grim darkness of the tunnel's wall.

I take a seat in front of him and Finn sits down next to me.

"What do you think they'll be like?" Peric's voice startles me, and I turn to look back at him.

"Who?"

"My parents. What do you suppose they're like? Nice? Or angry?"

"I don't know," I tell him. "But if they think they lost their son seven years ago, I imagine they're sad, more than anything else."

"Maybe they *wanted* to lose me. Maybe they left me behind on purpose."

"Peric, no one would do that."

"No?" He shuts his mouth and glares at his reflection in the window. "Parents in the Bastille give up their children all the time, just for a chance at a good life. Children, for them, are currency."

"They're just surviving," I say, surprised to find myself defending the Bastille's residents. "They're just trying to stay alive. Besides, most of them think giving their child to someone in the Arc means a better life for the children, too."

Peric shoots Finn a look and says, "Tell me, did you have such a great freaking life in the Arc, Davenport?"

"Depends. I had every material possession you could want. I had a great education. But I never breathed fresh air. I never saw mountains. I was controlled, monitored, expected to follow in my parents' footsteps. I'm not sure I could tell you it was a great life...but at least I wasn't targeted for slavery or murder."

"Yeah, I guess there's that," Peric says with a derisive snort.

I turn away from the two of them. Each is angry in their way, and both feel abandoned by parents who should have done more for them. But something tells me Finn got the worse deal. Peric's parents thought he was dead when they left. They were heartbroken.

Finn's parents knew he was very much alive, but still used him, still put him in harm's way purely for the amusement of the Wealthies.

The cruelty of it is immeasurable.

When the train finally starts moving, we go silent for a time. Finn reaches over and takes my hand, pulling it to his lips. But he still seems preoccupied, like there's something spinning around inside his head that he can't quite bring himself to say out loud.

After a time, I whisper his name.

"Hmm?" he asks.

"Talk to me. Tell me what's going on in there. Why are you so far away?"

He pulls his chin down and glances toward the floor. His inability to look me in the eye has become a knife, twisting in my side. It's like I repel him now, or worse.

"Have I done something wrong?" I ask, my voice catching.

"No, of course you haven't. It's nothing you've done. I just..."

"Just what?"

He finally turns his head to look at me. But the second our eyes meet, he presses his head back and closes his eyes, like it's pained him. "I told you, I just don't...entirely feel like myself. It's like I feel stronger than I ever have, but I'm slightly afraid of that strength. I feel like I could stop this train with a mere thought, and it's taking everything inside me not to let that happen."

As the train surges forward, I ponder what Finn's saying. "You're forecasting doom, but I don't know why. What's got you worried? Has something happened?"

He opens his mouth to reply but closes it, shakes his head, and presses back into the seat, silent.

"We all have the power to wreak havoc if we want to, you know," I say. "Most of us *choose* not to. That's what distinguishes good people from bad."

"Yeah? Well, I'm the son of a psychopath. *Bad* is in my DNA. Maybe the choice isn't as black and white as you think."

I rise to my feet. I don't want this conversation to

continue. I want the old Finn back, and not this gloomy creature who feels like he could snap at any second.

I glance over at Peric, who's sleeping with his head pressed against the window.

"I'm going to check on the others," I tell Finn. "I'll be back."

But I'm not sure I mean it.

19

THE JOURNEY

I FIND Rys, Illian, and Kurt gathered around the various screens in the tech car. Rys is watching what looks like the interior of the tunnel surging before us. Its walls seem to glow a strange, eerie blue, unlike what I see when I look out the windows.

"We're seeing the tunnel from Atticus's vantage point," Rys explains. "The blue is the reflection of his eyes against the tunnel walls. He's streaking ahead of us and so far, everything is clear."

"Good," I say absently. "That's good to hear."

Rys rises to his feet, takes my arm, and leads me several feet from Kurt and Illian, who are engaged in conversation about something involving weaponry. "Everything okay?"

I hesitate for a moment before telling him, "It's nothing."

Crossing his arms over his chest, he clicks his tongue against his teeth.

"Look, Ash—I know what's going on. I'm not stupid. The shimmer-wall, Finn's behavior, all of it. I know he's implanted himself with some kind of tech. I also know it's hurting you more than you're letting on."

Through gritted teeth, I reply, "It's fine, Rys."

"No. It's not." He reaches out and takes me by both shoulders, forcing me to look into his eyes. "If I were Finn Davenport, I'd take a knife and hack out every piece of whatever's inside me before risking losing you."

"He can't hack it out. He can't remove it. It's part of him now. There's no going back; he told me as much."

Rys narrows his eyes and scowls. "It's still just microchips and circuitry, whatever Finn may have told you. If it can't be removed, it can at least be reprogrammed or better still, disabled. It's just a matter of finding the hacker who knows how to destroy it."

A surge of hope overtakes me for a split second before my shoulders slump again, and I shake my head. "But Finn said…"

"I don't care what Finn said. He's brilliant, but he doesn't know everything. I know you love the guy—but if he loves you as much as I think he does, he'll find a way back to you. I promise."

I've never wanted to hug anyone so much as I want to hug Rys right now, but I resist. Instead, I just smile at him, thank him, and turn around to head back to Finn.

I find him pacing slowly up and down the aisle of the car where I left him. When he sees me, he strides over and takes my hand.

"Ash," he says quietly. "I'm sorry."

"You haven't done anything to be sorry for, so don't apologize." I glance over at Peric, who's still sleeping. "Can we go somewhere to be alone?" I ask quietly.

"Yeah. Let's."

We head for the next car, which turns out to be an old

freight car filled with sleeper bunks. Finn and I curl up together on one, my back pressed to his chest.

For a moment, I consider telling him what Rys said to me about hacking the nanotech, but something tells me he wouldn't listen. If Finn wanted to destroy it, I have no doubt he'd find a way to do it himself. But something is holding him back, convincing him that he needs to stay the course…even if it hurts us both.

"Remember who you are," I command, pulling his arm around me. "Remember *what* you are. You're more than a bunch of microchips or your mother's DNA, Finn. You're a person—and a very good one."

"I'm not so sure about that," he murmurs into my ear. "How can I possibly be as good as you think I am, Ash? I came from monsters. Parents who see me as a commodity, rather than a person. To them, I'm a political prop, a tool. Everything I thought, everything I experienced over the years, every moment I thought they were proud, or that they loved me—it was all fake. None of it was real. There was no affection—only greed."

I go silent, stunned that he's speaking in past tense about the Duke and Duchess as if they're dead to him now, his old life a thing of the past.

"Power can blind people," I say, my voice soft. "Your parents loved you when you were a child. I'm sure they did. They probably still do, in their way. Your mother never wanted you dead. Yes, she wanted to punish you, but she never wanted to lose you, whatever you might think. I don't think even *she* is capable of that level of callousness."

"Maybe you're right," he says. "But maybe not. I suppose we'll never know the truth, will we? It's not like either of us is about to sit her down and ask about her feelings."

"No. I'm not sure either of us wants to be in a position to speak to the Duchess anytime soon."

"Well," Finn says, tightening his arm around my chest. "You're my family now. You and Merit, and Kel. And I promise I'll do all I can to make sure I never fall into the trap that took my parents. I won't allow myself to harden in the way my mother did, no matter what."

I close my eyes and listen to his reassuring voice, his warmth promising that in spite of everything, he remains the Finn I fell in love with.

But I can't entirely convince myself of it. Not with the strange force that's pulling at his insides, at his mind, pelting him with a constant barrage of horror and devastation.

If he wasn't broken by what his mother did to him, the Aegis Implant might prove the final tipping point.

No, I think. *I won't let him disappear into an abyss of despair.*

With those words spinning through my mind, I drift off against him, sleep overtaking me.

That is, until the shrieking of brakes jolts me awake.

20

IMPEDIMENTS

"WHAT'S HAPPENED?" I ask as Finn and I storm into the Comms car.

The train is stopped dead on the tracks. The screen that showed Atticus's vantage point is still hovering above the desktop, but at first, I can't quite figure out what we're looking at. All I see is what looks like a shadowy void made of pure darkness.

"We're nearly at our the end of our journey," Illian tells us. "There's…a problem, though."

"What does Atticus see?" I ask.

"The blast door," Rys replies with a frustrated huff. "Which means we're at the end of the track."

"But that's good, isn't it?"

He nods. "The thing is…"

"There's no way to open it," Rys finishes, gesturing toward the screen. Atticus is on the move now, revealing what looks like an access panel embedded in the wall. Only it's been destroyed, its cover half-fallen off and cracked, its wiring exposed and mangled.

"Did the Directorate do that?" I ask, horrified to think they could have found their way into the tunnel...which would also mean they could have been perilously close to finding their way to the Pit.

"More likely rats. There are tooth marks on the wires."

My heart sinks. "So we're stuck? That's it? We just...give up and turn around?"

"There's no crowbar big enough to pry the damned blast door open," Illian says with a curse under his breath. "But turning around now, when we've come this far—it's not an option."

"Unfortunately, slamming into the door with the train isn't one either," Rys mutters under his breath. "Unless we all want to die horribly."

"Rys, you're a tech genius. There's no way you can, I don't know, rewire the panel?"

"Its wiring is fried, not to mention outdated. Even if I had the parts—which I don't—it would be a challenge. What we need are explosives, or..."

When his eyes land on mine, Finn steps forward, thrusting himself protectively between Rys and myself.

"No way," he says angrily. "Not a damned chance."

"She can do it, Finn. You know she can. She has the strength. She shredded the Directorate's steel cat—she can easily tear metal apart."

My voice is high-pitched when I cry, "Wait, what? You expect me to—" I stop the moment it hits me what he's suggesting, my hands shaking. "No. I can't. I can't. Please..."

"What are you talking about?" Kurt asks, pushing himself to his feet. "What exactly do they want you to do, Ashen?"

"They want me to use the Surge," I tell him. "To blast the door open myself."

Illian eyes me intently, as if he's seriously assessing the pros and cons if I were to go through with it.

"I nearly killed Finn. I don't know what it would do in an enclosed space like this. The train…"

"We'll back it up the track," Illian insists. "That should be enough to keep us safe. Right?" With that, he looks to Rys for an answer.

But Rys raises his hands. "I'm no expert, but…"

"I've only used it on people—and one robot cat," I interrupt. "Not huge, thick metal doors."

Rys looks at me, his eyes pleading. "It's no different, is it?"

"I don't know!" I half-yell. "I don't know what I'm capable of. But I could bring the whole tunnel down. It's not like I've honed the skill or anything."

"Ashen," Illian says quietly, rising to his feet and stepping toward me. "We need you to do this. For the Consortium—your father's organization. For all the people who have died, and for those who still live."

I glare at him, hating that he's right. I can't demand that we turn and go back to the Pit, not now, not after everything we've sacrificed to get to this place.

"Fine," I finally sigh. "I'll go out there. But you need to back the train up—a *lot*. Like I said, I don't know what the Surge might do in an enclosed space like this."

"Ash," Finn says, grabbing my arm. "You can't seriously be considering this."

Pivoting, I search his eyes for comfort. "I need to. We have to get to Santa Fe—we need to see if anyone's alive. Peric's parents, and the rest of them."

Finn narrows his eyes for a moment as if he's angry, and I sense that he's about to say something to try and stop me. But after a moment, his eyes lose their brightness, and the strange, insidious force inside him seems to take hold. He's staring through me as though he's looking at something else entirely.

Finally, he says, "You're right. It's the only way. If we're going to win the quiet war, it must be done."

"Quiet war?"

Finn simply nods, takes my hand, and kisses it. "It will be," he says mysteriously.

"You ready, Ashen?" Illian asks.

"Ready as I'll ever be."

I climb down from the train to see Atticus flapping in the darkness above me, his glowing eyes fixed on my face.

"You need to go with them," I tell him, nodding toward the train, which is already backing up. "I don't want to hurt you."

He lets out a quiet hoot of understanding and flies after the train, landing on the last car's roof.

When it's stopped two hundred or so feet away, I turn back to face the blast door.

"Appropriate name," I mumble under my breath as I fix my eyes on the darkness ahead of me. With Atticus gone I can't see much, only a grim, dark void in front of my eyes.

All I know is that beyond it lies daylight.

Crossing my hands over my chest, I close my eyes and issue a silent command. In my mind's eye, I see the blast door gone, blown into nothing but faint particles of metal scattered about the edges of the track.

I pry my eyes open and in one quick, powerful motion, thrust both palms toward the blast door. A bright blue flash blinds me, my body hurtling backwards through space as though I'm nothing more than a leaf carried on sudden a gust of wind.

I land hard on my back, grateful that I'm still wearing Finn's uniform as I struggle for breath.

After a few seconds, the blindness dissipates. The world above me is clear now— the tunnel's arched ceiling, the walls surrounding me. The terracotta-colored soil I'm grasping in my hands, dry as ground bones.

We made it. We're in New Mexico.

I push myself up onto my elbows to see sunlight pouring joyfully into the tunnel. Where the blast door existed a few seconds ago, there's nothing now but a few ragged edges, hinting at what once was. The tunnel's entrance looks like a giant's fist rammed straight through its center.

But I know better. *I am the fist.*

Behind me, I hear the pounding of excited footsteps. Whose, I'm not sure.

A moment later, Rys's hands are on me, lifting me to my feet.

"Are you all right?"

The words swirl through the air around my head, not entirely clear. It's like I'm underwater and the sound waves are coming at me from every possible direction.

I nod, pressing a hand to my forehead. "I didn't think I could do that," I confess as he takes me by the shoulders, looking to steady me. "I…"

Pulling away, I step over to the wall and press my hands to it, catching my breath as I double over in exhaustion and nausea.

"Is the train okay?" I ask.

"It's fine. Atticus is flying out to look at the city. We're waiting to see what he discovers."

I nod, straightening up. His voice is clearer now, as is my head. "Let's get back to the train, then. I want to see what Atticus finds out."

Rys supports me as we walk back. I stare at the train, now

visible in the shadows of the tunnel, and wonder why Finn didn't run out to make sure I was okay.

When we climb into the comms car, the answer comes quickly.

He's sitting in a seat in the corner, his face in his hands. As we step inside, he pulls his face up to look at me, but barely seems to register my presence.

"Finn?" I say, leaping over and crouching in front of him, my hands on his knees.

"I was…worried about you. Then something came over me. I saw the flames again. I…" He stops talking and shakes his head. "It took everything in me to push the vision away. I'm sorry—I wanted to come make sure you were okay…"

His skin is chalky and clammy, his hair soaked with sweat.

"It's fine," I lie. The truth is, it hurts to see him like this. That I'm losing him slowly, all over again.

But the thing that frightens me most is that his eyes, normally so expressive, so full of life, turn light gray as I look into them.

I've only seen eyes that color on one other face, and I'd hoped never to see them again.

ARRIVAL

WHILE ATTICUS SOARS into the open beyond the tunnel to scan the territory, I keep one eye on Finn, who sits stiffly to the side, staring into space as if focusing all his efforts on keeping his demons at bay.

But every now and then, my focus migrates to a screen floating in front of Rys. Illian and Kurt are gathered around him, watching intently, their breath tight in their chests as they anticipate the worst.

"A mile beyond the tunnel's entrance is Santa Fe," Illian tells us. "At least, it *should* be there."

The landscape spreading out in Atticus's field of vision settles on a long, straight road, broken and battered. The owl soars along it until, in the distance, the distinct outline of buildings begins to take shape.

Rys commands Atticus to rise into the sky, and he does, taking in a literal bird's eye view of the approaching city, which is surrounded by a tall stucco wall.

Atticus approaches the wall then flies over to reveal a close-up view of a welcome sight:

Houses, still perfectly intact. Green vines crawl up their walls, many covered in red or pink flowers.

On one wall, I spot graffiti, and Rys must spot it, too, because he sends Atticus in for a closer look.

As the image grows larger, I recognize it.

A circle, crossed by two swords. The sign of the Consortium.

"I don't see any evidence of attacks or battles," Kurt says, narrowing his eyes at the screen. "Looks like they left quietly, and probably in a hurry."

Dismayed, I sigh. "Any idea where they might have gone?"

"I have a few theories," Illian tells me, straightening up. "But in order to confirm them, we'll need to find some actual people. Which means leaving this tunnel."

"You think that's safe?" I shoot a look at Rys, then Finn, who's still sitting, feverish and pale, on a chair in the corner.

"Atticus will scan for drones," Rys says. "But he hasn't found any evidence of their presence. If the Directorate was ever here, it was a long time ago."

I nod, though I'm unconvinced. Walking out into the open seems foolish, at best. Those of us who aren't cloaked will be making ourselves vulnerable to any motion sensors or cameras the Directorate may have left behind.

But I can see from the resolute look in Illian's eye that I don't have a say in the matter.

"We head out," Illian commands. "No sense in waiting. Besides, they probably already know we're here."

"Who exactly is this *they* you're talking about?"

"Our allies. Those who run the Santa Fe sect of the Consortium."

"With all due respect, it looks to me like our allies turned tail and ran a thousand miles away," Rys protests.

"They ran," Finn says from the shadows, his voice raw. "But they're close."

Illian eyes him with a mix of concern and curiosity. "Why would you say that?"

"I've seen them."

I step over and crouch in front of Finn, taking his hands in my own. "Are you sure?" I ask him quietly.

He nods. "I know how insane it sounds, Ash. But it's true. I've seen them, just like I've seen the boy being taken. It's both clear and foggy—like the image is in my mind, but just beyond my reach." He stops talking and looks at Illian again. "We will find them if we leave now. They're waiting for us."

"I have no idea how you can be so certain," Illian says, "but I agree. We need to leave now."

Leaving behind Darryn and Mura to wait for confirmation that we've found what we're looking for, Illian, Kurt, Finn, Peric, Rys, and I head out into the open air as Atticus flies in high circles in the sky above.

The day is clear and warm, the land before us reflecting the sun in a blinding array of yellows and reds.

As we hike toward the city in silence, I stay close to Finn, whose eyes are locked on the horizon. His body is tense, though he seems to be feeling slightly better. Some of the color has returned to his cheeks, and his eyes have regained some of their brightness.

But I still sense the battle raging inside him, and wish I could say or do something—anything—to help him.

Let me take some of your burden.

Before long, we get to the city's outer wall, where we find a large set of double wooden doors standing open. Glancing around warily, we walk right in, and I admit tacitly that I'm grateful when the doors don't immediately slam shut behind us.

We're greeted by a broad street flanked by tile-roofed adobe houses tucked away behind trademark terra-cotta walls. Each property is quiet, idyllic...and utterly empty.

It's not until we reach the center of the city—the old tourist hub filled with small art galleries and shops—that we see any sign of life.

As we come to a restaurant called the Blue Ghecko, Rys holds up a hand, his eyes fixed on his small glass screen.

"Atticus just spotted something on the next street over," he says quietly. "Two people—a man and a woman—moving this way."

I find myself grasping the hilt of my dagger in my hand as Illian tightens and tells us to stop and wait.

"Shouldn't we go inside?" I ask, eyeing the restaurant's open door. "For cover?"

"Are the man and woman wearing Directorate garb?" he asks Rys quietly.

"No. Khaki clothing. Looks like old army fatigues."

Illian's face relaxes into a smile when he says, "We're fine."

It's only a few seconds before two figures emerge from around the bend in the street up ahead, each carrying a rifle in their hands. Atticus shoots down, swooping and startling them only briefly before they exchange a puzzled look and continue to head in our direction.

"Who are they?" a voice asks from behind me.

I turn to see Peric, who's been silently trudging along with our party like a sullen shadow.

"Friends," Illian says with finality.

He steps toward the pair first, followed by Kurt then the rest of us. Though I don't know who these people are, I find myself thankful that Rys isn't wearing his old Directorate uniform. If these *are* allies, I can only imagine their guns would quickly be trained on anyone stupid enough to display the golden rose on their chest.

"Illian, how nice to see you," the woman says, speaking first. "It's been years." She's smiling warmly, though the man next to her eyes us all warily.

"Emiline," Illian replies. "And Razh. I'm so pleased to see you both."

"Pleased and confused, by the looks of it," the woman chuckles. "You're wondering where the former population of Santa Fe is tucked away."

"I'll admit that I am. But knowing you, they're safe. You always were adept at protecting your own."

"Most of them are safe, yes," she says with a solemn nod.

"Most?"

"Some are long gone. Taken in the days of the Blight."

"Is that why you abandoned the city?"

"Partly. When we heard what was happening to so many cities—the arcologies, the cruelty—we decided to take matters into our own hands. If the Directorate wanted to take Santa Fe, so be it. Our most valuable assets aren't in the city, after all, but hidden under the hills."

"Of course."

"What's he talking about?" I whisper to Rys, who's standing next to me now.

"New Mexico is famous for its weapons," Rys tells me. "Nuclear and other kinds. I've heard there are secret labs out here too—for developing chemical weapons, running genetic experiments, you name it. The sort of thing the Consortium used to thrive on."

"You really think we'll find weapons out here?"

"I do. But I'm not sure they're the sort we really need. What we *need* is an army."

Nodding, I turn my focus back to Emiline and Razh.

Illian is in the process of explaining how we came to be here. "We only recently regained power, thanks to our resourceful friends here. We didn't know what we'd find if we headed in this direction, but I'm glad to see you both standing."

The woman called Emiline eyes our small group and says, "We should get out of the open. Come with us and we'll fill you in on our lives while you fill us in on yours."

Illian nods, and we begin a slow group march, following Emiline and her leery companion.

"It was my understanding the Directorate once considered building another arcology here," Illian says. "What happened?"

"They wanted to. Of course they did—they've built them all over the country. But Santa Fe was home to some powerful people—wealthy ones, who were able to use their powers of persuasion to steer the Directorate away. They claimed the place was too lovely to allow it to be marred by such a monstrosity."

"If only other cities had been so lucky. But surely that wasn't all that dissuaded them. Negotiations and the Directorate don't exactly go hand in hand."

"No, they don't," Emiline says with a sigh.

As we walk, I marvel at the properties that surround us. I was in Santa Fe once when I was little, and remember the stucco walls crawling with red roses. Walls that are still perfectly preserved. The roses, a symbol of the odious organization known as the Directorate, now seem to represent freedom.

"That's where we're headed," the man called Razh says, nodding to a building in the distance. Like the houses, it's an adobe structure of clay-colored stucco, but it's several stories high, a large, steel door standing open on its façade.

"Our old city hall," Emiline says. "It's now become something else entirely."

She leads us inside and Razh closes the door behind us with a loud, echoing clang.

Inside, the air feels dense and thick as if there's no circulation, and though the building is spacious, its ceilings high, I feel suddenly claustrophobic.

"The trains between our strongholds lost power years ago, as you know," Emiline tells Illian, "but there is one train here that still runs. It will take us to the Dwelling."

I've been silent until now but I can't help myself. "Dwelling?"

"Our homes," Emiline says with a smile. "Cliff dwellings. Rooms and entire tunnel networks carved into the rock itself. There are many in the area—some of them used to be considered historical sites, back when people cared about such things. Now the Dwelling is literally keeping us alive by shielding us from the Directorate's eyes."

She leads us down a staircase and a long corridor until we come to a locked door, which Emiline opens with a facial recognition panel to its right.

"Obviously you have electricity," Kurt comments. "I'm impressed."

"Limited amounts. Mostly solar. We could use more, to be sure. Our drones haven't been active in years."

"Drones," Rys repeats. "You have drones?"

"We do," she replies. "Quite a few, actually. Though they're currently unusable—our limited power is required for other things."

"Speaking of which, we brought you a gift," Illian tells her. "It's still on the train, but perhaps we could have our people transport it to the Dwelling."

"A gift?" Emiline asks, intrigued.

"Two, to be precise. Quantum Sources stolen from the King's level in the Arc."

At that, Razh raises an eyebrow, clearly impressed. "I'm not sure how you pulled that off. But it's encouraging to know you have such resourceful people on your side, Illian."

"Resourceful doesn't even begin to cover it."

"May I ask a question?" I ask as we begin walking again.

"Of course," Emiline assures me.

"Why didn't the Directorate destroy Santa Fe? It's not like them to leave things standing."

"Rumor has it that they're hoping to take the city back one day," Emiline replies as she guides us down another hallway, which lights up as we move. "As I said, some of the Aristocrats are fond of the city. So once they decide they're tired of being confined inside the Arc, some of them will no doubt try and lay claim to a perfectly preserved city. That is, if no one stops them."

I narrow my eyes at her. "Something tells me you'd like to."

"I would. Though it would be difficult without destroying the city ourselves. This was our home. It's been hard to let it go—but it would be even harder to see it in ruins."

She continues to lead us until we reach another locked door. Just beyond this one, we find a small, narrow train platform not unlike the one in the Pit.

"This will take us to the Dwelling," Emiline says. "Where

you'll stay with us while we figure out how to win the Quiet War."

Quiet war...

I look over at Finn to see if he's noticed her coincidental choice of words, but he seems entirely focused on the simple act of walking.

I ease over and touch his arm. "Are you all right?"

"I'm fine," he insists, though the perspiration on his brow begs to differ. "Just looking forward to getting to our destination."

As he speaks, the so-called train comes barreling into our sightline, screeching to a halt as it reaches us.

But unlike the one we took from the Pit, it's only one car—a sleek, bullet-shaped silver carriage. We climb inside, easing into comfortable leather seats before the train shoots us toward our mysterious destination.

Rys is sitting a few feet away, with Atticus on his lap. The owl's eyes are closed as though he's taking a well-deserved rest.

Fewer than five minutes pass before the train comes to a stop at another platform, this one embedded in a broad wall of red stone. Our surroundings, lit here and there by what look like halogen bulbs, are cavernous.

We climb down from the car and the two hosts lead us to a large glass elevator, which shoots us up several floors before we climb out.

I gasp when my eyes meet the sight before us.

22

SETTLING IN

WE'RE STANDING near the edge of a high cliff that overlooks a broad valley. In the distance, tucked between rolling green and terracotta-colored hills, lies the city of Santa Fe.

As high up as we seem to be, I feel no breeze on my face, no hit of fresh air as I step toward the cliff's edge. It feels almost like one of the Arc's illusions, the so-called "windows" in the Aristocrats' residences intended to make Wealthies feel as though they're staring at majestic outdoor views when in reality, the windows are nothing more than expensive, deceptive projections stolen from various camera feeds.

But something tells me the view before me is no projection.

I step forward, pressing my hand outward only to realize I'm touching what looks and feels like a thick panel of glass.

"Mirage Shielding," Emiline explains, stepping up next to me. "Invisible from the outside. It can resist bullets, grenades, even some smaller missiles. It's also retractable."

With that, she reaches over to the wall of stone beside her, pressing her hand into what looks like a cleverly disguised switch, and the window slowly slides downward, disappearing into solid stone. A warm blast of wind hits my face before Emiline reverses the mechanism and seals the window back up. "Welcome to the Dwelling's Surveillance Deck. It's impressive, isn't it?"

"When did all this happen?" Illian asks. "The construction of the shields, the underground train...How..."

"Years ago, thanks to a few of the wealthy Santa Fe residents I told you about—the ones who weren't on the Directorate's side. They set this place up while the Arc was being built. I suppose they knew our little corner of the world wouldn't be safe for long."

"I'm looking forward to the grand tour," Illian says with a quick, astonished exhale.

"I imagine you'll want to stay for at least a few days, both to see the place and to negotiate," Emiline says cryptically.

Razh, standing at her side, looks irritated and agitated at once, as if he's still not convinced it was a good idea to let us anywhere near the Dwelling.

"Negotiate?" Illian asks with a wry smile. "Just what are you implying?"

Emiline laughs. "You'd only come here for two things: Weapons and manpower. I know you, Illian. Nothing would bring you out of your hiding spot unless you had a plan hatching in that mind of yours. You intend to take down the Arc, and obviously you're hoping for our help."

"You do know me well."

Razh, who seems less pleased than ever, steps toward Illian, his hands tightening into fists at his sides. "We have no army to offer you. No militia, even. Every able-bodied young man or woman we had was recently sent to the east coast to join the rebels there."

"If they're planning to take on the Behemoth," Kurt says with a raise of his eyebrows, "they're on a suicide mission."

"They're helping the Dregs who are being systematically murdered in the Sectors *surrounding* the Behemoth," Emiline replies. "As penetrating that place is all but impossible. At any rate, it means we have no force to offer you—and even if we did, it wouldn't suffice. Storming the Arc isn't the way to take the Directorate down, Illian. There are other, more sensible ways." With a glance toward Finn and me, she adds, "We can discuss them once we get you all settled in."

She pulls a small device from her pocket and presses the button at its center. Moments later, a woman in a gray jumpsuit arrives with a smile on her face.

"Nora," our hostess says. "These guests have just traveled from the stronghold in Colorado. They're in need of rooms. Would you and the others please escort the younger ones to the south wing? I'll take Illian and Kurt to their quarters."

"It would be my pleasure," the woman says, clapping her hands twice. Instantly, three others—two men and a woman—appear, all dressed similarly. Silently, they guide Rys, Peric, Finn and me down several long hallways until we come to a corridor flanked by wooden doors.

"These are the guest quarters," the woman called Nora says. "Not that we have many guests, as you can imagine. You're the first in years. But we've always been charged with keeping the rooms clean and clear, just in case."

"You were *expecting* guests?" I ask.

"More like hoping," she tells us with a smile. "Emiline always said it was only a matter of time before Illian came calling."

"Do you have weapons?" Peric asks. A strange, direct question. "I mean, other than Emiline and Razh's rifles?"

"We have," Nora replies. "But we also have a few great minds, which are far more dangerous to the Directorate. Now, let's get you to your quarters and you can relax for a little."

Nora and the others show us to four different rooms, two on each side of the hallway of reddish stone. Each room is pleasantly decorated, with paintings on the walls and comfortable-looking double beds.

And each, to my delight, has its own bathroom.

When we've had a chance to scope out our individual quarters, I head over to Finn's room opposite mine and knock on his door.

"Come in," he calls out. When I step inside, he's lying on his bed, looking more like himself than he has since we left the confines of the train.

"You look better."

"I feel fine," he tells me with a grin. "Sorry to freak you out earlier. My mind just got a little addled. Honestly, I'm feeling pretty good."

Though I'm not sure how it's possible, he seems to be telling the truth. His eyes are bright, his skin glowing. For now, at least, he's fought off the demon that was eating away at his insides.

Still, I can't help wondering when it will come back with a vengeance.

"I'm glad to hear it," I tell him.

As if testing him, I lie down next to him. He passes with flying colors when he wraps an arm around me and pulls me close, kissing my neck. I revel in the sensation only for a moment before my mind begins to reel with troubled thoughts.

Finn seems to sense my mood, because his grip tightens. "What is it?" he whispers.

"Do you think we'll really find what we need in this place? It's so peaceful here—so quiet. It seems more like an escape than somewhere you'd come to start a war."

"I don't know what we'll find, but I'll admit I'm wary."

"Why?"

His breath strokes my skin for a few moments before he murmurs, "On the train...the vision I saw...it was different from last time. More real, somehow."

"You said you saw flames."

"I did. Vividly. I could feel their heat, like it was close to scalding my flesh."

"What was on fire?"

He pauses for a few seconds before saying, "Everything."

I want to ask him more questions, but a knock sounds at the door, stealing away my thoughts.

I leap to my feet and step over to open it, expecting to see Rys. But instead, it's Emiline.

"I came to make sure you were settling in all right," she says, throwing a glance toward Finn, who's still lying on the bed. "And from the looks of it, you are."

"I was just checking in on Finn," I tell her apologetically, aware of what she's probably thinking.

She waves her hand and chuckles. "Oh, don't worry about me judging. Around here, we don't care who's in whose room. Young love is an especially valuable commodity, and I'm the last person to want to discourage it."

My cheeks heat at her words and I quickly change the subject. "Actually, Emiline, I'm glad you came by. I have something to ask you."

"Oh?"

"One of the young men we brought with us is hoping his parents might be here with you. He's been through a lot, and it would mean everything to him to find them."

"Of course," she says, her tone gentle and kind. "I'd be delighted to help—particularly as I've just learned you're Oliver Spencer's daughter."

"You knew my father?"

"In name only. But I knew he was a very good man. I was so sorry to hear about his death. It's an honor to meet his daughter—I've heard incredible things about you already, from Illian and Kurt."

"I—thank you," I blush.

There's an awkward silence before Emiline asks, "This friend of yours—what's his name?"

I shoot Finn a glance before I reply, "Peric."

Emiline's face goes white, like she's seen a ghost. "You..." she breathes. "You said *Peric?*"

"Yes," I barely whisper, terrified of what she's about to say. "Do you know if his parents are..."

"Alive?" she asks with a nod. "Very much alive. And yes, they live here in the Dwelling with us. Take me to him—I'd be happy to reunite them."

Delighted, I turn to Finn. "Did you want to come?" I ask excitedly.

"No," he says simply, coldly, and I can tell that the veil that sometimes covers his mind is back, isolating his thoughts, his emotions from me.

For a second, I consider trying to persuade him, but I think better of it and leave the room with Emiline just behind me.

When Peric opens his door, she immediately cups his face in her hands, stunning him into silence.

"Why didn't you tell me who you were?" she asks as he gawks at her, baffled. "Your parents will be overwhelmed with joy to see you—to learn you're..."

"They're alive?" he says, pulling away and shooting me a sideways look.

"I hope it's okay that I told her who you are," I reply. "It wasn't my place, I know. It's just..."

There are tears in his eyes when he says, "No, no. It's fine. I just...I'd given up hoping..."

"Oh, you *should* hope," Emiline says. "Come. I'll take you to them."

I step into the hallway, intending to head back to Finn, but Peric asks me to come with them.

"Me? Why?"

"Honestly? I'm scared. What if they..." He lowers his voice to a whisper when he says, "What if they don't like me?"

I feel like I've stepped into a bizarre alternate universe. The Peric I know would never admit to being afraid, let alone that there's a chance someone in the world might not enjoy him.

"Of course they'll like you, you doof," I tell him with a chuckle. "You're their son."

"Even so," he adds, "I need some moral support. Please come, Ash."

I turn to look down the hall toward Finn's room before sighing, "All right. Yes, of course I'll come with you."

As we take off to follow Emiline, a door opens behind us. I turn and look to see Finn watching us, his eyes dull and cold. In his expression, I see an accusation—though I can't tell if it's aimed at Peric or at me.

But when I open my mouth to call out to him, he backs into the room and shuts the door.

23

REUNION

THRUSTING THOUGHTS OF FINN ASIDE, I follow along as Emiline guides Peric and me through a series of narrow, labyrinthine tunnels dug into the red cliffs. They remind me of the Pit's vast network of hallways—except that the Dwelling is more open and airy, a cool breeze caressing our faces as we move past a glassless window leading to the world beyond the cliffs.

The exposure to the outside instills a sense of quiet fear in me and I tighten as I look out over the rolling hills to the distant buildings of Santa Fe. My pulse calms as I tell myself there's not a drone in sight.

"I understand your concern," Emiline confesses when she sees me staring out the window. "The shields only cover certain sections of the Dwelling. Though we haven't seen a drone around here in years. There was a time when the Directorate lingered around the territory—they wanted to gain access to Los Alamos, mainly. But they gave up when they realized they'd never get through the blast doors."

"Los Alamos," Peric says, seeming to unlock something in his memory. "The nuclear weapons site?"

"That's right. Nuclear, and then some."

"Do you have access to it?"

"There wouldn't be much point anymore," Emiline replies, throwing him a knowing wink. "Anything that was of value in Los Alamos is in our possession, locked deep under the hills some distance from here—though if the Directorate knew that, the landscape would be crawling with them. Point is, we're well equipped to start a nuclear war, if we so choose."

"You're joking," I say.

"I wish I were. We thought about destroying the weapons some years back—getting rid of them once and for all. But too many innocent lives would have been lost. So we keep the most dangerous of them hidden far beneath the earth. Even our residents don't know where they are. It's a measure we've taken for their safety as well as our own."

"What about *other* weapons?" Peric asks a little too eagerly for my taste. "It sounds like there's more than just nukes in this place."

"Our most dangerous weapons are chemical and biological, and most of those are hidden away behind multi-layered security systems. They'll stay put unless we find an extremely compelling reason to remove them from their hiding spot."

Taking down the Directorate is as compelling a reason as any, I think.

But something tells me Emiline isn't the kind of leader to attack an organization like the Directorate without first knowing the odds are very much in her favor. As satisfying as it would be to blow the Arc sky-high, she's right; it would mean murdering multitudes of innocent people.

"Come on," Emiline says, gesturing ahead. "There's something far more interesting—not to mention pleasant—than weapons at the end of this tunnel."

Peric falls back, trailing behind me as our host guides us toward what looks like a large space divided up by walls that don't quite make it to the ceiling.

"This is the Dwelling School," Emiline tells us. "Each of the walls you see before you surrounds a small classroom. We believe in education here, so we hold classes for several hours a day."

"You have a lot of kids here?" Peric asks quietly, and I get the distinct impression that he's trying to stall, to delay the daunting reunion with his parents.

"A few kids, yes. But most of the students are adults. Your parents both teach here. In fact, I believe they're co-leading a course in Navajo History right now. Their room is just up ahead."

She stops when we reach a broad doorway leading into a small classroom that contains ten or so desks. Adults of various ages are focused on the front of the room, where a man and a woman stand before them. The woman is writing directly on the red adobe wall in chalk while the man looks on, clearly fascinated by what she's working on.

The man is tall and distinguished-looking, with a shock of gray hair. The woman has dark brown hair and laugh lines, though something in her eyes looks a little sad.

"The Navajo's method of firing ceramics…" the woman is saying, but she halts cold when she spots Emiline.

"This is unexpected," she says, shifting her gaze to me as her husband turns and eyes us. "To what do we owe this honor?"

Emiline reaches a gentle hand out, and, taking Peric by the shoulder, she guides him to stand in front of her.

When the woman's eyes land on Peric, she looks puzzled for a moment, then seems to suffocate, gasping silently for air as she presses back against the wall.

Her husband, seeming to understand, drops the coffee cup in his hand. It shatters as it slams into the ground, sending water splashing in every direction.

"I guess they recognize you after all," I mutter to Peric out of the corner of my mouth. "And here you thought they'd forgotten about you."

Peric doesn't reply. He doesn't even blink.

He looks like a prey animal trying to decide whether to flee or to freeze in place.

I've never seen him looking so vulnerable, so terrified—not even in the moment we shared near the chalet above the Bastille, when he thought a Directorate Guard was about to end his life.

The woman approaches first.

I look down at her hands—thin fingers, trembling with excitement or fear, or both. The man comes after her, and beyond, the students watch, curious, and I wonder if they have any idea what's happening before their eyes.

"June, David," Emiline says. "I'd like you to meet someone who traveled here from the woods near what used to be Breckenridge. It seems he's been in the Bastille all this time—though I suspect he would rather have been with the two of you."

With those words of confirmation, June drops to her knees on the ground, her face in her hands. She's shaking as her husband kneels down to take her in his arms. His face, too, is stained with tears as he looks up at his son.

Peric leaps forward and then he, too, collapses onto his knees. When he reaches his arms around both of them, the three of them seem to tremble as one entity, sobs of joy filling the air around us like a strange, beautiful chorus.

"I believe class is dismissed," Emiline announces to the enraptured students. "I think we should leave these three alone. They have a lot of catching up to do."

24

MIRACLE

WHEN EMILINE HAS LED me back to my sleeping quarters, I slip inside and lie down on the bed. My heart is telling me to go across the hall and knock on Finn's door, but I choose instead to isolate myself.

The way he was looking at me when I accompanied Emiline and Peric—with those dull, emotionless eyes—I'm not sure I could stand such a glare again right now.

When I've rested for half an hour or so, a knock sounds at my door, and I open it to see Illian standing before me.

"It's time for dinner," he says. "You interested?"

When I glance toward Finn's door, he adds, "I'm afraid Mr. Davenport won't be joining us."

"Why not?"

The muscle in Illian's cheek twitches as he says, "He came to find me a little while ago, Ashen. He was...agitated. He insisted there was a threat against the Dwelling—that an attack was coming. I told him he was wrong, and when he insisted on seeing for himself, I took him to one of the

Dwelling's Comms rooms and showed him the camera feeds. The sky is perfectly clear, and there's nothing remotely threatening out there. He seemed frazzled when I presented him with the facts—as if reality was contradicting something in his mind. But he gathered himself, apologized, and said he needed to clear his head. So I escorted him back to his room. He's resting now."

"That's good," I tell him, searching my mind for some kind of excuse for Finn's behavior. "He's had a hard time lately. He—"

"Ashen..." Illian says my name with all the sympathy the two syllables can possibly contain. "He's not well. I can see that as clearly as my hand in front of my face. You don't need to cover for him."

"He's fine most of the time," I insist. "He just has these moments when he..." I bite my lip, scolding myself for coming so close to revealing Finn's secret. I don't know how Illian would react if he were to learn about Finn's self-inflicted nanotechnology, given that Finn has admitted himself how unstable it is. "He's just exhausted, I think," I add with as much nonchalance as I can muster. "He's been through a lot."

"Look, I know he's a fine young man, and that whatever is happening with him may pass with some rest. But we can't afford to risk this mission. We're here to strategize, to plan. Having one of our own people ranting about nonexistent attacks is no help, to put it mildly. If it comes down to it, I'll be forced to take action."

"Action?" I retort defensively. "What's that supposed to mean?"

"It means whatever it needs to. I won't hurt him, of course

—I would never do that. But we're living in a very fragile moment right now. We need all hands on deck, all minds focused. Finn is a distraction to you, most of all—and we *need* you."

I pull my eyes to the floor when I say, "I understand. But Finn is…"

"He's all right. I have no doubt he'll be asleep for hours. Honestly, he looked like he could use the rest."

I want to go to him, to make sure Illian's right. But instead of insisting, I simply nod and say, "Thank you. I…I think I'm ready for dinner, then."

In silence, I accompany him to a dining room with a table large enough to accommodate twenty or so people. Around its perimeter are Razh, Rys, Kurt, and Emiline.

Peric and his parents are absent, and I can only assume they're still catching up on their lost years. As tortured as I feel to know Finn is suffering, the thought of a family's pure joy brings a smile to my face.

"Two others will be here soon to join us," Emiline explains as we seat ourselves. I'm assuming she's talking about Darryn and Mura, who have probably already wheeled the Batts to Santa Fe to meet Emiline's escorts. "In the meantime, we can begin talking strategy." She looks around the table, then fixes her eyes firmly on Illian. "We are not a community of scrappers here. There are exactly three-hundred-and-thirty people left here, and as I've already told you, we can't offer you soldiers. We have weapons, some of which are incredibly powerful, but given that you aren't setting out to blow the Arc to pieces, we need to cast them aside and consider other tactics."

"You're telling us everything we *can't* do," Illian replies, his tone betraying his frustration. "What exactly do you suggest?"

"We approach the Arc's residents from the standpoint of what I call Verity Warfare."

"Verity?" Rys asks. "As in truth?"

"Exactly. We impart the truth to those who live in the Arc under false pretenses. We expose their leaders for the murderers and liars they are."

"You do realize the Directorate is a powerful propaganda machine, right?" Illian replies, his tone almost patronizing. "They manipulated millions of people into leaving their homes behind and moving into arcologies to feed into the coffers of the wealthiest members of society. They're *masters* of deception. If we reveal the truth, they'll simply call us liars."

"I'm not so sure," Rys interjects.

"What do you mean?"

For a moment, Rys looks self-conscious, as if he wishes he hadn't said a thing. But he speaks up, raising his chin high as if assuming the role of a military strategist. "Word has begun to circulate in the Arc. Before Ash and Finn's fight, even, there were rumors about a rebel Dreg who had fought the King's son and won. To the people in the Arc who are growing disillusioned with the directorate, Ash is a hero—and I can only guess her fight with Finn led to more rumors spreading."

Emiline nods. "As gifted as the Directorate is at deception, their tactics can be used against them. What we need to understand is that our most powerful weapon—or *weapons*, rather—reside inside the Arc. They're the people themselves. The ones who have begun to feel controlled, imprisoned. The ones who are craving what we have to show them."

Illian and Kurt exchange a look, and I watch as Illian's hands clench into fists on the table. Tension overtakes his face, the irritability of a man who's waited for years for an opportunity that, as it turns out, doesn't exist.

There is no army for him here. No weapon of mass destruction.

Only…*words.*

"Fear will not turn the tide in our favor," he growls. "Fear is what has torn our nation apart."

"You're disappointed that we aren't offering you an arsenal of brutal weaponry or a battalion of blood-thirsty fighters," Razh says. "But we do have options. Truth is only our starting point."

"And after we've told them the truth?" Illian asks.

"We figure out just how far we're willing to go to win this war."

"You're proposing that we fight a war using little more than facts," Kurt protests. "But facts don't take down the powerful—if they did, most Aristocrats and the entire Directorate would be in prison."

"Now you're beginning to get it," Emiline says with a cunning smile. "Prison is exactly where they belong, and we have every intention of putting them there. But first, we need to gain the upper hand."

"How?"

"Recently, someone came to us. Someone who has lived inside the Arc since almost the beginning. She brought us a valuable gift, as well as the man who knows how to use it—a man some of us have met before. I propose that we spend a few days working toward a plan of action and then figure out how to land the death blow."

"I'm not entirely sure we're in any position to land even the *weakest* blow," Kurt sighs, reaching for Illian's hand. "But I suppose if we don't try, we're guaranteed to lose, aren't we?"

Illian leans forward and narrows his eyes at Emiline. "This contact of yours—how did she manage to escape the Arc?"

"The same way she managed to acquire a vehicle to travel all this way without being pursued. She managed to pose as Directorate Guard, thanks to a little help on the inside."

Rys and I exchange a look, and I almost want to laugh. After nearly being bombed into oblivion on the road out of the Arc, it's a wonder someone else managed such a smooth escape.

"Is your contact a spy or something?" I ask, pondering who it could possibly be. "She sounds kind of incredible."

"I suppose she is, though until recently, she was something else entirely. And I believe you know her, Ashen."

Emiline rises to her feet and strides over to open the dining room's door. A moment later, a young woman strides into the room, her hair darkly twisted into an array of intricate braids on top of her head. Her smile is warm and inviting, her eyes bright.

And the first thing she does is sprint over to throw her arms around me.

"Diva..." I gasp, unbelieving.

"Surprise!" she sings, entertaining us all with a little dance of triumph.

I can barely string my words together as I stammer, "The last time I saw you..."

The last time I saw you, I was about to fight Finn...and my whole life was about to change.

"You two know each other?" Illian asks with a confused smirk.

"We go way back," Diva says. "Ashen is my hero. She's the one who opened my eyes to the Directorate's horrible treatment of Dregs. God, I still hate using that word, even after all this time."

"Okay, you're going to have to explain this to me," I tell

her. "Because right now, I'm just…stunned. How did you end up here? How did you even know about this place?"

"The professor told me all about it," she beams.

"The professor?"

Diva seats herself next to me, taking my hand in hers. "Where do I begin?" she asks. "Let's just say you inspired me to get out of the Arc. Well, you and the guards who looked like they were ready to shoot a giant hole in my chest every time I walked by them. I had a…*friend*—one I'd made some time ago—in the Directorate Guard. He implanted me with a Directorate Guard Identification unit that gave me permission to do what they call Long Distance Surveillance, which means I could come and go as I pleased. He also got me a vehicle and introduced me to the man who directed me here. Funny old guy—he's a scientist. He knows more about the Arc than anyone I've ever met. About other things, too. Can you believe I had to hide him in the trunk for half our journey?"

"You brought a scientist here—someone from the Arc. Who?"

"He's super-smart. And the wild part is he told me he knows you."

"Knows me? I don't know any scientists from the Arc, other than the Duke—and there's no way *he* would ever have helped you get here."

"All I know is that the professor told me he's spoken to you before. He said you were neighbors for a time."

"Neighbors…" I echo. A memory floods my mind of sitting in a cell in the Hold, the Arc's desolate prison system. I had a neighbor—a scientist who told me about the Directorate's plans to develop potent biological weapons that would make the Blight look like child's play.

"I never even saw his face," I say softly. "But he was kind. He saved Kel when he was taken by the Duchess. He…" My eyes lock on Diva's again. "What's his name?"

"Professor Astrum Lyon," a voice behind me says. "At your service, Ashen Spencer."

25

THE SPY

THE PROFESSOR IS a short man with a round face, glasses, and a neatly-trimmed white beard. He's dressed in a slightly ratty-looking tweed jacket with elbow patches, a stained white button-down shirt and corduroy pants that remind me of my father.

I freeze, unsure if I should hug him or be terrified of him. But as I look into his eyes, I'm immediately comforted by a kindness and a wisdom I'm not entirely accustomed to.

"Let's eat," Emiline says cheerfully. "We can talk about our plans another time, when these two have had a chance to reunite."

Our companions seem perfectly content to delay our strategy session in terms of filling our stomachs. Diva rises to her feet to offer Lyon her chair before seating herself next to Rys, who looks both intimidated and delighted to find himself in such close proximity to the attractive young woman.

As the professor seats himself, the Dwelling's staff bring us plates of food and we feast as we chat.

"You really are the one, aren't you?" I ask. "The man who

talked to me through the wall in the Hold, and who helped Kyra when Kel was taken."

"I am."

"How did you get out? No one escapes that place."

"You're not wrong." Lyon smiles. "Normally they would have tortured me. Or offered me a Champion, who would have died on my behalf before the Directorate murdered me. You know, the usual song and dance. But I managed to work my way out easily enough. Amazing what people will do when made offers they can't refuse."

"Meaning?"

"One of the guards in the Hold had a wife who was terminally ill. I offered him a cure in exchange for my freedom. He jumped at the chance."

"What was her illness?"

"Cancer. It was spreading, and he was desperate. The guard found out through the grapevine I'd been on the team who developed the Xenocell technology responsible for curing every case among the Aristocracy in the last decade."

"Xenocell?"

"Microscopic, organic bots introduced into the human body. They act like cells—they replicate, they morph and adapt, changing the human body from the inside out. And they can kill cancer cells within hours of their introduction into our systems."

"They can kill cells..." I half-whisper. "Tell me—could they kill other things, too?"

"Dare I ask what you're talking about?"

I hesitate, then clamp my mouth shut. "It's nothing. I just..."

"I do hope you know you can trust me, Ashen. I'm here to

help the Consortium. To fight the only way I know how—from a distance." At that, he chuckles.

"I know," I assure him. "After what you did for Kel—getting him out of the Davenport residence—I owe you so much."

"You owe me nothing. Your father was a good man who didn't deserve the legacy he was ultimately saddled with. It's my pleasure to help."

"Thank you. Really."

Lyon waves his hand as if to assure me it was all in a day's work. "Tell me something," he says. "Young Mr. Davenport—is he all right?"

"Finn? You've met him?"

He shakes his head. "Not exactly. I was doing some quiet work in the Comms room when he issued Illian his warning of things to come. To be honest, I was quite interested in what he had to say—and in his irises. Light gray is not a color one normally sees in human eyes."

I tighten at those words. Each time Finn's eyes change to gray, a piece of him seems to die. The thought is a knife in my heart.

"He's been through a lot recently—his parents..."

"Yes, I know. The Duke and Duchess are horrid people, which in itself is enough to traumatize any child." He lowers his voice when he adds, "But you and I both know this isn't about his parents, or even his exhaustion. It's about nanotechnology."

My eyes go wide. "So, you know what he did to himself."

"I know he's implanted, yes," he nods. "I've seen this sort of thing before, albeit on a more experimental level. Geneticists have attempted to implant nanotech in humans a multitude of times over the years, always with...mixed results. I'm sure you've seen the Duchess's monstrous Cyphers."

"I have," I reply. "But Finn isn't like them."

"No, thank God he's not." Lyon clears his throat, his gaze intent on mine and filled with a kindness that nearly brings tears to my eyes.

"He's struggling," he says. "Fighting to hold onto what makes him Finn. There's a powerful force inside him, combatting his human side and struggling for supremacy. Nanotech is powerful, insidious. It plays with the mind, unless it's perfectly calibrated to complement the individual."

I nod, hesitant to reveal that I'm also implanted—but that I haven't exhibited any of Finn's symptoms. If anything, I feel more balanced, more powerful, more *me* than ever before.

"Tell me," Lyon says, "what sort of enhancement does he have?"

I look around to make sure no one's listening before replying, "He called it an Aegis Implant. It allows him to create a sort of shield around him, and shimmer-walls that are so strong even charging horses can't get through them."

"Ah." Lyon looks as if his mind is going a thousand miles a minute, processing what I've just told him. "That explains a good deal, both about him and about you."

"What could it possibly say about me?"

"Well, let's see." Lyon smiles. "You've looked at the door no fewer than twenty times since I sat down next to you—not because I'm dull company, but because your mind is constantly on him. You know Finn is resting, so your worry isn't for his immediate well-being; it's for the future. You feel him growing distant from you, like you're losing him slowly. And in a way, you are."

I want to protest, to tell him he's wrong. But I'd be lying.

I nod, defeated. "Every time I try and reach out to him, he ends up shutting down. It's like this thing inside him is taking over, steering his mind away from me, from us, from everything. Except for..."

"Except for?"

"He sees things—horrible things. I think that's why he told Illian this place was in danger. He gets this feeling that something is going to happen, and it's all he can think about."

"Interesting," Lyon says, stroking his beard. "Tell me, do you know what intuition is?"

I shrug. "It's a feeling. A hunch. Like you know without thinking if someone is good or bad, or if a situation is potentially dangerous."

"Yes. But it's more than just those things. Intuition is a form of self-preservation, an evolutionary instinct deep inside our minds. A mental shield, as it were, to protect us from danger. When we have those hunches—those feelings—it's because our minds are processing information so rapidly that we're unaware it's even happening. Our brains scan like computers through a multitude of scenarios, through every piece of data we've been given, until we establish a conclusion."

"Okay, but what does that have to do with—" I begin to ask, but Lyon cuts me off.

"I suspect that Finn's brain moves faster than most people's. He's always been a highly intelligent young man, as far as I can gather. But with the enhancement from the Aegis Implant, there's more to him than the simple ability to conjure a physical barrier. He protects himself emotionally, too. Which means he shuts down when confronted with a harrowing situation or a terrifying thought. He pulls away— or rather, the nanotech forces him to pull away as it runs through its multitude of scenarios, using his mind to scan them like a powerful computer."

"They're more than just thoughts," I whisper, leaning in close. "He has dreams, although I'm not sure I should call them that, because sometimes they happen when he's awake, too. Visions of some apocalypse that hasn't happened yet. He's seen a young boy being taken by some enemy. He talks about fire, about people screaming. It's almost like he's seeing snippets of the future. But when I say it out loud, it sounds insane."

"Not insane," Lyon says, taking off his glasses and cleaning them with the hem of his shirt. "Predicting the future is entirely fathomable."

"No, it's not," I protest. "It's impossible."

"Is it? Can we not forecast rain or snow days in advance? Can we not predict how an illness will spread through a person's body?"

I lower my chin and shoot him a dubious look. "Those things are based on science. On what we already know. Not on nightmarish visions."

"Ah. But what you're forgetting is that what Finn sees in his visions—what his mind is processing when he sees the images—it's all based on what he already knows. The difference is that his mind is working faster and harder than we can conceive, processing an incredible amount of information at a highly accelerated rate. Think of him as a watchdog who barks madly before the intruder is anywhere near the house. Did the dog hear the intruder, or simply *sense* that he was coming?"

"So you're saying the things Finn is seeing will definitely come to pass?"

"Not necessarily. But I am saying they *could*—and that no

one would know better than Finn himself." He pushes out a hard sigh. "Still, he's not a soothsayer. No one is. He is merely a forecaster of danger. It's a curse he's inflicted on himself in the form of the Aegis Implant—a curse he probably never expected."

When I lower my eyes, Lyon reaches a hand out, placing it gently on mine. "I know it hurts to see him like this. It hurts that he's altered. There are ways to bring him back, you know, if he *chooses* to come back."

I raise my chin and stare him in the eye. "What ways? How?"

"You asked earlier if the Xenocells can destroy other entities inside the human body, and the answer is yes." He reaches into his pocket and extracts a small vial of clear liquid, which he hands over. "I brought a supply with me when I left the Arc —as well as other compounds. I don't travel anywhere without them."

"If Finn injects this...it will destroy the tech?"

"Yes. It would be hard on his body, make no mistake. He would suffer something like withdrawal symptoms for a time, but I'm sure he'd be just fine in the end."

I gaze at the vial in my hand before reaching out to hand it back to Lyon.

"I can't take this," I tell him. "I couldn't inject Finn. It's not my choice."

"No, of course not," he says, but he doesn't take it. "It's his choice. He has to decide who he wants to be, and if the nanotech is as powerful as I suspect, his mind will have to fight a long, hard battle before it can emerge victorious. In the meantime, take every piece of him you can get, savor every moment when he manages to fight off the effects of the tech.

Count yourself fortunate to have him in your life in the limited capacity that you do."

I suck in my cheeks as I slip the vial into my pocket. "I am fortunate," I tell him. "I only wish I could do more to help him."

"You're helping him by supporting him," Lyon says. "And as unlikely as it sounds, maybe one day soon, you'll find yourself grateful for his abilities."

LOST

WHEN I'VE BID Lyon and the others goodnight and headed back to our corridor, I knock gently on Finn's door, half terrified of what I might find inside.

When a hoarse voice calls out, "Come in," I push the door open, closing it behind me and pressing my back to it.

Finn is sitting up on his bed, a distant look in his eyes. But there's no trace of the irrational wildness that Illian described, at least. No evidence of the strange, frightening gray irises Lyon and I have both seen on his face.

"You all right?" I ask, daring a few steps toward him.

"I'm fine," he tells me. "Except…" He turns to look at me. "I know I freaked Illian out. I can't quite remember all of it—all I know is that I was ranting like a madman. He must have wanted to lock me up."

"He knows you're going through a rough patch." I exhale, staring down at my feet, apprehensive about how he might interpret my next words. My hand reaches instinctively for my pocket, where I finger the small vial the professor gave me. "I met someone tonight. Professor Lyon."

"The man with the beard and glasses," he replies with a nod. "Don't ask me how I know his name; I don't understand much about my brain these days. He was in the Comms room when I..." He flinches. "He must think I'm nuts, huh?"

I smile faintly and shake my head. "He knows about the Aegis Implant. He also seems to understand what's going on inside your mind—at least, he has a theory. And a possible solution."

A look of quiet irritation slips over Finn's features as he says, "Does this *solution* involve hurting me?"

"What? No, of course not. It's just...look, Finn—there's a way to get rid of the nanotech. If you want to, I mean. You could go back to being yourself—you could get rid of the visions. It would mean you couldn't create a shimmer-wall, but..."

With that, I extract the vial. "According to Lyon, this will destroy the Aegis Implant, break it down until it's harmless. He said it might be hard on your body, but..."

Finn shakes his head violently. "I don't want it," he growls, his eyes robbed of their color as the entity inside him rises up to challenge me.

"That's fine, of course," I tell him, putting the vial back in my pocket. "But when you're ready, it's here for you."

"You're not hearing me." He presses his hands to his temples and shakes his head violently, trying to fight off an invisible foe. "Take it away. Now! I want no part of it."

His voice is rising, frantic and hostile. Thrusting a hand out violently, he leaps off the bed.

"Finn!" I shout, raising my hands protectively in front of my face.

They collide with something hard and cold to the touch. I pull back, horrified to realize a near-invisible shield stands mere inches from my face. A barrier, dividing the room in two and separating me from Finn.

He raised a shimmer-wall to defend himself against...me.

"You're trying to control me," he snarls in a voice that sounds like it's coming from another person, another place. "You want to alter me to suit your needs. It won't happen. I won't allow it."

He paces back and forth on the other side of the barrier, his breath heavy.

"I'm not trying to control you," I insist, my voice pleading. "I just wanted you to know there are options."

"Options?" he asks with a snicker. "Maybe I don't *want* options. Maybe this version of me is the best possible one. Maybe this happened to me for a reason, and maybe I *like* it. I need this power. *We* need it." He stops and presses his palms to the shimmer-wall, staring at me with cold eyes. "War is coming to this place, whether you see it or not. It is coming for us all. There is no safety in the Dwelling. No safety anywhere. They see us, Ashen."

Ashen.

Finn hasn't called me that since the earliest days of our relationship.

But this person isn't Finn. I'm not sure he's a person at all.

"There won't be a war here, Finn." I use his name in hopes of bringing him back, of banishing the stranger who's taken up residence inside him. "This place is hidden from sight. You know as well as I do that if the Directorate knew about it, they would have destroyed it years ago."

"They will know soon enough. And when they do, there's little chance for any of us. Do you hear me?" He begins pacing faster now, his hand raking violently through his hair. "I have to stop them. I have to find a way. But no one will listen—no one believes me. The screaming—I can hear it like it's happening right now, in this very room." He stops, looks into my eyes, and says, "This isn't the only place where there will be suffering and death."

"Where else?" I ask, my voice pleading. "What are you talking about? What's going to happen?"

I back away, tears streaming down my face. There's something so alien in his voice, so terrifying, yet I can't bring myself to leave him. As long as the smallest piece of Finn still exists inside his mind, his body...I can't abandon him.

"So much pain, so many voices silenced. Some of them are cruel, but it's not for us to decide whether they live or die. We should not be allowed that power, and yet it will be ours soon enough..."

"I don't understand," I murmur. "What are you saying?"

He pulls his eyes upward, as though he's searching the sky through solid stone. "When they come, we must be ready. Now, leave me. I need to think."

"Finn..."

"Go!"

I spin around, open the door, and rush into my room, slamming the door and throwing myself onto the bed.

I don't know who I was just speaking to—the young man with the wild eyes, a feral rage growing inside him like a threatening, all-consuming wave.

But it was not the young man I know and love.

THE CAVES

I'm desperate to go back and speak to Finn, to try and reason with him. But I tell myself there's no reasoning with someone whose mind has been stolen away.

I fall asleep on a tear-stained pillow, mourning the boy I've lost for the second time. He's still in there, I know he is. But I'm not strong enough to go searching for him.

When morning comes, I find myself surprised to realize I've actually slept.

Just as I manage to pull myself up to a sitting position, a knock sounds at the door and Rys pokes his head in.

"Oh...sorry," he says when he sees my puffy eyes and blotchy cheeks. "Emiline...wants to show us around the Dwelling this morning. I thought you might be interested, but..." He steps closer. "Are you okay?"

"I'll be fine," I tell him, lying in the hopes of reassuring us both. "But maybe I should check on Finn before—"

"Finn's not in his room," Rys stammers. "I...I thought you knew."

Those words are enough to jolt me into alertness. "Where is he?"

"The infirmary. He's been there since last night. He's been sedated."

"Sedated?" I climb out of the bed, ready to go tearing out the door. "Where's the infirmary? I need to go see him. I have to…"

"Ash—he's not conscious. At least, as of half an hour ago he wasn't."

"But he needs me. He's…"

But Rys shakes his head. "Look, he came to my room last night. He looked like crap, honestly. He said he needed to get himself somewhere isolated—that he wanted to be sedated so he could calm the visions for a while. He told me he'd hurt you and that he didn't want to do it anymore. Honestly, at first, I thought he was saying he'd hit you or something. I was ready to murder him."

Shaking my head, I say, "No. He would never hit me."

It's the truth. Still, if Rys knew Finn had once wrapped his hands around my throat, I have little doubt that he *would* try to kill him.

But it wasn't Finn who did that to me. His eyes, overtaken by the force inside him, looked through me, icy and unseeing.

"I need to shower and get dressed," I say, in sudden dire need of solitude. "I'll meet you in the hallway in a minute, okay?"

"Sure. I'll keep an eye out."

A few minutes later, after I've had a chance to calm down, Rys guides me to large room where we find Emiline awaiting us. The space is bright and open, with an oval window to one side that looks out onto the broad valley below. In the distance I can just make out the low silhouettes of Santa Fe's adobe buildings, undisturbed and idyllic.

On the chamber's curved stone walls are a series of paintings of New Mexico's signature houses, the desert, the mountains.

"Welcome to the gallery," Emiline tells us both. "We managed to bring these from the city. It's hard for this community to imagine life without art."

"Is everyone in the Dwelling an artist?" Rys asks, and I'm grateful he's taken the lead. Right now, I don't trust my voice not to break if I should try to speak.

"No, but everyone here sees value in art. People used to flock to Santa Fe to be part of the scene. Our population in the Dwelling is a mixture of former Wealthies and artists—and some are both."

"*Former* Wealthies?" Rys asks. "Are you saying they lost their money when they left the city?"

"I'm saying money means nothing in a place like this. Our world has advanced beyond it. Even in the arcologies, the only currency that truly matters now is power. And power is not of great importance to us."

Perusing the wall of paintings, Rys says, "You know, I like it here. I wouldn't mind staying."

"Something tells me you'd be a useful addition," Emiline tells him. "If that owl of yours is any indication, at least. You do seem to have a way with drones."

"I do. But for the record, if you want my birds transporting nukes, you'll have to give me danger pay," Rys laughs. "Even if money *is* meaningless around here. Or a bit of property would be nice. I'm just saying."

"One day, we would happily pay you in land. There's lots to be had around here, if we can only find a way to reclaim it."

"Land is good." Rys's tone is wistful when he adds, "It's all I've ever wanted, really."

It's true. Rys has always been ambitious, but there's a part of him that craves the simple life, too. Somewhere he can live in peace, surrounded by people he cares about—preferably with a house large enough to host his multitude of pastimes.

"And you, Ashen?" Emiline asks, eyeing me. "What would make you happy?"

The question takes me by surprise, and my eyes fill with tears as I contemplate the answer.

The truth?

Getting Finn back. The real Finn—not the one who's turned into a nightmare machine bent on predicting a horrifying future for us all.

But I tell her, "Finally letting the people know what the Directorate truly is. Winning this Quiet War, as you call it, so we can get on with our lives. And moving my brother somewhere safe and beautiful where he can grow up without the Directorate's constant threats lingering over his head."

"Which is precisely why we need to find a way to beat them," Illian says, stepping into the gallery. "For people like Kel."

"Where's Kurt?" I ask, glancing around.

"He's gone with Razh to have a look at the toys," he laughs. "He's enthralled with this place." He turns to Emiline when he says, "I hear your drones are exquisite."

"How many have you got?" Rys is practically drooling as he asks the question.

"A hundred or so, of various shapes and sizes," Emiline says. "Most are in a state of disrepair after years of neglect. But come, I'll show you the one that's the pride and joy of the Dwelling. I'm curious to know what you think of it, now that we've successfully connected one of the Quantum Sources and powered it up."

She guides the three of us to a nearby elevator, which shoots us downward for what feels like an eternity before finally coming to a stop.

When the doors open, we're greeted by a small, motorized vehicle just big enough for the four of us to sit in. When we've climbed in, Emiline drives us down a long tunnel until we come to a cavernous space whose ceiling must be a hundred feet from the floor, at least. People in white lab coats are milling about, some of them fiddling with small electronic devices on table tops, others testing small drones as the machines hover in the air around them.

"This is the Silo," Emiline tells us as she pulls the vehicle to a stop. "They used to test-launch missiles from here. Now, we use it as a launching area for our flyers."

After scanning the intricate ceiling mechanism, my eyes land on the object at the center of the room. Kurt and Razh are standing next to what looks like a small, beautifully streamlined jet plane painted reflective orange, red, and yellow. Its beak is pointed like that of a bird, its wings decorated with bright flames.

"This is the Phoenix," Emiline tells us as we begin to walk toward it. "It can firebomb an enemy's army out of existence."

"That sounds horrible," I reply, my mind reeling with thoughts of Finn's visions.

"Which is precisely why it's never been used, and most likely never will be. I have no desire to torch innocents—or even the Directorate, for that matter. And it's no way to gain favor with potential allies. The Phoenix is a last resort. Still, we're proud of the design. She's the only one of her kind in existence."

As Rys and Illian stride over for a closer look, I turn Emiline's way, studying her face. She's intelligent, empathetic, and a little mysterious. She has an arsenal of weaponry at her fingertips, but doesn't seem to have a vengeful bone in her body. She could blow the Arc sky-high from the sound of things, but is far too reasonable a person to consider such violence.

"When you talked about Verity Warfare, what exactly did you mean?" I ask her. "How do you propose to teach the Arc's residents the truth?"

"An excellent question," she says, calling out to Razh, Kurt, and Rys. "Come with me, all of you. I have a surprise for you all."

She leads us out of the Silo and down a long, uneven corridor of red stone until we arrive at another elevator, which shoots us back up to the main level high above the valley. Emiline guides us along a corridor until we reach a locked wooden door embedded in the wall—one of the few locks I've seen since our arrival. When she removes a key from around her neck and unlocks it, we're met with the sight of a large, brightly lit room filled with what looks like surveillance equipment.

Rys steps forward, curious about two floating screens hovering near the wall on the far side of the room. Each screen displays a rapidly scrolling wall of text in some sort of code that I've never seen before.

"This looks like an Encrypted Bi-Path," Rys says with a tone of wonder. When he sees the confused look on my face, he clarifies. "A two-way system. They're receiving information from the Arc and transmitting it, as well—but they're doing it without risk of detection."

"Diva's friend in the Directorate Guard helped us to access

the Arc's systems a few days back," Emiline says with a nod. "It's how our contacts send us the Directorate's classified information. It's all in code, of course, but we've decrypted their language and can quickly make sense of all of it."

"I'm impressed, honestly," Rys replies. "I've constantly got my eyes on everything in the Arc—at least, I *thought* I did. I never detected this infiltration."

"We're very careful," Emiline chuckles. "As you can imagine. Our contact is gifted at bypassing the Directorate's security, though he's risking a great deal by doing so. He manages not to leave a trace behind, but I can only imagine what would happen if they caught him."

"Impressive," Illian says. "So you're saying there's nothing to trace us back to this location, even if they knew we were rifling through their classified intel?"

"Nothing," Emiline says with a shake of her head. "We're ghosts."

"Tell me something," Rys says pensively. "Could we broadcast video to the Arc's screens from here?"

"I'm counting on it, actually." Turning to me, she adds, "Ashen, you asked how the Arc's residents will learn the truth. Well, now you have your answer."

"You're going to tell them?" I ask.

"No. You are."

ASSIGNMENT

"WHAT? NO," I say, shaking my head and backing away. "No way. My face was plastered all over the Arc's screens when the Directorate was calling me a murderer. I can't imagine anyone in that place is about to believe I'm some great Bringer of Truth."

"I beg to differ," Rys protests with a warm smile. "You haven't seen what's been going on in the Arc over the last several days. But I've been watching."

He spins around in his seat and, with his fingertips, enlarges the screen in front of him, tapping it once, twice, until a bustling crowd appears before us.

"The Escapa?" I ask, leaning in to look. "So what?"

He zooms in again to show me the front window of an expensive-looking clothing store. A poster is pasted onto the glass, and two Directorate guards are busying themselves trying to remove it.

As Rys zooms in, I see why they're so set on taking it down.

At its center is a red rose hanging upside down, a menacing trickle of blood dripping from its petals.

Above the rose, bold words scream out:

Death to the Directorate!
Death to the Traitors!
Ashen Spencer Reigns!

The guards manage to peel the poster off the glass, crumple it up, and toss it into a nearby bin. But as Rys zooms out, still more posters fill my sightline, plastered one after the other along the walls and storefronts.

A sudden memory floods my mind of one of the last things Diva said to me before my battle with Finn:

Rumors started spreading a while back. Rumors about a girl who defied the King and Queen of the Arc...

"Ashen Spencer," I say, tasting my own name on my tongue as if for the first time. "They can't be serious."

"Of course they are. Word has made its way around about your victories, about what you did to the King's son, to Finn, even."

"They think I'm his killer," I protest with a bitter laugh.

"They *like* that you're his killer," Rys counters. "No offense to Finn, but murdering him does make you look like a serious badass."

"He's not dead. And anyhow, what would I even say? I'm garbage at public speaking, I always have been. It scares the hell out of me."

"Your life has been on the line a thousand times since you first left the Mire, Ash. Are you telling me that talking to a camera scares you more than what you've already been through?"

I narrow my eyes at him, wishing I could come up with some brilliant retort.

But he's right. A few months ago, speaking to a couple of million people would have seemed like the greatest horror imaginable.

Now, it feels almost trivial.

"Just tell them the truth," Rys says, his eyes lighting up when he realizes I'm not putting up much of a fight. "Drop hints about what the rebels need to do, how they need to organize to take the Directorate down. Then, when we're ready, we'll move in and help them land the final blow. It'll be fun. You'll be a *famous* badass."

"Being famous is literally the last thing I want."

"I'm afraid it's too late for that. Look—we don't have an army of thousands. We don't have the means to go blasting our way into the Arc. Whatever we do, it will require subterfuge. Allies on the inside. This is the Quiet War, remember? Look—the only way to secure the allies we need is by communicating with them directly. They already worship you; just think how they'll love you when you talk to them face to face. And think how much it'll piss off that bitch, the Duchess." Even as Rys finishes speaking, he mutters under his breath, "With apologies to Finn for being a dick about his mom."

"We can help, Ashen," Emiline adds with a proud smile. "We'll set you up with a plain backdrop so no one will know where you are."

"I don't know…" I moan, looking over at Illian, who's standing quietly a few feet away. He locks his eyes on mine and says, "I'm sorry, but they're quite right. Much as it pains me to say, we don't have an army. What we *do* have are a lot of people inside the Arc who are just waiting for an excuse to throw off the shackles they're only now realizing are clamped around their wrists and feet." He nods toward the screen. "They've finally realized their overlords aren't entirely benevolent. We need to strike this particular iron while it's red-hot, and get the crowds on our side."

"But they'd be insane to speak out against the Directorate!" I snap. "The Cyphers—the new militia the Duchess is building —they'll kill the protestors. I've seen what they can do. They're not even human."

"No," Rys says. "They're *not* human. Which means they can be subdued in ways a human can't. Leave them to me— Professor Lyon and I have a plan for how to deal with them. Right now, though, let's focus on the *actual* humans. What do you say?"

I'm about to protest some more when a single syllable cuts its way through my mind:

"Please."

It's Illian who says the word. I turn his way, my shoulders slumping in defeat.

"We're weak," he says. "But we don't have to be. Once we reveal the truth, many of them will turn. You know it as well as I do, Ashen."

I sigh.

He's right. The Arc's population doesn't yet know the worst of the Directorate's lies.

Even if they are indifferent to the plight of the Dregs of the Mire, they *will* pay attention to what I tell them— because the Dregs are far from the Directorate's only victims.

"It's hard to argue with your logic," I say with a reluctant nod. "They have a right to know the truth."

"We'll get ready for broadcast, then," Emiline says almost

gleefully. "And we'll get Diva to help you prepare. I'm sure she'll be delighted by the task."

The thought of spending a few minutes with Diva sends a frisson of joy shivering through me. There's something so pleasant, so luxurious about being pampered by her, if only because she derives so much pleasure from making me look and feel my best.

It's frivolous, I know, but sometimes all it takes to evade the grim reality of our world is a few minutes of luxury.

"Why don't you head to your rooms, then?" Emiline says with a joyful clap of her hands. "We'll meet back here in an hour or two."

I nod and head to the elevator with Rys by my side.

"If we can get enough people on our side, we can win this thing," he assures me when the doors have closed, unflinchingly confident as usual.

"I wish I believed that," I tell him. "But right now, I can't see it."

Rys smiles down at me. "You'll do great, you know. You're made for this, even if you don't know it."

"What if I fall on my face?"

He shakes his head. "No *what ifs*, Ash. Not now. You need to believe you can do this, for the sake of millions of people."

"But no pressure, right?"

He winces, and for a second, his gaze goes distant in a way that reminds me eerily of Finn.

"I know it's a lot," he says, "the weight that's on your shoulders right now. But I promise I will be by your side every second, no matter what."

It's been a long time since I last hugged Rys but I do it now, holding him tight before finally letting go. "Thank you," I breathe. "That means a lot."

When he's turned and left, I step into my room and close my door.

I miss Finn more than ever—the *old* Finn, the calming, soothing version who never fails to instill confidence, to remind me that he thinks I'm amazing even when I'm convinced of the opposite.

Feeling entirely alone, I sit down on my soft bed, staring at nothing while I contemplate what I can possibly say to an audience of millions of enemies and potential allies alike.

How the hell does one start a war?

BROADCAST

AFTER A FEW MINUTES of quiet contemplation, I'm startled out of my thoughts by a loud knock at my door.

Hoping to see Finn's face, I leap to my feet and bound over. But I'm greeted by another face altogether, albeit a pleasant one.

It's still surreal to see Diva in New Mexico of all places, her effervescent energy infiltrating this strange, otherworldly network of cliffside apartments.

"Emiline told me I'm to get you ready for the broadcast," she beams, leaping into my small room with her kit in one hand and a garment bag in the other. "I can't tell you how happy that makes me."

"It makes *me* terrified," I chuckle. "But knowing you're going to set me up helps a little. Maybe you can make me look like someone else, so I can stop feeling so self-conscious."

"The only person you should look like, Ashen Spencer, is you," she scolds, laying her kit on the small wooden table by the door before handing me the garment bag. "I knew the first second I met you that you were someone special, and it turns out I was right, *as usual.*" She adds a wink for good measure.

"What's in here?" I ask, holding up the garment bag.

"Unzip it and find out."

I do as she says, only to discover a long, sleeveless red dress made of the same shade of silk I saw in Vittorio's fabric shop in the Escapa.

"It's beautiful. Where did it come from?"

"Emiline said it was hers once, but she has no occasion to wear it here in the Dwelling. All I know is it looks like it would fit you perfectly, so I snatched it up. Red always pops on camera."

"You don't think I should keep my uniform on for the broadcast? I'd look more...official."

She shakes her head. "Emiline doesn't want you going for the military look. She insists on elegance, and I agree. You don't want the Arc's people to see you as the leader of an invading force—you're supposed to be their liberator. At least, the *face* of their liberation. Of course, before you free people, you have to convince them they're actually prisoners. That's your job today."

I chew on my lip for a second. She's right. The most difficult part of my task will be convincing the brainwashed that they've actually *been* brainwashed.

"I'll put the dress on, then," I finally sigh. "A little color would be a nice change, anyhow."

"That's the spirit!" she chirps.

As she seats me and begins to sort out her gear, I ask her to tell me more about her contact in the Arc. "Are you sure the Directorate Guard—your friend, I mean—won't tell his bosses about this place? You totally trust him?"

She nods. "He's a good guy. He risked his life helping me get here, all because he was worried I'd be killed." Under her breath, she adds, "He's a secret rebel. He knows all about you—says the whole Directorate Guard knows the legend that is Ashen Spencer. They're terrified of you after what happened in the Arenum with…" She purses her lips. "Finn. Is he actually…?"

"He's okay," I assure her. *I wish I could say he's totally fine, but that would be a lie.* "He's…resting."

She nods. "I'm glad to hear it. You scared a lot of people that evening, you know. They say you had an army of birds fighting alongside you. If you were anyone else, I wouldn't have believed it…but I've always said Ashen Spencer is a miracle."

I let out a chuckle. "Not a miracle. And the army of birds is Rys's, not mine. I guess I just have talented friends."

"So, our clever friend Rys is cute *and* brilliant. I don't suppose he's single?"

With a laugh, I reply, "Very."

Once I've slipped the dress on—which, as Diva promised, fits perfectly—I take a seat in front of her. She turns my way with a collection of cosmetics in hand and slips over to stand at my side. "Now, let's get you ready for First Contact with those assholes in the Arc, shall we?"

She doesn't take long to prep me, my hair included. But when we're done, instead of showing me my reflection in her mirror, she leads me out of my room. "Can you find your way back to the surveillance room?" she asks.

"I think so," I say with a nod, and when she's given me a quick hug and told me I'll do great, I make my way back to the chamber where Emiline, Illian, and Rys are already waiting for me.

"You look amazing," Rys tells me with a grin. "Finn will be sorry he missed this."

I smirk awkwardly and thank him, kicking myself for not delaying the broadcast until Finn is feeling better.

Then again, I think with a sudden twinge of sadness, *there's a chance he'll* never *feel better.*

"We've set you up with a backdrop," Emiline tells me as she gestures toward the far wall, which is covered in a plain off-white cotton sheet. "It should be enough to hide your where-abouts. The rest of the hiding will be up to Rys."

"We'll be fine," he assures her. "My whole life is spent concealing things from the Directorate. I'm a freaking virtuoso at it."

I nod, too overcome with terror-induced nausea to say anything.

"When we start filming," Emiline tells me, her voice delib-erately calm to counteract my fear, "go ahead and begin. Don't think too hard—just let the words come. Speak directly to the people. Accuse the Directorate. Be angry, if it feels right. Tell them what you know, and you can be sure the Arc's residents will listen."

"Okay," I reply through tremulous vocal cords.

The others watch silently as she guides me over to a chair positioned in front of the white sheet and tells me to take a seat.

"Where should I start?" I ask, twisting to glance at Rys. "How much should I say?"

"All of it," Rys tells me. "Everything. Don't show any mercy. The Directorate wouldn't."

"He's right," Illian agrees. "Just unleash the truth. It's time the people knew what's been done to them."

My hands shaking, I turn toward the camera. I still haven't

seen Diva's hair and makeup job, but when Emiline turns the camera on, a projection of my face crops up in the air above her.

My newly polished appearance is an unfamiliar combination of pretty, elegant, and professional. For the first time I can remember, I genuinely look like an adult. My cheekbones are prominent, my chin strong, my hair pulled back in just the right way to accentuate my features. It's as if the last remnants of youth have deserted me over the past few months.

Not surprisingly, Diva was right about the red dress, which jumps out like a violent yet oddly appealing wound against the white backdrop. I feel strangely empowered by the color.

The crimson shade of the blood shed by all those the Directorate has wronged so cruelly.

"Whenever you're ready," Emiline says. "Give me a nod, and we'll go live."

"Live?" I gasp. "But I thought we were recording for a later broadcast."

"Yeah, um," Rys says apologetically. "About that—it won't work. If I want to bypass the Directorate's systems and keep our location undetected, we can't afford to give them a pre-record. I'm sorry, Ash. But don't worry—you're going to do great."

Throwing him a final, petrified look, I turn to Emiline. "I suppose I'm ready, then. It's now or never."

"Excellent," she says, flicking something on the camera, which causes a red light to flash just above the lens. "I'm going to count you down. In three...two..."

She shows me the "one" silently with her finger, then signals that we're rolling. I find myself staring into space for a moment before focusing on the camera's lens, a million thoughts racing through my mind at once.

"My...my name is Ashen Spencer," I finally muster, my voice shaking, hands clasped tightly in my lap. "You may have heard of me. I am a Dreg from Sector Eight in the Mire, and it's my understanding..." My voice cracks, and I clear my throat before repeating, "...my understanding that the Directorate has told you I'm pure evil. That I've risen up against them despite their alleged benevolence and kindness. But I'm here to tell you the truth—not just about me, but about all those who rule the Arc. About the monsters that they really are."

Out of the corner of my eye, I see Rys beaming, his arms crossed over his chest as the others quietly watch and wait.

"I was brought to the Arc days after my seventeenth birthday, as so many Dregs were," I continue. "We were told before we left the Mire that the Arc was our path to the Cure and to salvation. The Directorate said they would protect us from the illness known as the Blight...and that we'd be offered the chance to protect whatever family we had left. But what they didn't tell us..."

My voice turns bitter in my mouth, and I tell myself to embrace the sensation of growing rage.

"... is that the Blight is a lie, and the so-called Cure is nothing more than a curse. The moment we step foot in the Arc, our lives are stolen from us. We are imprisoned, made to serve the Directorate loyally. And if we don't, we die."

I take a deep breath, collecting myself before continuing.

"But I know most of you couldn't care less about Dregs like me. And why should you? We're nothing to you but memories of the past. Remnants of those who dwell in the Mire, in the shadows of the Arc. We're not wealthy or powerful. But I'm here to tell you we're far from the only victims of the Directorate. You're victims, too. *Each and every one of you."*

Emiline nods, a smile on her lips, and gestures me to continue. I mull over my next words, choosing to start at the beginning.

"You were told years ago that the Blight is a highly contagious disease that spreads like wildfire, killing anyone and everyone over eighteen. But that's a lie. The Blight is a biological weapon transmitted deliberately and maliciously via micro-drones controlled by the Directorate, the very people you've learned to trust. The ones who like to tell you they're your saviors."

I take a deep breath before continuing.

"I know all this because...because my father, Oliver Spencer, was the man who invented the Blight. He never meant for it to be used on our own people, and when he learned the Directorate's intentions, he tried to stop them. But he was killed for resisting, for wanting to reveal the truth. They've killed many others since that day. You've seen it with your own eyes—you've watched innocent people succumb even as you scurried for shelter in the Arc, where the murderers welcomed you with open arms."

With another surge of anger swelling inside me, I narrow my eyes at the camera, setting my jaw.

I don't care at this point how many people I'm scaring or shocking. I don't care how frightened I may make them.

All I care about is that they learn the truth.

I keep talking for I don't know how long—about how the Directorate kills Candidates for their own entertainment, how they steal young women and children from the Bastille to distribute to the Aristocracy because the so-called "Cure" causes mass infertility.

"You don't have to choose whether or not to believe me," I tell my unseen audience. "You already *know* it's true. You've seen the evidence firsthand. How many of you have had children since you came to the Arc years ago? How many have been told by the Directorate's doctors that your infertility is caused by stress or a simple change of environment?"

My jaw tight, I fix my eyes straight ahead. "The Directorate is playing you for fools. They are no leaders, no benevolent overlords. They're nothing more than abusive prison wardens profiting off your suffering. Ask yourselves what would happen if you chose to leave the Arc—if you wanted to take in a single breath of fresh air. It's not the so-called Blight that's keeping you locked inside—it's the bastards pretending to be your caretakers, the ones who stole your homes, your money, and your families from you."

With the same haughty lift of my chin that I've so often seen from the Duchess, I add, "It's time to rise up against them! Don't let them rule your lives. It's up to you to take back control of your own destinies. You are not at the mercy of the Directorate—they are at *yours*. Fight them. Bring them down. Reclaim your freedom!"

With that, Emiline signals me to stop and shuts the camera down.

"That was amazing," she tells me. "Thank you, Ashen."

"But I had more to say," I reply, my chest heaving as adrenaline courses through me. "So much more."

"I know you did. That's why I want you to save it for tomorrow."

"Tomorrow?" I ask, my voice suddenly meek as my heart sinks, my excitement morphing into a new hit of fear. "I have to do it again?"

Nodding, she chuckles. "We'll keep it going. Every day

we'll broadcast a new message. We'll take you from infamous to famous, Ashen. You will be the shining face of a rebellion desperately in need of hope. We need them to keep thinking about you, talking about you. We need their anger to flourish, to ignite into a flame that burns the Directorate where they sleep. Their rage is our weapon—*you* are our weapon. You are the truth that will bring the Directorate to its knees. And if you can inspire the rebellion to take hold, we've already won."

"She's right." Illian, who has been silent, steps forward with a nod. "Each word out of your mouth has the potential to land a lethal blow. Each revelation is a dagger held to the Directorate's throat. You did extremely well, but we need more from you. Much more. Are you up for it, Ashen?"

I want to say no, but I glance over at Rys, whose lips are curled up in a proud smile. As much as I wish Finn were here, I'm endlessly grateful to have my old friend by my side.

My old friend.

"Yes," I tell them with a smile of my own. "I'm up for anything that will end the Directorate's reign. Even if it takes a thousand broadcasts."

THE C. D.

SEEKING a little solitude after the stress of the broadcast, I wander to the Surveillance Deck, where I find Peric sitting quietly on his own.

He smiles and leaps to his feet when he spots me. "Ash!" he calls out. "I was hoping to see you. You did great!"

I feel my face turn scarlet as I reply, "You watched?"

"My parents have a screen in their room with access to the feed. I hope it's okay—Emiline told us we could watch."

"Of course," I reply, swallowing down my embarrassment. "But...I'm not exactly an expert at bringing down authoritarian governments with nothing more than words."

Peric laughs, and it's the laugh of someone without a care in the world. He looks so relaxed, so effortlessly happy. "I beg to differ. You were amazing. Hell, I was shaking in my boots watching you, so I can imagine you freaked out at least a few Directorate members. But then, I've seen your wrath first-hand. I know what you're capable of."

"You have no idea," I tell him with a chuckle. "And hopefully you'll never find out."

Desperate to change the subject, I ask, "How are things going with your parents?"

"Really well. Like, *freakishly* well. It's almost like we were never apart in the first place. It's so weird to think I went from Veer, who's constantly scheming and conniving, to my mother and father, who are the most docile, gentle people you could ever hope to meet. It's almost jarring, but in the best possible way."

"I'm really happy for you," I tell him, and I genuinely mean it.

"Thanks," he replies with a surprisingly bashful grin.

We seat ourselves on a couch by the Mirage Shield, looking out at the view of the valley below.

"So, what are they like?" I ask. "I haven't had much of a chance to talk to them."

"My mother is quiet. Sweet, too. She's baked me about fourteen different kinds of cookies since we arrived, in an oven carved into the stone. She keeps telling me about the clothes she sewed for me when I was little, about how she kept making more even after they lost me—after they settled in Santa Fe. She made larger and larger sizes over the years, like she was anticipating that I'd show up some day. It's almost like she knew."

"Maybe she did know, somehow," I reply.

"Maybe. She told me she used to have dreams about me where she'd see me wandering the woods. How weird is that?"

I think of Finn then, of his dreams and visions, and wonder if I've underestimated the human brain all my life. Maybe predicting the future is more common than I've ever known.

"And your father? What's he like?"

"He's reserved. I get the impression that losing me at the

same time he lost so many friends and family did something to him—hurt him in a way he can't quite talk about. But he's a good guy. He wants to take me fishing someday, after all this is over."

"That's so great. You look so...I don't know, different. So happy."

Peric's former arrogance and bluster have fallen away, leaving behind someone kind and warm, almost innocent. It's like his hard outer shell has been removed to reveal pure softness underneath.

"I am, Ash. Happy and grateful."

He reaches out and puts an arm around my shoulders, pulling me close. But for once, it feels more like a gesture of friendship than an intimate, romantic one. I hug him back. Much as I crave Finn's touch, I find myself grateful to feel the support of Peric's powerful arms. There's something both reassuring and hopeful in his embrace.

When we pull apart, I force myself to my feet. "I'm going to go rest," I tell him with a yawn. "The broadcast took a lot out of me. I'll see you around?"

"Of course."

When I get back to our hallway, Rys leaps out of his room to greet me, a grin a mile wide on his lips.

"What's going on?" I ask as I push my door open. "You look like you won the lottery."

"I feel like I did." He's practically bouncing off the walls as we step inside. "*We* did, rather."

"What could possibly be this exciting?"

"I've been watching the inside of the Arc via my drones," he tells me, his tongue working to get the words out at record speed. "I've got a lot of birds on the go right now, tracking down Cyphers, watching Directorate movement, and the thing is..."

He pauses as if for dramatic effect.

"Spit it out!" I try to say the words calmly, but the truth is, my heart is pounding.

"Let's just say there's been a...favorable reaction to your broadcast."

"Define favorable."

"Protests. No, not protests—that's the wrong word. We're talking *riots*. People throwing chairs through shop windows, others trying to storm the Conveyors to force their way to the upper levels to confront the Aristocrats and Directorate members. There's been a lot of angry shouting. And the best part..."

I raise my eyebrows, terrified he's going to tell me someone has burned the Arc to the ground.

He almost shouts the words. "You have a *nickname*."

"What?" I sputter. "What do you mean?"

"They're calling you the Crimson Dreg. You know—because of..."

"The dress. Yeah, I get it." I want to roll my eyes, but instead, I start laughing. "I like it, actually. Has a nice ring to it."

"Ash, it's working," Rys says, leaping onto my bed and inter-twining his fingers behind his head as he lies back. "This insane plan of ours is *working*. We have an army of thousands fighting our battle for us while we relax in sunny New Mexico. I mean, it's not quite how we pictured the war playing out, but..."

I press my back to the wall and cross my arms.

"I can't quite believe it," I say quietly. "But it seems you're right."

"It's like Emiline told us. We don't need to storm into the Arc, guns blazing. Turns out all we needed was a girl, a red dress, and a whole lot of rage."

✕

I ask Emiline at dinner if there's a chance I could go visit Finn in the infirmary, but she tells me he's still resting and that the doctors advise he be left alone for a little.

"They say he should be back up and about by morning," she assures me. "By the time of your next broadcast."

The thought invigorates and frightens me at once—as much as I want to see him, to talk to him, our last meeting was so tense, so unnaturally hostile, that I'm not sure we can find our way back to how we once were.

Still, when I get back to my room, I manage to fall asleep feeling hopeful and excited about what tomorrow may bring.

✕

In the morning, I'm just about to change into the red dress that's already come to represent our rebellion when a gentle knock sounds at my door.

I open it to see Finn's face, looking relaxed, healthy...and deeply apologetic.

He lingers in the hallway, hands behind his back as if deliberately restraining himself from touching me.

"I'm happy to see you up and about," I tell him, my tone more formal than I'd like. The truth is, I'm not entirely sure what to say to him right now. The last time we spoke, he—or some entity inside him—was snarling at me to get out of his room. I know better than to hold it against him, but it's not exactly the easiest thing in the world to pretend it didn't happen. "Are you...okay?"

Eyeing me like he knows exactly what I mean, he nods. "I'm feeling much more like myself. Dr. Lyon came to me and gave me a pill—something to counteract the effects of the nanotech, at least temporarily."

"I'm just glad to see you looking so relaxed," I say, my tone hopeful.

He nods. "As I said, the professor's drug is only temporary relief. But it means I can talk to you without fear of...a resurgence." He glances toward my room's interior. "Could I..."

"Come in? Yes, of course," I tell him, backing away to let him enter.

He seats himself in the small chair by my dresser and looks into my eyes. "I know I was horrible to you the other night, and I'm sorry. I don't really even know what I was so angry about. Hell, I'm not even sure it was *me* who was angry. It was like someone was speaking through me, trying to control my thoughts, my feelings."

I brace myself as I ask, "Do you remember anything specific?"

The shimmer-wall? The fear in my eyes? Any of it?

Finn shakes his head. "I remember seeing fire and hearing screams. An attack from above."

I sit down on the edge of the bed and look at him. "You told me we need to leave this place. You said we're all in danger. Do you have any idea why? There's been no sign of any potential attack, but you seemed so sure..."

His brow furrows as he stares back at me and shakes his head. "No. I...I don't remember saying that. This thing inside me, it steers my mind, like it's taking control of my thoughts, only not quite. I don't know how to explain it. It's like..." He tightens for a second then looks away, his jaw clenching, and says, "You suggested I get rid of the nanotech. That's why I went off, isn't it?"

I brace myself as I nod, waiting for another onslaught of anger.

But it never comes.

Instead, Finn puts his face in his hands and lets out a groan before pulling his chin up again. "God, Ash, I'm so sorry. You must hate me. I can't explain what it's like to be inside my head right now. I know you want me to destroy this thing inside me—but for some reason, it feels like you're asking me to hack off my own arm. This voice inside me keeps telling me I *need* it—like something horrible will happen if I let it go. There's something I have yet to do, but I'm not sure what it is. Does any of this make sense?"

I lower my head, fighting back tears. *No, it doesn't make sense. I don't want you to change into a stranger. I don't want to lose you when I've only just gotten you back.*

I swallow before saying, "Whatever is happening to you, we'll work through it together, okay?"

He nods and reaches a hand out, and rising from the bed, I take it in mine. When he pulls me toward him, I allow myself to collapse onto his lap, his arms wrapping possessively around me.

"Together," he whispers in my ear.

I hold onto him, the word echoing in my mind.

Three of the most exquisite three syllables I've ever heard.

"Now," I tell him when I finally pull away, "I need to change for the next broadcast. I don't know if you've heard, but the rebels in the Arc are calling me the Crimson Dreg. I have a whole new identity since we last spoke."

"Do you?" Finn asks, one eyebrow raised. "I'm looking forward to this."

I try to suppress the hope in my voice when I say, "So you're coming to the broadcast?"

"Wouldn't miss it. I'll let you get dressed and meet you in a few minutes."

When he's left, I change into the red dress that's come to symbolize me after just one wearing. A few minutes later, as if she's read my mind, Diva shows up with a jaunty knock on my door and prepares me for the camera once again. This time, instead of pulling my hair back, she leaves it flowing in waves around my shoulders.

"I hear they're calling you the Crimson Dreg," she says as she fills in my eyebrows. "I like the sound of that."

"It sounds like the name you'd give a bandit," I laugh.

"I see nothing wrong with that. You're a rebel. A leader. A symbol. But right now..." she says, turning me toward the mirror, "You look like a lovely rose."

"Ironic, considering the enemy wears the rose on their chests."

"Appropriating symbols is a clever strategy," Diva insists. "It takes away their power. Now, one last touch, then I want you to go kick some Directorate ass, C. D."

Her last touch, as it turns out, is to apply blood-red gloss to my lips.

"There," she says, backing away. "You're beyond perfect. Now go incite some rebels into action and send that Duchess bitch into total hysteria."

I head to the surveillance room, where I find the white sheet still pinned to the wall. Razh and Emiline are the only ones in the room when I arrive, but after a few minutes, Rys walks in with Finn at his side.

My heart pounds a little faster when I lay eyes on Finn, who looks preoccupied, but smiles when he spots me.

"Everything all right?" I ask him, daring to reach for his arm.

"Fine," he assures me. "Now, tell me what you're going to talk about today."

"Actually, if it's okay, I thought I'd mention you."

He looks bemused when he says, "Me?"

I nod. "Are you up for it?"

He stares down at me, his lips parting as if he's about to say something. But he simply wishes me luck as Emiline calls me over to tell me she's ready to go.

I seat myself in front of the sheet, adjusting my hair slightly before shooting Finn a final glance.

"The answer is yes," he mouths with a sly smile.

"Looks like I'm ready, then," I tell Emiline, who starts her countdown once again.

"The rebellion inside the Arc is raging," I begin when the camera is rolling, my voice authoritative and bolder than I feel. "The Directorate is beginning to understand a brutal truth: that there will be consequences for their lies. And I—the one you call the Crimson Dreg—am here to fight along at your side." I smile when I add, "The Directorate and the Aristocracy want you to think I'm nothing more than a criminal. A murdering monster. You all know they've accused me of slaying Finn Davenport. But that's another of their lies. I didn't kill Finn. I would never do such a thing."

Glancing over at him, I continue.

"Finn is the best person I've ever met. Aristocrat blood may flow in his veins, but his heart is on the side of the rebellion."

He watches me, his chin raised, his eyes focused and bright.

"In fact, it may surprise some of the Directorate to learn," I say, my eyes locking on the camera lens once again, "that he is here with me right now."

I gesture to Finn, who steps over to stand next to me.

As Emiline redirects the camera to focus on him, he looks relaxed as he scoffs, "What's the old quote? The *reports of my death have been greatly exaggerated.* But I'm still very much alive, despite your efforts to the contrary...*Mother.*" He narrows his eyes, and I can feel his rage igniting the air around us as he addresses the Duchess directly, his gaze piercing and cold. "Maybe the Arc's residents would be interested to learn what you did to your own son. You used me as a pawn in your sick game, hoping I would kill Ashen and suffer for it. Hoping it would break me, even if it didn't kill me. But Ash and I have prevailed, as you can see. As of today, your reign of terror is over. The people of the Arc will not stand for your lies anymore. A force has been unleashed more powerful than anything you could possibly muster."

His voice is bitter, acrid, low and deep. A chill runs along my skin to hear him like this—so angry, so ready for violence.

But at the same time, my chest is on the verge of bursting with pride.

"The rebellion is here," Finn announces. "It will grow and flourish even as you and your kind cower in fear. I have seen the end of this war, and I want you to know, it does not end well for you."

At those words, I tighten.

I have seen the end.

Finn's visions. Fire, screams of agony. A young boy, taken by force.

Was he seeing the downfall of the Directorate? Will the Arc burn?

What, exactly, is the end?

When he's finished speaking, he steps away, and the camera once again focuses on me. My chest is heaving, my skin flushed. "If you are a resident of the Arc," I say, struggling to steady my voice, "it's time to rise up against those who have stripped you of your homes, of your families. Fight the Directorate. Don't let them destroy you as they've destroyed so many others. The war is here, and it's yours to lose, my friends. Do not comply. Do not let them break your spirits. We are with you, and we won't stop fighting until each and every one of you is free. Long live the Resistance!"

With a nod, I signal Emiline to stop filming. When the camera is shut down, she lets out a whoop and steps toward me, grabbing me by the shoulders as she shoots Finn an approving look.

"That was exactly the kind of instigation I was hoping for!" she says, beaming. "You're the best kind of troublemakers. Both of you."

"Thanks," I reply with a crooked smile, looking over at Finn. "Sorry for putting you on the spot like that, but you *were* kind of amazing."

"It's all right," he tells me, though I can see from the tightness in his neck that he's still fighting off the anger roiling inside him. "I can only hope my parents are now feeling a fraction of the pain they've caused so many others."

With that, he turns on his heel and leaves the room.

CONSEQUENCE

THAT EVENING, Rys gives me some news as we sit at the dinner table, a generous spread before us. Finn is seated across from me, his body still tight from the morning's broadcast.

I'm grateful when I notice Professor Lyon strike up a casual conversation. I can only hope he's trying to assess Finn, to see if his nanotech-suppressing drug is still having a positive effect.

"Things are...progressing...in the Arc," Rys whispers, leaning in close to me. I can't tell from his expression if he's pleased to be divulging this information or not.

"Progressing?" I ask, trying to decipher his tone.

"You've obviously freaked out the Duchess. She's implemented a new rule: All 'Traitors' are to be publicly shamed on the floating screens around the Arc."

"*Publicly shamed* doesn't sound like much of a punishment. But something tells me that's not all she's doing."

"No. It's definitely not all." He holds up his small handheld monitor and pulls up a video feed from one of the Arc's many marketplaces.

A young woman's face appears, hovering ghost-like and miserable above a crowd in a public marketplace. Under the projection are the words,

Unlawfully gathered with a group of Rebels.

As I watch, a large red X paints itself over the so-called traitor's face, and I can only guess what it means.

My suspicion is confirmed when the word "Terminated" appears in large letters where her face was a moment ago.

"So, it's out in the open now," I say under my breath. "No more pretending. No more 'The Directorate is benevolent' crap. They've ripped the masks off."

"Probably not literally, but yeah," Rys agrees. "Fear is their most powerful weapon, and they intend to use it. The Duchess's boasting about Cyphers is meaningless—she doesn't have enough of them to hold back hundreds of thousands of rebels. The new rule is that gatherings of more than three people are no longer allowed under any circumstance, outside of official Directorate business. Any groups who assemble are assumed to be rebels."

I would laugh if I weren't so angry. "The Aristocracy won't be pleased with that. No more parties for them. No more Trials, even."

"_They'll_ still gather. We all know the rules never applied to them." Finn's voice is strained as he interrupts. I cringe when I hear the anger I've witnessed in him so often over the last several days. "The Aristocrats will get together in their private spaces and shirk any and all rules, because they can. They were probably delighted when that woman was murdered.

This is their dream come true—the official return of the guillotine."

Instead of replying, I simply nod as Finn excuses himself and leaves the table, telling us he's heading to his room.

"Do you want me to come with you?" I ask.

"It's best if you don't," he replies, throwing me an attempt at a smile. "For your own good."

I nod, saddened as I glance over at Professor Lyon. When Finn's gone, he leans forward and tells me, "He'll be all right. He just needs to calm himself down."

I can tell from the brutal honesty in his eyes that he doesn't entirely believe his own words.

"You can't give him another pill? Something to ease his pain?"

He shakes his head grimly. "I gave him a nano-inhibitor hours ago, but too much of it could do permanent damage. Best to let him fight his demons on his own, I'm afraid."

My heart sinks to think Finn's seeming respite was so brief. For a few hours, he seemed almost like his old self, and I felt hopeful that we could find our way back to one another.

Sensing the tension in the room, Rys announces he's going to follow suit and head to bed.

"Come knock if you need me," he tells me, the words full of meaning. I can tell he knows how much it hurts me to see Finn like this. How much it eats away at me to know I can't do anything about it.

I only wish he could take the pain away.

When I go to bed that night, I stare at the vial Lyon gave me as it sits on my nightstand.

Part of me is tempted to steal a hypodermic needle from the infirmary, to sneak into Finn's room and inject him as he sleeps. But it would be a violation. A cruelty beyond imagining.

I'm not selfish enough to rob him of what he's become— even if I don't fully understand it. Even if it frightens me.

I try to justify my desire by reminding myself that Finn gave me a power without my consent. After all, the Surge isn't something I ever asked for.

But in the end, I was the one who chose to press the needle to my flesh. I accepted what he was giving me without question, hoping it would save one or both of us.

It was my choice.

And destroying the invasive nanotech that swarms through Finn's body is *his* choice, not mine.

I can only hope he'll eventually choose to find his way back to the boy I once knew.

In the morning, Rys comes to me to once again report the latest goings-on in the Arc.

He looks excited. Happy, even, and for a moment I let myself forget the emotional turmoil that's been eating away at me almost constantly for days.

"What is it?" I ask, inviting him in.

"The Directorate's 'punishments' aren't working," he says. "They're not having the effect the Duchess wants. It's the opposite. It's incredible, Ash!"

"Which means what? What's happened, Rys?"

"On almost every level below Two-Fifty, rebel groups are forming. *Big* ones. They meet under the eye of the Directorate, in full view. In the middle of markets, malls, parks, you name it. It's like they're flaunting it. This morning, I counted over three-hundred individual meetings. The Directorate Guard is overwhelmed. They've arrested a few people, but there aren't enough of them to take everyone down."

"What about drones and Cyphers?"

With a smug grin, Rys reaches into a pocket to extract a small silver egg like the one Klondike the sparrow emerged from when we were in the Palace Grounds. This one, though, is smaller—no bigger than a grape.

When Rys slips a finger over it, the egg cracks open. A bird barely larger than a bumblebee shoots out faster than my eyes can register, hovering next to Rys's head, its wings flapping with impossible speed. Its beak is shaped like a narrow dagger, deadly sharp as it glints in the light.

"It's the darnedest thing," Rys says. "Somehow, there's an infestation of Needlebeaks in the Arc. Seems the little rascals keep injecting the Cyphers with a cocktail the professor designed."

"The Xenocells, you mean?"

"A modified version," Rys says, whistling low. Obediently, the Needlebeak back shoots inside the silver egg and he seals it back up. "I've always wanted to find a use for these guys, and here we are. I've got hundreds of them hidden in the Arc, so I remotely programmed them to retrieve the necessary ingredients from Lyon's old lab, then sent them on a mission. Most of the Cyphers are now...*incapacitated*. They won't be hurting anyone ever again."

"Wait—the Xenocells are *killing* them?"

All of a sudden, my hope for Finn's eventual recovery is shattered.

"Not the Xenocells," Rys says. "They only neutralize the

nanotech to render the Cyphers powerless. The killing is done by another drug entirely."

I shudder, horrified to think of the former humans the Duchess has turned into Cyphers. They once had minds of their own, and agency. For all I know, some of them might even have been decent once.

And now, they're being killed, and for what?

"There's so much more," Rys says. "Below Level Two-Hundred, the Arc is utter mayhem. There's constant talk of the Crimson Dreg and her Aristocrat Boy. You two are the golden couple—the saviors of the Arc."

The Golden couple.

I look away, chewing on my lip. *I'm not even sure we are a couple. Not anymore.*

"There is a little bad news, though," Rys says.

"Oh, God." My stomach clenches as I brace myself. "Tell me."

"The Directorate is on the hunt, Ash. They're desperate to get your head on a pike. Finn's, too."

"Is there any way they might find us?"

Rys shakes his head. "Not from any trail left by our broadcasts, at least. I checked the system myself—every signal is jammed, encrypted or twisted to redirect their efforts. If they do manage to trace us, they'll end up convinced we're broadcasting from a bunker in Siberia. We'll be fine out here. The people in the Dwelling have managed to hide themselves for years, just like the ones in the Pit. I don't think we have anything to worry about."

"No," I say, "You're probably right."

But a nagging sensation has taken up residence in my mind. Finn's warning about an attack, however unlikely it may have sounded, probably came from the pervasive worry that his mother is constantly on the lookout for us both.

I wouldn't be worried if she weren't so intent on punishing us for loving each other.

"Now come on," Rys says. "Let's get some breakfast. We have planning to do. Soon, it'll be time to take the bastards down for good—which means making our way back to the Arc."

When I open the door to accompany him to the dining room, Finn is standing in the hallway, his hand in mid-air, ready to knock. His lips are pulled into a frown, his eyes narrowed.

"Could I come in?" he asks.

"Of course," I tell him. "I…"

Rys throws me a shallow smile, raises an eyebrow, then excuses himself.

When he's stepped inside and shut the door, Finn begins to pace. I seat myself on the bed, nervous at how agitated he seems. It feels like minutes pass before he finally stops moving long enough to look me in the eye.

"Yesterday was hard for me. The truth is, every day is hard. But addressing my mother in that broadcast—it felt like a severing of any last traces of the bond we once shared. It feels like an end."

I find myself holding my breath. It's difficult to understand anyone having a bond with the Duchess, but she's still Finn's mother, still the woman who raised him, regardless of how cruel and cold she may be. And somewhere along the line, she must have done something right, to produce a son who's as strong and principled as Finn is.

"I know," I finally reply. "And I'm really sorry you had to go through that."

"It's...difficult for me to *feel*," he tells me mysteriously. "Hard to let the emotions come. Each intense feeling is a shock to my system, a blast from a weapon that hits me square in the chest and hurls me backward. Those shocks hurt more than they should, so I push away the feelings as if I'm trying to kill them."

"You're saying you shield yourself," I reply. *Just like Lyon told me.* "I wish you wouldn't. I wish you'd let me in. Not all emotions have to be painful ones, Finn."

"No. That's very true."

Seeming to calm down, he steps toward me and crouches down, taking my hands in his and kissing my fingers as he's done so many times, before pressing his face to them. I feel him breathing against me, absorbing my love for him, as if by osmosis.

As if he has no love of his own to give.

"You still have a family, Finn," I say. "You still have Merit to think about, even if you've severed ties with your parents. He needs you. He needs you to be capable of caring about him. And as selfish as it sounds, I need you, too."

"You still want me to destroy the nanotech. And I can't blame you for it. We both know it's the cause of all this." He looks into my eyes and I see it then—a desperation, a need that brings all his humanity soaring back to him, swirling in the air around us. He's fighting this thing inside him— whether it's the Aegis Implant or something more insidious— and it's taking all his strength to hold it back.

"I can't possibly ask for that," I tell him. "I can't tell you what to do. It's just that I miss you—the *real* you." With a sigh, I add, "But I understand why it's hard to give it up better than you might think. The truth is, you gave me a power, and even though it scares me, it would be hard for me to give it up. If it can help us to fight this battle and win, I have to live with it—at least for now. Maybe in the future, when things have settled, when we've won this war…"

He nods his understanding, and the truth comes to me then. *We've become something other than ourselves. We're two weapons on the same side of a battle, focusing our aim solely at the enemy…despite the damage it's wreaking on our hearts.*

"I came to the Arc for my family," I say softly. "To protect my mother and Kel. Every Dreg who walked through those doors on day one believed the same thing—that our mission was to earn the Cure for our families and ourselves. It was all a lie, but that doesn't mean we can't protect people, you and I. We can still help Kel and Merit, and so many others."

"And we will," he says. "We will help them, because we have to. And then…it will be over."

"Maybe."

I offer him a wistful smile and put my hands around his neck, pulling him close and pressing my forehead to his. "I wonder sometimes if it will ever truly end."

"It will. I'm not sure how or when, but it will. Like I said, I've seen the end. It wasn't entirely clear—it was a mess of rapidly moving images. I saw violence, I saw destruction and cruelty. But I know there is an end coming."

"I believe you. And I hope we can face it together."

"Me too." Pulling back, he looks at me and smiles. "I still feel them, you know. The butterflies. Despite everything happening in my mind, I still get that jolt when I look into your eyes." With a kiss that soothes me more than I can say, he adds, "I promise, I'll find my heart again. And when I do, it will be yours alone."

32

STRATEGY

OVER THE NEXT SEVERAL DAYS, the spark we've ignited with our broadcasts erupts into a full-on conflagration.

We watch via Rys's feeds as civilians battle the Directorate Guard in the Escapa and other public areas. The Royal Gardens are destroyed when a small militia of torch-wielding Candidates shows up and hangs Consortium banners in the trees before burning the hedge maze to the ground. In the marketplaces and malls, rebels hang massive posters praising the Crimson Dreg or showing a golden crown slashed with angry strokes of red paint.

Each day, I broadcast a new message to offer my support and to let the rebels—and the Directorate—know I have my eye on them.

To no one's surprise, a small but fierce group of loyalists has also joined the fray, supporters of the Directorate unwilling to surrender the luxurious lifestyle they've enjoyed between the Arc's walls. With golden roses made of silk pinned to their chests, they do battle with the rebels.

But the rebels respond by confronting them in still greater numbers, pushing the loyal forces back.

And before long, it becomes obvious whose side is winning.

In a meeting one afternoon in the dining room, Lyon tells us triumphantly that it's time for the next phase of our mission.

Peric, Rys, Finn, Emiline, Razh, Illian, Kurt and I sit around the table, listening intently.

It's strange to see the Professor taking control. He's not a military leader like Illian or Emiline, but he's determined, angry, and apparently has a plan of action up his sleeve.

"Civilians can only do so much," he tells us. "There's an enemy that still needs to be taken down, and we—the Consortium—are the only ones who can do it. The Directorate remains too powerful so long as they're able to communicate among themselves and to move about the Arc freely."

"Yes, but the Directorate's greatest weakness," Emiline interjects, "is that, in creating a prison for their millions of residents, they've imprisoned themselves. They're locked inside the Arc, which makes them vulnerable. There is a two-headed snake leading them, and its heads need severing. The King. The Duchess. Take them down, and the Directorate begins to collapse."

"Why take off the heads when you can kill the whole snake?" Lyon asks. His tone is ominous, filled with a quiet malevolence. "There is not a single individual in the Directorate who deserves to live in peace. They've destroyed too much of our former world. Killed too many innocents. They need to be punished for it."

"So what do you propose?" Illian asks. "That we storm the Arc and politely ask them to lock themselves in the Hold?"

With a grim smile, Lyon shakes his head. "Not at all." He waves a hand in the air, summoning a holo-screen which shimmers to life above the table's center. "Tell me something: does any of you know what a buffalo jump is?"

Those of us seated around the table exchange puzzled looks before Finn finally speaks up. His voice is tight as he struggles more with each passing day to fight the unrelenting force inside him. "It was a method once used by Native Americans to herd buffalo off a cliff—to make them jump to their deaths. Thousands of buffalo could be killed with one successful jump."

"Exactly. And do you know, Mr. Davenport, how those buffalo were persuaded off the cliff?"

His cheeks pale, Finn shakes his head.

Lyon summons an image on the holo-screen that shows a field of long, swaying grass. Leading into the distance are two parallel rows of small rocks, set out like the edges of a road.

"All it takes is a little bit of steering," he says as a video shows us a reenactment of a massive herd of buffalo tearing along the makeshift highway until they begin leaping off the edge of a cliff in the distance. It's a horror to see that such enormous, powerful animals can so easily be manipulated.

"May I ask what the point of this is, Professor?" Illian asks impatiently.

"Simple," Lyon says with a smile. "I propose that we steer the Directorate back into their homes, where we seal them inside. Much of the Aristocracy has already been sensible enough to isolate themselves from the violence in the lower levels, locking themselves into their own residences. We simply need their overlords to follow suit."

"To what end? By all accounts, the Directorate's homes are

beautiful, enormous, and luxurious. What sort of punishment would that be?"

"You didn't let me finish," Lyon chastises. "Getting them locked in is only the beginning. Once we have them snared, we have only to unleash the weapon I designed before I left the Arc."

"What weapon would that be, exactly?"

Lyon reaches into the inside pocket of his jacket and extracts a bottle filled with brown liquid. Holding it up for all to see, he asks, "Have you heard of the Ubiquity Formula?"

"You can't be serious," Razh chides. "You're talking about mass murder."

"What's the Ubiquity Formula?" Kurt asks, a look of horror on his face.

"The one weapon we need to take down the entire Directorate—and a fair few Aristocrats, if we so choose. It's not unlike the Blight, though it's more potent and less risky. A biological formula precisely calibrated to target individuals based on their genetic coding. Once introduced in aerosol form into a residence, anyone pinpointed for termination dies —while those who are not targeted survive without a single symptom."

I glance at Finn, who looks like he's mulling the same question that's swirling through my mind. *Would Merit survive such an attack?*

"Hidden inside the Arc," Lyon continues, "is an ample supply of the Ubiquity Formula. I also happen to possess a database that contains the genetic code of every single member of the Directorate. I stole it just before Diva and I made our escape from the Arc."

I sit back in my seat, breathless. The very notion is

extraordinary—the possibility of taking down the masked, soulless monsters who have been responsible for so much pain and suffering.

And we wouldn't even need to set foot in the Arc.

But Illian snaps me out of my dark fantasy when he snarls, "We aren't murderers, Astrum. We have no intention of employing the same mass-killing tactics the Directorate used against our people."

"Of course not," Lyon replies with a wave of his hand. "We would only *threaten* to use it. Fear of death is a powerful means of convincing an enemy to comply. We herd them into their homes, then we issue our threat."

"You're saying you want us to blackmail them."

"I am simply offering you a potential means of persuading the Directorate's individual members to choose the right side. That's all."

"What then?" I ask. "What happens after we 'persuade' the Directorate? They get up and leave the Arc, and let everyone live in blissful peace? I'm sorry, but I don't see that happening."

"You'd be surprised by how many Directorate members forget their loyalty when they have a figurative gun to their heads, Ashen. They are people without integrity, after all."

"We know as well as you that the Directorate will never let the Arc's residents live in peace," Illian protests. "They will never cease to try and control them, their minds, their lives. But if we can find a way to *dismantle* the Directorate, piece by piece, there is some hope. It seems to me our best shot—our most likely chance at success—is to lay siege. Shut down their levels. Lock them in, cut off their food supply, as well as their communications. We could even cut off their water. It would take some time to force them to come around, but in the end it would mean fewer casualties. And it would give us the upper hand without making us into monsters. As grateful as I am to you, Professor Lyon, for the offer of this incredible weapon, I don't have it in me to use it, even as a means of manipulation. It goes against everything I stand for."

"I thought you stood for survival," Lyon replies, his voice gentler now. "You just admitted the Directorate will never let the Arc's residents live in peace. Now that there's been an uprising, I can guarantee they will seek revenge on everyone who has stood against them. Give them an inch, they will take a thousand miles. It's time their power was quashed, once and for all. A slow-moving siege will not have the result you desire."

Illian shakes his head. "My people have suffered in darkness, in damp, in cold, for years. Our resources have been few. We've suffered illness from eating food tainted with bacteria. Many of those who live in the Pit have lost their eyesight, even. We didn't go through all that only to emerge into the light as cold-blooded psychopaths."

Overcome with admiration, I watch as he sits back in his seat, his hands on the table.

Illian has the air of a true leader—a noble man, patient, thoughtful, and wise. He doesn't act on impulse, tempting though it must be. And as much as I've dreamed of murdering the Directorate myself, of taking each one of their lives with my silver dagger, I know he's right.

We can't descend to their level of inhumanity and still call ourselves human.

"I understand your feelings," Emiline says, "But if we use the weapon Lyon has offered, we'll have the leverage we need—"

"No," Illian snaps, and I can tell by his tone that his decision is final. "We'll find another way. We have to." He pushes himself to his feet and says, "We thank you for all you've done for us, but we cannot lower ourselves. If we become the thing we despise, there's nothing left to fight for."

With that, he turns and heads for the door.

33

DANGER

AFTER OUR MEETING, Finn tells me he needs to lie down for a little. I'm not entirely surprised that he's agitated. After what we just discussed, we should *all* be agitated.

The end of the battle for the Arc is in our sights. But how we choose to proceed will be the difference between a few deaths or tens of thousands.

Hoping to calm my frayed nerves, I find myself wandering alone to the Surveillance Deck to stare down at the large valley below. In the distance, I spot the faint silhouette of Santa Fe.

According to Emiline, the Dwelling is almost eight-hundred years old. It's strangely pristine and, unlike so much of the rest of the country, untouched by the ravages of war. A beautiful simplicity defines every chamber and every rough-carved window.

In the distant sky, I spot Atticus circling overhead, his silver feathers reflecting the sun in flashes of blinding light as he scans the area. From here, he looks like a solitary vulture, searching for carrion on the ground far below. A peaceful, if bleak, sight.

"It's a pretty amazing view, isn't it?" says Peric, who has crept up to stand beside me.

I try not to let on that he's startled me out of a trance-like state, or that I was enjoying my solitude. "Very," I tell him. "Like another world."

"It feels like another time, too. One before everything went to hell."

I glance over to study his face. In spite of his words, he looks at peace. Calm, collected, as if all traces of his former life have melted away.

"I'm curious to know what you think of the Professor's idea," he says quietly, looking at me sideways.

"I think it's insane," I tell him. "But that doesn't mean I don't dream of killing every one of those bastards with my bare hands." As I study his impassive expression I ask, "What do you think?"

"I think enough people have died," he says softly. "I think it's time to stop embracing violence."

"Okay, who are you and what have you done with Peric?" I ask, drawing a snicker from him.

"Peric's turned into a pacifist," he tells me. "At least, as long as he gets to live in this place."

A thought occurs to me then, one that makes me oddly sad. "Do you think you'll stay here when we leave?"

He shrugs. "Maybe. Maybe not. It depends on a lot of things." With that, he gives me an odd, cryptic look.

We're interrupted by the sound of someone clearing his throat behind us. I turn around to see Rys staring at us both, a grave expression on his face.

"What's happened?" I ask, immediately tightening.

"I just went to my room to check my private surveillance feeds," Rys says. "I was running through my daily review of my birds' views—specifically, the ones out in the wild who surveil the Pit's location and the woods around it."

"And?"

"It's the Bastille." Rys fixes Peric in his gaze, a look of apprehension taking hold of his features when he adds, "It was…attacked last night."

My stomach tightens with the memory of something Finn said to me a while ago. *This isn't the only place where there will be suffering and death.*

A sense of horrible foreboding fills me to think what Rys's next words might be.

"What do you mean, attacked?" Peric asks, every ounce of joy stolen from his eyes.

"I mean it was bombed. I'm so sorry, Peric. I know you had friends there."

I reach for Peric's arm, as much for my own comfort as his. Those people were his family for so many years.

There was even a time when *I* called the Bastille home. Many of its residents were kind, welcoming.

They didn't deserve this.

"How bad is it?" Peric asks, his voice quavering.

"Not good. The southern half of the town is still burning. Some of the buildings on the main street remain intact, but I'm honestly not sure how many survivors there are. I'd say it's the work of some very angry Directorate members."

"Veer had a bomb shelter," Peric says. "If she saw the attack coming, chances are she herded people inside. There will be survivors."

"I hope you're right."

"Why would they attack the Bastille?" I ask, shaken. "The

Directorate had an agreement—the children..." My heart sinks as I think about the toddlers and babies being raised by young mothers—the ones offered to the Directorate in exchange for their ongoing truce.

"I can guess why." Peric's voice is darkly confident. "They knew you'd be watching, Ash. They knew you'd care. They did it to hurt you, to prey on your emotions. Maybe they were hoping to pull you out of hiding."

The weight of it is more than I can bear right now. Brushing away the tears streaking down my cheeks, I turn to Rys. My nausea is quickly morphing into rage. "I'm not going to cower or hide in the shadows. We're officially at war now, and I have every intention of fighting."

"Well, right now, we're losing, Ash. If they're willing to mob their own allies in the Bastille, there's no telling what they'll do next."

"Then it's time for a counter-attack." I chew on my lip for only a moment before I say, "It's time for another broadcast."

⊗

Finn's reaction to the news of the bombing is unreadable and cold, though I can feel the quiet rage bubbling under the surface of his skin when I touch his arm.

Within half an hour, I'm once again in front of the camera in the red dress that feels more appropriately symbolic than ever. Finn stands a few feet from me, watching intently. His brow is beaded with sweat, the veins in his neck prominent. He looks physically spent, like he's just raced through an obstacle course only to realize he's about to begin another.

"It was my mother," he says under his breath. "Wasn't it?"

"I can't say for sure. But it does sound like her work."

"Only my mother would issue the command to bomb a town filled with children. No one else is that heartless."

I can't deny he's right. I may not be intimately acquainted with many members of the Directorate, but I can't say I've ever met a human as cruel and calculating as the Duchess.

"We have to tell the Arc's residents about this. And not just with words this time." Finn growls, turning to Rys. "Do you have footage of the aftermath?"

Rys nods. "As much as you'd like. But I should warn you, it's graphic."

"Graphic is what we need," Emiline tells us as she readies the camera for filming. "The Arc's residents need to see that no one is safe from the Directorate bastards, not even the innocent children who were supposed to find homes with the Aristocrats. Put together any footage you have that shows what monsters they are. Not only the bombing of the Bastille, but the cruelty within the Arc, as well. Let's rip their masks entirely off."

When Rys has isolated the footage he plans to use, Emiline signals me to begin.

"I come to you today with dire news," I announce, struggling to keep my voice in check. "It gives me no pleasure to tell you what the Directorate has just done to innocent civilians—people who lived peaceful, quiet lives outside the Arc. People who were willing, even, to give you their beloved children in return for a chance at survival."

I nod to Rys, who links his feed to the broadcast and begins to roll the footage of the bombings. In mid-air before us, we see it for the first time: Burning houses and shops torn to pieces by the Directorate's bombs. Charred, blackened corpses, victims of every age.

On one street I see what look like the bodies of a mother

and a small child, though they're burnt beyond recognition. I heave when I see the image, pulling my eyes away.

I steel myself against the imagery, harnessing all my strength to keep my face from revealing my pain. I may have known some of those victims. Whether any of them is Cyntra, the girl I once called a friend, or Veer herself, or Piper—none of it matters. The victims were human beings, and they shouldn't be dead.

When Rys's bird pans to what is clearly the corpse of a baby lying on the road, I cup my hand over my mouth to stifle the scream that wants to explode from my chest.

It's not quite horror that I'm feeling—I've seen death. I've seen brutality, violence, cruelty. I've been part of it.

What I feel in this moment is nothing short of the purest rage. I want to blast my way through every wall between myself and the Duchess, and take her down with my bare hands.

When Rys asks me if I'm ready to speak again, I nod. He cuts the footage, signals me, and I begin.

"It is our understanding," I say in a hoarse snarl, "That the Aristocracy has isolated themselves in their palatial residences on the Arc's upper levels. They're sealed off, but they have access to all the food, water, and oxygen they could want. Meanwhile, you in the lower levels remain as vulnerable as those in the Bastille who were murdered in cold blood. You know by now that you are expected to abide by the Directorate's rules, their twisted, dictatorial rule—or they'll kill you, too."

I clear my throat and narrow my eyes.

"I know you're watching, Duchess. I know you're hunting me."

I glance at Finn, who is stone-faced as I mention his mother.

"You attacked the Bastille, despite years of loyalty to you. I can only guess what you would do to those inside the Arc who are not willing to serve you. Which is why we're coming for you, Duchess, and for the entire Directorate. We intend to put you on Trial for your crimes. Justice is coming for you—but you're fortunate. The Consortium is fair, which is far more than I can say for your cruel, so-called *government*."

I nod to Rys once again and he plays more footage, this time of a Trial that took place several months ago. The victim is a girl of seventeen who's strapped to a chair in the center of the Arenum. As the Arbiter reads the charges against the accused, who steps forward and pleads Not Guilty, a large pendulum descends from the ceiling, swinging slowly back and forth. At its end is a sharp, curved blade, which edges closer to the girl with each menacing swing.

She is given the opportunity to go free, but only if she can name every state in the country in alphabetical order.

Flustered and terrified, she struggles, her eyes locked on the blade as it moves closer and closer.

She makes it as far as Massachusetts before she lets out a final scream.

When the camera focuses on me again, I say, "*That* is justice in the Arc. That is how they treat those they deem unworthy of life among the rich. But it ends now. We're coming for you, Duchess, and when we do, you'll wish you were dead."

Emiline disconnects us, and I breathe a heaving sigh, looking to Finn for support. He steps over and puts his arms around me, but even as he holds me, he tightens, his spine straightening, his breath going shallow.

"She's coming," he whispers.

"What did you just say?" I ask, pulling away.

His eyes have turned light gray, his skin pale. He looks into the distance, at something far beyond the walls of the Dwelling.

"There's no stopping her. I don't know how she knows where we are…but she knows."

He shakes his head hard, as if he's trying to clear it of thoughts. Just then, the sound of crackling static meets our ears.

I let him go and spin around to see the floating screen swirl to life.

"What is that?" I ask Rys. "Are you playing back what we just recorded?"

He shakes his head. "I…no. I didn't do anything…" Frantically, he scrolls through a series of commands on his control panel, but he still looks baffled. "This is coming from inside the Arc."

I pull closer to Finn, taking his hand. His skin is burning hot, and out of the corner of my eye I see his shoulders rising and falling, each breath an ordeal.

"What's hap—" I begin to ask.

But when I see the Duchess's face, the question is answered.

34

ENEMY NUMBER ONE

THE DUCHESS CAN'T SEE me—I'm sure of that much. But it doesn't matter. She knows she has my full attention. It pleases her, energizes her. She's torturing me and loving every second of it.

"Does she know where we are?" I ask quietly.

Rys shakes his head. "No. Someone in the Arc just reversed the signal—but doing so doesn't give them any geographical information."

"I must say, Ashen, your little game amuses me," the Duchess says, her eyes somehow staring directly into mine. "But your tactics are just that: *a simple game*. Don't get me wrong—I'm more than delighted to have learned my Finn is alive, not that I ever doubted my son's strength. I will admit I'm a little disappointed that he disappeared with you, rather than come home to those who truly care about him. But then, we all know how teenage boys are. Mercurial, fleeting. One second, they think they want you. The next, they toss you aside in favor of the next great thing. Finn will soon realize you are nothing to him, and that his true calling is with the

Directorate. He's meant for far greater things than running around with a Dreg girl who's fool enough to think she can possibly alter the course of the world."

I glance at Finn, stone-faced as he stares daggers at his mother. He doesn't return my gaze, doesn't offer me a reassuring smile. He's pure ice.

"As for your kind offer to come for me, let me save you the trouble. We will find *you*. And when we do, we will not show the mercy we showed the Bastille's residents. So if I were you, I'd consider turning myself in before this goes any further. Spare the people around you the pain that so many others have had to endure."

With that, she signals to someone off-camera, who shoves a girl in a Candidate's uniform in front of the Duchess.

When I see the girl's face, my heart begins to pound mercilessly inside my chest.

"I know her," I breathe. "That's Lucinda—one of the Candidates from my Training Sessions. We called her Rat-girl, because of the symbol on her uniform…"

I feel numb, like someone's anesthetized my insides. It doesn't matter what we called her, or why. All that matters is what's about to happen to her.

"Did you like her?" Rys asks, and I don't need to inquire as to why he's using past tense.

"Yes. I did," I say, turning from the screen even as a shot rings out. Slamming my eyes shut doesn't prevent me from hearing the horrid thud as Lucinda falls dead to the ground.

The screen fizzles away, and I'm left breathless.

"I did that," I say quietly. "I killed her. Just like I killed those people in the Bastille. She's doing it to get to me."

"No," Rys assures me. When I pull my tear-filled eyes to his face, he turns to Finn, his brows meeting. "Your *mother* did all of it. Whether she pulled the trigger or not just now doesn't matter. She's a monster. You know that, right?"

"Rys," I mutter. "Don't."

But he steps over to Finn and grabs him by the collar, shaking him. "What's wrong with you? Why aren't you reacting?" he shouts. "Why are you so freaking cold?"

"It's too late," Finn says in a monotone. "If I could stop her, I would. But it's too late. She's already found us. The wheels are in motion...I wish I could do something, but I..."

With a look of despair, he pulls away from Rys and, excusing himself, strides out of the room.

I want to stop him, to tell him everything will be okay. But his mother just had a girl killed for the sole purpose of hurting me.

There's nothing Finn or any of us can do to change that.

A few minutes later, when I push Finn's door open, I find him lying on his bed, his eyes fixed on the ceiling. He's devoid of expression and doesn't so much as turn to look when I enter the room.

"I'd offer you a penny for your thoughts, but something tells me it would mean nothing to you," I tell him as I cross my arms and lean against the door frame.

"They're coming," he says, his voice deep and ominous. "And when they do, I have to protect you."

"No one is coming, Finn."

"But they are. Don't you see?" In a trance-like state, he rises to his feet and steps over to me, taking my shoulders in his hands. He looks down at me before raising his head. "Outside," he says, but he doesn't explain his meaning.

He steps into the hallway and I follow, baffled by his strange, halting way of speaking. It's like a robot has taken over Finn's body. He's still beautiful, still strong. But his soul is gone, wiped clean.

Whether temporarily or permanently, I can't say.

"Finn, you're freaking me out."

"Come with me," he orders, unsympathetic. "You'll see soon enough."

Reluctantly, I follow as he leads me down several hallways to the large Mirage Shield I was looking out earlier. Staring out, he points toward the valley.

At first, I don't understand why we're here. But after a few seconds of searching, I spot two figures far below us. Small children, from the looks of it.

It's not the first time I've seen children out in the valley. Emiline told me she likes to let them run around for a few minutes here and there once the Dwelling's guards have established that there are no drones in the vicinity. "So they can experience what it is to be free," she said with a smile. "We keep an eye on them, of course."

I've never thought much about it. We're far enough from any major city that it's never occurred to me there would be any danger for a couple of children who would be virtually invisible to any high-flying drone.

But right now, seeing the two small moving targets so conspicuous on a sea of red earth, I'm terrified. All I can think of are the charred remains of the young children in the Bastille. The innocent victims of the Duchess's cruelty.

Overhead, I see something circling, and it takes me a moment to determine it's an actual vulture this time, not one of Rys's birds.

"They probably shouldn't be out there," I say, pulling my

eyes to the sky. "But it looks like they're safe."

I pull my eyes down to see that the children are playing with a couple of sticks. They're forming shapes on the ground, creating drawings of people, a house, a dog.

I call out to them, aware that it's futile. The Mirage Shield is too thick; they'll never hear me.

"The children are beacons," Finn says.

"Beacons?"

But his eyes aren't fixed on the kids. They're locked on something in the sky, far in the distance.

I squint, trying to figure out what he's looking at when something draws my eye down to the ground once again. Far below us, I see Rys charging across the clearing toward the children.

"What's he doing?" I cry out, but he's already halfway across, running at full speed. "Why does he look so desperate to get to them?"

"He's trying to stop what's about to happen," Finn says, his tone eerily calm.

As I watch Rys go, my eyes move up to focus on an object rapidly approaching from the south—small at first, but growing larger with each passing second.

Rys grabs the two children by the arms and pulls them back toward the Dwelling just as the drone comes into firing range.

He sprints toward the entrance even as two of the Consortium guards leap out to take the children in their arms. I watch as Rys follows them in and the doors seal shut.

I turn my attention back to the drone, which hasn't fired a single shot. I tell myself I should feel relieved. It looks like it's only a patrol drone, after all. Unarmed and virtually harmless.

But instead, I'm terrified.

The drone is hovering in the air above a drawing I hadn't noticed before.

A circle, crossed with what look like two messily drawn swords.

The Consortium's symbol.

The drone stays in place for a few seconds, descends toward the symbol, then turns and flies away. Even as it moves, the Mirage Shield in front of us lowers into the floor to leave nothing protecting us from the outside.

"What's happening?" I cry, turning to Finn.

When he doesn't reply I spring away from him, leaping down the nearest staircase until I find Rys talking to Illian and Emiline about what just happened.

"Can't you send Atticus or another bird after the drone?" I ask. "To intercept it?"

He shakes his head. "It wouldn't matter at this point."

"Matter? The drone will send the Directorate an image of the Consortium symbol! They'll know…"

"Ashen," Emiline says. "They already know. They've already hacked into our systems."

"The Mirage Shield," I reply, turning to see Finn walking toward me from the stairwell. "*They* did that?"

"All the Dwelling's shields have been tampered with," Illian says with a nod. "We're sitting ducks if they come at us with assault drones."

"But we have weapons," I retort. "Don't we?"

Emiline and Rys exchange a concerned look.

"The missile silo has been hacked, too," Rys tells me. "We can't open its doors. We can't access the drones, either."

"There are guns in the Dwelling," Emiline says, "but not enough people who know how to use them. We have no choice but to leave."

My voice is frantic as I look at Rys. "How did this happen? I thought you said they couldn't tell where we were!"

"They couldn't. Not from the camera feed. But the Directorate has gained remote access to the Dwelling, somehow. They know we're here, and someone has figured out how to get into our security system. I've tried to push them back, to override what they're doing, but I can't. Someone out there is a more sophisticated hacker than I am."

"So what do we do?"

"We should have a few hours," Rys says. "It would take a while for the Directorate's assault drones to make it here from the Arc, but we need to leave as soon as possible."

"How did we not see this coming..." I begin, but I stop short of finishing and turn to Finn. *"You* saw it coming," I say. "You knew."

He looks through me, his eyes light gray, his mind a million miles from my own.

"You should have warned us," Illian says angrily, taking a long step toward him.

"He did," I remind him. "Days ago. He warned us over and over again, and we didn't listen."

Illian shuts his mouth, shamed into silence.

"We need to evacuate, *now,*" Emiline says, trying in vain to keep her voice calm. "We'll gather as many supplies as we can. It will be fastest to cut across the valley toward the train. It will be dangerous, but we have no choice."

"There's no point in standing around and discussing it," Illian snaps. "What's done is done. It will take at least an hour to gather everyone and everything we need. We have to get going now, or there will be nothing left of the Dwelling to save."

35

FLIGHT

WITHIN AN HOUR, every man, woman, and child inside the Dwelling is standing by the doors that lead out to the valley, ready to make a dash toward the train that will take us all back to the Pit.

The distance is only two miles or so, but right now, staring out into the open, it feels like an insurmountable distance.

"I'll lead the way," Razh announces, his voice booming as he addresses the evacuees. "First group, follow me in an orderly manner. We'll move fast, and we'll head directly for the tunnel. Carry only what you can safely manage—material possessions aren't as important as your lives. Understood?"

I scan the first group, noting that Peric's parents are among them. My heart breaks for Peric to think how happy he was to have found a new, welcoming home in this place.

Wondering where he is, I look back to see him helping some of the older evacuees getting their things together. "You're not going with your parents' group?" I call out to him.

"I'll catch up with them!" he tells me. "I wanted to make sure everyone got out safely."

After a few more shouted commands, Razh begins to move into the open at a jog, urging those behind him to hurry.

He, Emiline, Illian, and Kurt have already decided to take the Dwelling's population in groups of fifty, and each to proceed when the other has made it to the center of the valley.

I wonder at first why we don't all file out together, but a morbid thought sends a shiver of horror down my spine: *they're sending smaller groups to make it more difficult for the Directorate to kill us all at once.*

As I watch Razh's group move out, Finn says, "We need to evacuate faster. This isn't going to work."

His voice sounds more even now, more human. But when I glance over at him, he's still oddly laser-focused, and though his eyes have returned to their usual hazel , they still seem to stare at something in the far distance.

"They're almost at the mid-point!" Emiline shouts, turning to the panicked crowd behind us. "Group two, get ready to move out!"

But just as Razh's group reaches the valley's center, Finn grabs Emiline's arm. His tone ominous and frightening, he says, "They're going to die."

"Why do you say that?" I ask, my eyes peeled for any threat in the sky, but I see nothing. When Finn doesn't reply, I turn to Rys. "Has Atticus seen any drones?"

"No," he says with a shrug. "Nothing."

I can see Atticus in the sky high above us, circling as he always does when he's programmed for surveillance. In the distance, dark storm clouds are rolling our way, but there's little else to trouble us.

"It's okay, Finn," I say, but it does nothing to calm him. He takes a step outside, his eyes fixed on the clouds. When I reach for his arm, he evades my grip.

"Next group, we're leaving!" Emiline shouts, stepping around Finn to lead the next fifty residents outside.

They've gone fewer than twenty feet when Finn shouts, "Stop!"

Emiline turns to look, but she keeps moving. "We can't afford to wait!" she protests.

"You have no choice!" Finn yells, pointing to the sky.

In the far distance, the storm clouds seem to break apart into small, dark wisps.

It takes me far too long to realize the wisps aren't clouds at all.

"Drones!" I shout. "Hundreds of them!"

"Oh, God," Rys cries out, quickly inputting a series of commands on his sleeve-panel. "How did they get here so fast?"

"I suspect they've been here for some time," Illian says, leaping over to scan the horizon. "If they knew we were in the Dwelling, they've probably been gathering, waiting for their chance to strike."

"We have to stop them!" Animated and frantic, Finn is on the move now, running across the open land. I chase after him, hoping with every ounce of strength I have that we can somehow stop the attack.

"Get back inside!" I scream at Emiline as we sprint past her. She locks her eyes on the swarm of drones before halting and signaling her group. Shouting, she turns them around, and they dash at full-speed back into the Dwelling, tripping over their feet amid shouts and screams of terror.

I dash after Finn, who's trying desperately to catch up to Razh before the drones can reach his group. But by now, we can both see that it's futile. The sea of fast-moving machines is a wave on the wind, already slipping into attack position. A giant, menacing flock of predators.

The first shot hits Razh in the back. He stumbles forward, falling face-first to the ground as howls of terror and panic erupt behind him. His group, scattered and confused, is instantly disoriented, running in every direction.

Another shot rains down, then another, taking down a woman and a child. Then more fall.

Five.

Ten.

Twenty.

I don't have time to process who's still standing or who's been lost.

With a swell of nausea, I remember seeing Peric's parents. *Where are they?*

But I can't find them. All I see are bodies lying face-down on the ground while a frantic group huddles some distance away from me.

As Finn and I leap over the bodies to get to the thirty or so who are left standing, Finn thrusts his hands, palms out toward the sky, forming a shimmer-wall over the survivors' heads.

"Mommy!" a small boy screams some distance away, stumbling among the dead. I run to him, sweeping him into my arms and dashing to join the group under Finn's protective barrier, even as a hail of bullets rains down toward the terrified onlookers.

"I have to try and stop the drones!" I shout to Finn, whose face is glistening with sweat, his muscles taut from the effort required to keep the shimmer-wall intact.

Slipping away from him, I sprint until I'm just beyond the

perimeter of his shield, cross my hands over my chest, then thrust my palms toward the sea of weapons in the sky.

Anger and despair explode from me in one violent blast, larger by far than the one I thrust at Finn in the Arenum. The entire valley lights up a bright, blinding shade of blue, reflecting off the blood-soaked bodies as a tidal wave of energy assaults the drones, sending their shattered pieces raining down on Finn's barrier.

I drop my hands to my sides, exhausted but confident that the threat is gone for now.

And that's when the low, menacing rumble of what sounds like distant thunder meets my ears.

"What the hell is that?" I shout, turning to Finn, my eyes wide with fear.

"The Phoenix," he says evenly, his eyes closed.

"You mean the Dwelling's drone?"

Finn opens his eyes, locking them on mine, and nods. "The Directorate has taken possession of it."

I spin around to look toward the Dwelling and signal those left behind not to step outside. But still, a lone figure runs at us from the doorway, crying out in pain and anguish.

Peric.

In slow motion, I pivot to look toward those Finn and I managed to save. But I still don't see Peric's parents among them.

I watch helplessly as he sprints over to land on his knees next to two of the bodies. He weeps as he struggles to turn them over, to look at their faces. He sweeps his mother's hair from her face as it clings in red strands to her pale skin.

"Peric..." I whisper, but I don't have time to run to him before the Phoenix reveals itself.

Rising up from beyond the cliff face, an object the size of a jet positions itself above the valley, its wings glowing with orange, red, and yellow flames.

"Finn!" I cry.

Once again, he thrusts his hands skyward and, with the last of his strength, he summons another shield just in time to stop the first fire-bomb.

The flames explode with devastating force as they collide with Finn's barrier. He collapses to his knees, struggling to hold the shield in place.

I look around, desperately trying to figure out what to do to save those who remain. The survivors scream and wail on the ground, clinging to one another as if convinced these are their last few seconds on earth. As strong as Finn is, he can't hold on forever.

And then, in a moment of clarity, it comes to me.

"Finn," I say calmly. "Let the shield down."

"I can't," he says.

I shake my head. "She's watching. She knows you're here—that you're in the middle of all of us. She won't hurt you. Not like this. This isn't how it ends."

Finn stares at me, his hazel eyes clear and focused as he pulls his hands down, the shimmer-wall bursting into thousands of tiny points of light, then disappearing entirely.

"You feel it too, don't you?" I ask.

He nods, his gaze shifting to the Phoenix as it hovers eerily quietly in the air above us. "I can feel her eyes boring into us both," he says. "You're right. She won't attack as long as I'm standing here. It's the last vestige of her humanity."

I step close to him and pull my chin up to lock my eyes on the aircraft.

"Duchess!" I shout. "You've lost!"

With that, I thrust my palms at the massive drone, every

ounce of hatred I feel for Finn's mother channeling itself into the blast that explodes from my body. The entire sky lights up in a blinding flash as the Phoenix shatters into thousands of confetti-sized shards that fall harmlessly to earth.

But the effort steals away the last of my strength, and with one final gasp, I collapse onto my knees, and the world goes dark.

EXIT

WHEN I COME TO, I'm lying in a cot in the train's sleeper car. We're not yet moving, and I can only assume our traumatized passengers are still being escorted on board.

Finn is crouched by the cot, a hand pressed to my cheek. He smiles when I look up at him and for the first time in what seems like days, I see him—the *real* Finn—looking back at me.

His eyes are bright, his skin flushed. When I push myself up onto my elbows, he leans down and kisses me fiercely, passionately, and I feel his body tremble as though he's managed to numb the demon inside him, pushing it away so that he can feel, if only for a few precious seconds.

"Are we safe?" I ask when he pulls away.

He nods. "We are, thanks to you. "

A distant explosion rings through the air then, and in the surrounding bunks, people cry out in panic and fear.

"They're collapsing the tunnel behind the train," Finn explains, "so no one can follow us."

I push myself up to a sitting position, a hand pressed to my forehead.

"The Phoenix—they hacked it just like they hacked the Mirage Shields?"

Finn nods. "Rys thinks the Directorate found its way into the Dwelling's systems a couple of days back—though he's still not sure how they figured out where we were."

"Is there a chance there's a traitor among us?" I whisper, looking around. "Or that Diva's connection in the Directorate Guard…"

"Emiline has her suspicions, as does Illian."

"And you?" After all, I've learned to trust Finn's instincts more than anyone else's.

"No. I don't think there's a traitor. After everything my mind has told me—every confusing, incomplete message—I think I'd know if someone among us had betrayed our group."

"The Professor…" I say. "Is he all right? Did he make it out?"

"He's fine. He was concerned about you—he helped get you onto the train, in fact."

I lie back, a spell of dizziness overtaking me.

"I'm glad he made it. But Peric's parents…" My voice trails off as I remember the wretched sight as my friend clung to the two people he loved most. "Oh, God," I murmur. "I feel sick for him."

Finn wraps his arms around me and holds me tight as the tears come. His touch only makes me cry harder.

"I thought I'd lost you back there, too," I breathe. "I wasn't sure if I'd ever see your eyes again."

He pulls away, pushes my hair behind my ear, and presses his lips to mine. I kiss him back hungrily, terrified that he'll disappear on me again.

"I'm touching you now," he tells me, his forehead against mine. "But…I understand more now, Ash. I understand what I was seeing. The flames—the people. I only wish I'd stopped them before they ever stepped into the valley. I wish I'd understood my vision more clearly…"

Shaking my head, I reply, "You saw what the rest of us didn't. You saved so many lives out there."

"I didn't save them. *You* did." He pulls back, his eyes wet with tears. "I would have collapsed with one more explosion from the Phoenix. It turns out I'm not as strong as you are."

Stroking my fingers over his cheek, I shake my head. "You tried so hard to warn us. We should have listened."

"The voice speaking to you through me belonged to someone else. It's understandable that you wouldn't trust it."

"Well, right now, I hear *your* voice. And I promise I'll never lack faith in your words again, no matter what."

"Good. Because I need you to believe me when I tell you I love you."

"I know," I tell him, kissing him again. "I know, I know, I know. I love you, too. Please—stay with me as long as you can."

Wordlessly, he climbs into the cot and holds me, his warm breath stroking my skin.

Around us, I hear the whispers and quiet sobs of survivors who have filed in and taken up residence around us.

They've lost friends, family. They've just lost their homes for the second time.

And though I know their pain all too well, I also know there's not a thing in the world I could say to help them.

$\otimes$

Sometime later, when Finn has fallen asleep next to me, I climb out of the cot and make my way through the sleeper car to the next one, where I find Rys and Diva sitting together. Both look shaken, angry, and sad all at once.

"Atticus?" I ask Rys apprehensively.

"He's in the back of the car," he says, nodding toward a large, closed storage unit. "Resting and recharging. He wasn't hurt in the attack. I only wish I'd had my entire army of birds at the ready. He didn't see the attack coming. His power was fading. I should have charged him sooner…I…"

"It's not your fault," I tell him. "None of this was."

"I haven't been as vigilant as I should have been," he says with a shake of his head. "I should have known how vulnerable the Dwelling's systems were. There were red flags and I was so content, so relaxed, I didn't even see them."

"We're all at fault, then," I tell him. "We've all been distracted. Maybe we've all been over-confident, too. I felt safe in the Dwelling, just like you and everyone else did. After everything we've been through, it felt like heaven."

I close my mouth as I glance over at Diva, whose forehead is pressed to the window as though she's trying to soothe a raging fever. "I knew the Directorate was cruel," she says softly. "But I've never had to watch. I didn't know how bad it could…"

She can't bring herself to finish.

"They did it to get to me," I tell her. "*Because* of me."

She pulls away from the window, shakes her head, and wipes a tear from her eye. "No. They did it because they're cowards who are scared of what you represent. They're frightened of your power, and you're a reminder of their weakness. Every second you're alive is a second they lose strength. You're hope, Ash. Living, breathing hope."

This time, I'm the one who looks away, my jaw clenched so tight it hurts. I know she's right—the Directorate sees me as the errant wrench wreaking havoc on their very large machine. But how many lives have to be lost before our side finds a way to bring them down? How much suffering do mothers, fathers, children have to endure before we say *Enough?*

"We have to take the war to them," I say softly. "They keep coming for us, but we need to come for them."

"We will," Rys says. "But first, I think we need to talk to Illian and Kurt about the Bastille."

"What about it?"

"It's in ruins. The people there will die if they stay. Veer was the only thing keeping them alive, and now she's lost her clout with the Directorate. It's only a matter of time before another attack rains down on them."

"What do you expect Illian and Kurt to do?" I ask coldly. "Veer betrayed them ages ago. She doesn't deserve their help."

"Maybe not. But don't you think the other survivors might?"

I want to tell him no. That they're all brainwashed sheep, following the Directorate's commands, handing over their children, handing over teenage girls to breed like livestock.

But the truth is, those of us who lived in the Mire were brainwashed too. I thought when I walked into the Arc that I was starting a new life with the potential to rise up in a beautiful, idyllic society filled with smiling, happy people.

Instead, I found something close to Hell.

"Veer is a traitor to her people," says a voice from somewhere behind me.

I twist around to see Peric moving down the aisle toward us.

His face is pale, his eyes red.

"Peric," I breathe, reaching a hand out to him. But he pulls back, averting his eyes. "I'm so sorry for what happened," I tell him, my voice breaking. "If we could only have gotten to them sooner—"

"It's not your fault," he replies, his voice as tight as a wire ready to snap. "But I know whose it is, and I intend to deal with them." Setting his jaw, he stares straight ahead when he says, "When the time comes to head into the Arc, I'm coming with you. I want to help bring the Directorate to its knees."

I nod solemnly, glancing at Rys, who says, "We will, Peric. We have them where we want them. You have my word that we'll win this."

"I don't need your word," he retorts, his brows meeting. "I already know it. Every single one of them will pay for what they've done. And when it's happened, I'll be the first to dance on their graves."

ARRIVAL

OUR TRAIN PULLS into the Pit sometime after midnight.

Finn wakes from his long sleep looking bright-eyed and alert. What happened in the valley seems to have cleared his head and purged his mind of the grim swirl of torment that had overtaken him in the hours preceding the attack.

He looks more like himself now, serious, determined, focused as he helps survivors off the train.

"Do we have space for everyone?" I ask Illian quietly when I've stepped onto the train's platform. Kurt and Emiline are ushering the crowd into the Pit while Darryn and Mura steer them down various hallways to empty living quarters.

"There are wings in the Pit we haven't used in years," Illian tells me. "They were practically inaccessible when we had no power, but we're opening them back up. There's plenty of space for everyone from the Dwelling, and then some." His shoulders slumped, he watches the forlorn masses trudge by, still shell-shocked by what they witnessed in New Mexico. "There's something I should tell you, Ashen."

"What?" I ask.

"On Rys's recommendation, I've decided to contact Veer. To invite the Bastille's survivors to come live with us. They have weapons and some food, and more importantly, human lives. I want to invite them to join in our fight."

"I'm not sure that's a good idea," I tell him with a shake of my head. "Veer allied herself with the Directorate for years. And are you forgetting she decapitated one of your men?"

"I know what Veer is. But she would have no power here. She would be nothing more than a civilian living among us, one with no weapons and no power. It's her choice, of course. She can opt to keep her people in the Bastille, where they would be vulnerable, or she can swallow her pride and find safety with us. If she cares about her people, it will be an easy choice."

"You have far more faith in her than I do," I tell him, recalling the last time I looked into Veer's eyes. She reminded me of a predator ready to strike. An only slightly less aggressive version of the Duchess.

"I'm thinking of Peric, as well," Illian says. "He's lost everything and everyone. Perhaps it would help him heal to have some of his old acquaintances around. I'm sure there are some survivors in the Bastille who still count him as a friend."

I let out a sigh. "I've had the same thought," I confess. "But I'm not sure there's any helping Peric. He's angry with the Directorate, and he's not feeling any love for Veer at the moment. I still don't think it's a good idea to invite her anywhere near the Pit."

"Point taken." Illian raises a hand, ending the conversation. "But I only told you of my intentions out of respect. Please, don't forget who runs the stronghold."

Sucking in my cheeks, I nod sullenly and head into the now-bright corridor leading away from the platform. My jaw clenched tight, I wind my way to my old room, where I find Finn waiting for me on the bed.

"You look surprised to see me," he says, a slow smile teasing its way across his lips as he watches me step inside the room and close the door. "I needed to get away from people for a bit."

"I feel the same, truth be told. As much as I want to help, I can't seem to push the images of what happened from my mind. The flames..."

I slam my eyes shut, fighting back tears.

"Come here, Ash."

I open my eyes and step forward, and when he reaches a hand out, I take it. He pulls it to his lips then guides me to the bed. I study his face, his demeanor, searching for clues as to which Finn I'm looking at right now.

"I'm in here," he says quietly. "I feel strong, for once. It's as if what happened in the valley—the pain of it—made me human again. Look—if you want me to, I'll inject the professor's Xenocells right here and now. I'll destroy the nanotech once and for all."

I pull my hand away from his and stare at the floor.

"Of course I want you to," I say, tears streaming down my cheeks. "You don't know how badly I need you to stay like this —to remain the Finn I love. How badly I want..." I stop speaking and shake my head. "But what you did out there for those people—they would be dead, every one of them, if it weren't for you."

"And you," he reminds me. "We make a good team, don't we?" He looks away, the muscles in his jaw tightening. "Together, we could do a great deal of damage."

"We could. But I want to be more than a weapon. I want a life, Finn. Otherwise, what are we fighting for?"

"Then it's settled," he says with a sigh. "I'll do it."

I shake my head and reach a hand out, laying it on his arm. "No. You didn't let me finish. I want a life with you, but for that to happen, we need to make it to the end of this. The Directorate may be running scared, but they're still fighting. I don't know how, but they found us in New Mexico. We need to end this—we need to cut the heads off the snake, like the Professor said." I rise to my feet and step toward the door, turning back to face him. "As much as I want the intimacy we once had, as much as I want to feel you close to me…I can't be selfish, not now. It wouldn't be fair to those who have died, or to those who are still living."

He pushes himself to his feet, a pained look in his eyes. "Do you want me to leave?"

"No. It just…hurts to be around you like this. For a long time, I've felt like I was losing you little by little. And if I get my hopes up—if you kiss me again the way you did on the train—I may break."

He steps toward me, a dark look overtaking his features, and presses me to the door. One hand locks itself in my hair, the other slips around my neck.

I'm frozen, my eyes locked on his. But my chest heaves under his touch as Finn's breath strokes its way over my skin.

"You would give me up," he says quietly, inching closer, his lips on the verge of touching mine, "for the greater good. You would sacrifice your own happiness if it saved a single life."

He doesn't look distant now, or lost. He's intense, focused, as if his mind is melding with my own, his emotions twisting possessively around mine. My skin heats under his touch, my thoughts spinning out of control.

"Yes, I would give you up," I say, trying to convince myself the words aren't a lie. "I would surrender you if it saved a single life. And I hope you would give me up, too."

His eyes flash, his features softening, and he kisses me hard, one hand still gripping my hair, the other slipping around my waist. I feel myself losing all my strength, all my resolve, my muscles and mind weakening at once under his touch.

His lips stroke my cheekbone, my neck, my collarbone. Fumbling for only a second, he pulls my silver uniform open, yanking it away from my shoulders and kissing them needfully. Falling to his knees as the uniform drops, his lips meet my stomach. I gasp at the sensation, my resolve shattered, ready to surrender fully.

I'm about to tell him so when a knock sounds at the door.

As if shocked out of a beautiful dream, Finn leaps to his feet, stepping away, and I pull my uniform up over my shoulders, calling out.

"Just a second!" I shout as I fumble with my zipper.

I yank the door open to see Kyra and Kel standing in the doorway.

Kel leaps at me, throwing his arms around my neck. "I'm so happy you're back!" he cries out as Kyra offers up an apologetic shrug.

"So sorry to…interrupt," she says, eyeing Finn knowingly. "Kel saw all the strangers coming into the Pit and wanted to make sure you were okay."

"It's fine," I assure her, squeezing Kel. If anyone else had knocked at that moment, I might find myself outraged.

But my little brother is the reason I get up in the morning. The reason I fight.

The reason I'm willing to push the boy I love away, even if it means breaking my own heart.

I turn to Finn to see how he's feeling. His eyes are still intense and warm, but that warmth is now accompanied by a look of sadness, and I don't have to ask what he's thinking about.

Merit.

His brother, still trapped with the Duke and Duchess inside the Arc.

"You were gone for so long," Kel says. "I was wondering if you'd ever come back. But it's cool that you rescued all those people."

"I only wish we could have rescued more," I tell him, my voice threatening to break as I pull him in for another hug. "You don't know how much."

PARLEY

After this brief visit, Finn tells me he'd like to check in with Illian to see how things are progressing.

"I'll go with you," I tell him, looking to Kyra and Kel, an apology lifting my brows. "I hate to ask but…"

"You want me to babysit Kyra?" Kel interrupts with a giggle only a child is capable of. "Done!"

"Exactly," I chuckle. It feels good to smile, and right now, my brother is about the only person on earth who could possibly coax a laugh out of me. "But I'll catch you later, okay?"

Kel nods, taking Kyra by the hand. "Come on then," he commands, "I need to make sure you've cleaned your room before I can let you play with the other kids."

As we watch them go, Finn tells me, "Your brother is amazingly resilient."

"He is, isn't he?" I sigh. "I'm grateful for it, if only for his sake. He's been through so much."

"I can only hope Merit proves as tough," Finn murmurs as we pad down the corridor in the other direction.

I hesitate before asking, "Have you had any more visions of him?"

"Every single night," Finn tells me bitterly. "I see him in my dreams, whether I'm awake or sound asleep. Someone takes him, but I can't see where he's going. I try to reach for him, but he's so far away...it haunts me, Ash."

"We'll find him. I promise."

Finn shakes his head. "The thing is, it hasn't happened yet. Right now, he's in my parents' residence, safe."

"But you said..."

"He hasn't been taken yet. But he will be, and when it happens, I have to find him. It may sound like madness, but something tells me he's the key to winning this war. As much as it pains me to say, I have to let this play out. I have to let him go."

"Let him go? What if someone hurts him? What if..."

"Those who will take him won't hurt him," he says mysteriously. "He's too valuable a commodity."

There's something final about his words, so I choose to let it go. Finn understands his visions far better than I do, and as much as they frighten me, I've begun to grow strangely accustomed to them.

When we reach the Central Chamber, Illian tells us that he and Kurt are headed out for a parley with Veer and Piper in the woods.

"I've sent word via one of Rys's birds that we want to talk. We'll be meeting the two women shortly."

"One of you should stay in the Pit," I warn. "Veer could easily have her snipers in position, waiting to take you both out. It would leave the Pit without a leader."

His voice eerily calm, Finn says, "Veer won't hurt them."

Shooting him a sideways glance, Illian nods. "He's right,

it's unlikely. She has nothing to gain by killing Kurt or me, except isolation and death for her people. But if it makes you feel any better, we'll be bringing weapons. And remember, we have Atticus watching over us. He'll warn us if there are snipers among the trees."

When they've left us, Finn and I head to find Rys, who's in his room, monitoring their progress through Atticus's eyes.

"It's so strange to watch," I murmur as I stare over his shoulder at the image of Kurt and Illian making their way through the woods. "To think that's how you stalked me for so long when I was out there."

"A bit creepy, isn't it?" Rys replies sheepishly. "Sorry about that again. But also...not sorry."

Our eyes remain locked on the screen until Illian and Kurt reach a small clearing about twenty minutes away, where they find Veer and Piper already waiting for them. Atticus flaps down to land on a nearby branch and I stare through his eyes, breathless and apprehensive as I listen in on the conversation.

"Illian," Veer says in her velvety voice as she steps toward him. She looks strong, unharmed by the recent attack on the Bastille that killed so many. "How nice to see you and your...um..."

She eyes Kurt up and down, a look of cold judgment on her face.

"My *partner*," Illian says, his tone curt.

"Partner, yes," she replies as if the word is so foreign to her it should be obvious why she didn't think of it. "So tell me, why is it that you wanted to see us? We have nothing to offer you. But I'm sure you already know that."

"I'm well aware. And I'm sorry for your losses; what happened to the Bastille was an atrocity. I hope you see now that the Directorate was never deserving of your loyalty."

"The Directorate punished us for our failures," she says matter-of-factly, and I half expect her to shrug. "Had we managed to deliver Ashen Spencer and your man, they would never have hurt us."

"Ashen Spencer and our man were never yours to deliver. I need to know you understand that before we proceed."

Veer exchanges a glance with Piper, who nods her head slightly.

"We understand perfectly," Veer says, her tone sickly-sweet. "We aren't here to sing the praises of the Directorate."

"Good, because we have a proposition for you."

"I'm all ears."

Illian proceeds to fill them in on his offer to accept the Bastille's survivors into the Pit. "You may live among us. We will provide you with food, water, shelter. But there are conditions."

"What might those be?"

"That your snipers turn in their weapons. They—and you —live as civilians in the Pit. We protect you, we feed you. But you, Veer, are not an authority figure anymore, nor will you try to overthrow our existing hierarchy. You will simply be one of the group. Your time as a liaison with the Directorate is at an end."

Veer smiles. Piper, as always, looks coldly obedient.

"I could have chosen to join you in the Pit years ago," Veer tells Illian. "What makes you think I want to now?"

"Your town is in ruins. You have no power, no influence over the Directorate, and you know they could strike again at any time. You're hobbled, and if you don't take me up on my offer, I fear you'll be killed. The Directorate is unwilling to risk any sort of rebellion at this point, and that includes you and yours."

Veer raises her chin and stares at her rival, but says nothing. After a few seconds, she says, "Fine. We accept your offer. We will gather our people, and we will bring everything we can with us to the Pit. Food, clothing, supplies. We'll have to do it when night falls, of course."

Illian nods. "We have ways of ridding the sky of the Directorate's drones," he tells her without explaining his meaning. "Your people will be safe if we move quickly and quietly."

"Of course. Meet us here tonight. Ten p.m. I will have the survivors with me, and you can lead us to your so-called *Pit*." With that, she turns to walk away.

"Veer," Illian says, his tone sharp.

She stops, but only turns her head.

"If you betray me again, I will kill you myself."

That night, I watch as the first of the Bastille's residents come filing into the Pit through the Central Chamber. Silent and ghostly, they move heavily as the Pit's workers guide them toward the various residential wings that remain unoccupied.

Last to enter is Veer, who looks with disdain upon the Central Chamber, her eyes narrowing as they land on the large holographic fireplace.

"It will do, I suppose," she sneers.

As I watch from a distance, Peric sidles up to me, his expression grim.

"Are you sure you want to be here right now?" I ask him.

"After all her years of lying to my face, I want Veer to look me in the eye. I want her to admit what she did to me."

When Veer spots him and steps over to us, her expression is as proud and haughty as ever.

"I'm so sorry about your parents," she tells Peric in a failed attempt at warmth.

He braces next to me. "Which is it? You're sorry that you lied to me for years about their death, or that they're dead now, thanks to your psychotic friends in the Arc?"

Instead of replying, she simply smiles and turns to me. "Ashen Spencer. I thought *you'd* be dead by now."

"I have nine lives," I tell her, wishing I had retractable claws and could shred her face as a cat might. "No thanks to you."

When she's stepped away without another word, I find myself scanning the remaining group of Bastille residents for a face I haven't seen yet.

"Where's Cyntra?" I mutter under my breath.

But just as I ask the question, the girl I once called a friend steps into the room in one of her flouncy dresses, looking as though she's about to attend a young child's birthday party.

She bounces toward us and throws her arms around Peric, but he remains stiff, unwilling to return the embrace.

"Per!" she purrs. "I'm sooo happy to see you!"

"I wish I could say the same." The pain in his voice is palpable as he pushes her away, turns, and leaves the room.

"And Ash!" she coos, unfazed as she spins to face me. "My gosh, look at you in your silver. It suits you, with your pale skin. So, where's this handsome fellow of yours I've heard so much about?"

I'm about to tell her I don't know where Finn is when I turn to see him striding into the room, his eyes locked on Cyntra. Though they've never met, I can tell he's deduced who she is.

He steps over to stand next to me.

"Cyntra, I take it," he says, slipping a possessive arm around my waist.

"Finn, right? You're as handsome as Ash always said you were." She puts a hand out to lay it on his chest in a far-too-familiar gesture, but he grabs her wrist and pulls it away, squeezing hard enough to make her wince.

"You'd do well not to touch me. And if you touch Ash, I'll kill you. If you betray her or any of us, I'll kill you for that, too. That's a promise."

"Feisty," she sings in her most flirty tone before skipping over to Veer, who's talking to Piper on the other side of the room.

"Thanks," I say softly. "I didn't expect that."

"I don't think the Bastille's people will try anything," Finn replies. "But I want them to know what will happen if they do."

LAST NIGHT

OVER THE NEXT FEW DAYS, the former residents of the Dwelling and the Bastille settle into the subterranean stronghold, their faces pale and drawn, their eyes overtaken by a profound sadness that will never fully heal.

But no one among them looks more devastated than Peric, who resembles a ghostly version of his former self. His spirit is sapped, his shoulders slumped, all hope stolen from him in one single, horrifying moment.

I try to speak to him occasionally to ask how he's faring. He puts up a strong front, trying his best not to collapse under the weight of all that's happened. Each time Veer comes near him, I see rage simmering near the surface of his skin, but he says nothing.

She may as well be dead to him now.

In a meeting one afternoon with Illian, Kurt, Emiline, and Professor Lyon, Rys tells us that the upper levels of the Arc have gone largely silent. Now that he has disabled or taken over most of their drones, the Directorate has entirely ceased to enforce its rules, isolating themselves from anyone below Level Two-Fifty.

Riots have broken out in several of the lower districts, resulting in shops destroyed by angry mobs, Directorate Guard members beaten to within an inch of their lives. New de facto leaders of various of the Arc's sectors have begun to emerge here and there, Consortium symbols emblazoned proudly on their clothing.

"We're nearly ready to infiltrate," Rys informs us. "As soon as Illian gives us the go-ahead, I say it's time to move in."

Move in, I think. *Interesting choice of words.*

Never again do I want to live in the Arc. I have no desire to subject myself to that awful place, regardless of how exquisitely beautiful parts of it may be. I'd sooner take my chances foraging in the woods for the rest of my days.

"How can you tell the Directorate hasn't been gathering and preparing for a major attack?" Illian asks Rys. "For all we know, they're meeting behind closed doors to strategize, just as we are."

With a smug grin, Rys shakes his head. "There are secret cameras in every one of those residences—probably installed by the Duchess's private cabal of miscreants. And I have eyes on all of them."

"And?"

"The Directorate members are moping around, pacing through their residences like restless zombies. They don't know what to do with themselves. Not to mention that a lot of the Guard has taken to wearing civilian clothing in public places for fear of reprisal. Basically, the entire organization has collapsed, without so much as a gunshot fired by us."

"There's something I don't understand," I interject. "What happened to the cat-bots like the one we saw in the Palace

Grounds? There must be more of them. Why isn't the Directorate Guard using them?"

"They belong to the King's forces, and the King ordered them disabled for transport some time ago. There are none in the Arc at this point."

"Transport?"

Rys nods. "He's sending them somewhere. I haven't been able to track their trajectory, but I suspect they're headed to the Behemoth."

"The arcology in Manhattan? Why?"

Rys bows his head for a second, chuckling. "I haven't told you the best part. The King and his family have fled. They took one of their jets east. I was only able to track them as far as Missouri before I lost the signal. My theory is that the King needs something to offer in exchange for refuge, and the Behemoth's Aristocracy is just sadistic enough to embrace feline killing machines. So, any bots or other tech the King had in his possession is probably in the Behemoth as we speak."

"One head of the snake has severed itself," Professor Lyon says with a smile. "What about the Duke and Duchess?"

"They're still in the Arc," Rys replies. "Though the Duchess is clever, and has disabled every camera in the Davenport residence by now."

"How do you know they're still there, then?" I ask.

Rys pulls out his small glass screen, flicks a finger tip in a rapid shape over its surface, and shows me a video feed of the Duchess sitting in the Davenports' living room, stewing.

"How are we seeing that?" Illian asks, impressed.

"Nano-drones," Rys says. "They're smaller than gnats— almost invisible. I have them follow her almost everywhere."

"Excellent," Illian says with a chuckle. "Well, I'd say the Arc is well and truly secured, and ready for new leadership. We'll be heading out in two days' time. Emiline will be in charge here while we're gone."

I turn to look at Emiline, whose expression is stoic. I haven't seen her show any emotion since Razh was killed—since so many of her people died in the valley. I suppose the mark of a true leader is the ability to suffer loss and go on leading without crumbling. But I wonder at times if she's as close to her breaking point as the rest of us.

"Is Peric coming with us?" I ask, refraining from revealing just how concerned I am for him.

With a nod, Illian explains. "He came to me this morning and asked that he be included in our party. I couldn't say no—he's been through too much, and the thought of leaving him here felt like a cruelty. Much as I'd hoped having the Bastille's population close by could help, I believe I was wrong on that front. Peric needs a purpose, a distraction. And I think a trip to the Arc might help him to heal."

I shoot Finn a look and bite my lip when I see the same question in his eyes:

Is Peric strong enough for what's to come?

$$\otimes$$

The night before we're to leave for the Arc, a knock sounds at my door.

When I open it, Finn is standing before me in a white t-shirt and jeans, a strange, almost wild look in his eyes. Like a red flag of warning, his gaze burns into me as he steps forward, locking the door from the inside and pressing a palm to my cheek.

He pulls me close and kisses me hungrily, all his former

coldness melted away by an intense surge of heat. When he unzips my uniform and pulls it away from my shoulders, I allow it to drop to the floor. I step out of the garment, vulnerable as I brace for whatever is to come.

The Arc is a dangerous place, and I'm all too aware this could be my last night with Finn.

And I want every bit of him.

Instead of guiding me to the bed, he pushes me against the wall, his lips on my neck. I gasp, laughing at how cold the Pit's solid stone is against my bare back.

When Finn pulls me close, I bite his lip just hard enough to induce a small cry of pain, and he returns my laugh. I feel his smile against my lips. A mischievous grin, one I haven't seen from him in far too long.

My fingers are tangled in his hair now, their tips clawing their way down to his neck, possessive and greedy as I kiss him deeply, a feral need rearing its head somewhere inside me.

Finn lets out a sound akin to a growl before dragging his teeth along my neck, my shoulder.

When he steps back and yanks off his shirt, a memory floods my mind of our day spent by the chilly pond in the mountains before Illian and his people first found us. He's beautiful, his chest hard and tight, his arms braided with taut muscle.

When I first laid eyes on him at the Introduction Ceremony in the Arc, he was still a boy.

But there's no denying now that the past months have made him a man.

Tall, strong, and powerful, he speaks only with his eyes, his emotions written on his face as he wards off the power that's so often taken hold of him over the last days.

He takes me in his arms again and trails kisses along my skin, his tongue tasting my flesh as though I'm the greatest meal he's ever savored. As his lips move down my body, my breath hitches in my throat and I wrap myself around him, eyes tightly shut as I hold onto the sensation, trying to etch it into my memory.

My nails scratch at his flesh, taking possession of him, as starved for this moment as I've ever been for anything in this world.

"I need everything from you," I whisper against his skin, my mind swirling, devoid of thoughts yet filled with them, all at once. "I *want* you."

"I want you." He presses himself against me, his body fever-hot, his breath coming in fits and starts. "I've never wanted anything more."

But the second he utters the last few words, he lets me go and leaps back so quickly that my eyes and mind hardly register his movement.

"No," he says, shaking his head even as his eyes shift from hazel to light gray.

The power inside him is back, fighting with his emotions, his desire.

Tears stream down his cheeks as he tries to push it away. I step toward him, hoping to calm whatever torment has taken up residence inside him, but he holds his hands out to stop me.

"I can't," he says. "It's too strong."

My legs weaken under me as I ask, "What's too strong? What are you seeing, Finn?"

"You," he says. "Hurt. But by what, I can't see."

"Nothing is hurting me," I assure him.

Except for you pulling away when we were so close.

"I can't, Ash," he breathes. "This isn't how I want it to happen for us."

"But I want—"

He shakes his head. "I want it, too. But not like this—not feeling like I'm feeling right now. There's enough humanity still inside me left to know it wouldn't be right."

His eyes flash bright in the darkness. He's angry at the world, at fate, for putting us here.

He steps toward me and reaches for me, pulling me tight to his chest. I bask in the sensation of his skin against mine, of the hunger I still feel in him.

"I'm so sorry," he tells me. "But I don't want to associate loving you with the darkest of thoughts. I can't do that to us. I need to be free of this—I need to be free to love you. When we've won our fight—when we've taken the Arc—I promise, we can be together."

I nod, tears streaming down my cheeks. But I know, deep down, that it's not a promise I can ask him to keep. Our world is full of obstacles and enemies. It's not like Finn and I will suddenly be able to buy a small cottage in the mountains and live in peace for the rest of our days.

Someone will always come for us...and the thought fills me with fear.

"Stay with me tonight," I say softly. "Don't go. Please."

"I won't."

I guide him to the bed and we lie down, Finn on his back and me with my tear-stained cheek pressed to his chest. As he holds me, I can feel him fighting against the force inside him that wants to shut down his emotions, to pull him selfishly away from me.

My voice quakes when I ask, "Do you think we'll ever have a normal life?"

"I don't think there's any such thing as normal. Not anymore." He kisses the crown of my head, his arms tight around me. "If I could give you anything in this world, though, it would be a normal life, one without killing and cruelty."

I think about those words, both beautiful and sweet.

But they're only words.

"A life without killing or cruelty doesn't exist," I murmur against his skin. "Not in our world. And we're foolish if we try to convince ourselves otherwise."

I pull my head up and look into his eyes. They've regained their color, all traces of gray disappearing "But I do know I love you. Even the version of you who tears himself away from me and shuts down—the one I can't get close to. Because inside him is a person who would sacrifice himself to save the world."

DEPARTURE

As PROMISED, our party prepares to leave for the Arc the following morning.

Rys and Atticus, Finn, Illian, Kurt, Peric, and I are each equipped with cloaking garments, weapons, and enough food to sustain us on the long hike ahead.

When I say goodbye to Kel, it's with tears in my eyes. Kyra has assured me a thousand times that she will keep an eye on him for me, but I can't help feeling a pang of something more than sorrow when I tell him I'll see him soon.

"You promise?" he asks.

"Of course," I murmur, though I'm terrified that it's a promise I'll have to break. "The Arc is already secured. I'm not going to war or anything—we won't be doing anything super-dangerous."

I tell myself the last part isn't a lie. The mere act of leaving the Pit is a massive risk. There will still be Directorate Guardsmen looking for us in the woods, and maybe even the occasional errant drone.

As we begin our hike in silence, it's the Duchess I think of

—her cold eyes, her tight lips, a look of perpetual disdain. I wonder with a heavy heart whether either of us will survive our next confrontation.

Carrying a large pack, Peric walks just ahead of me, his head low. There's a determination in his stride as he keeps up with Kurt, who's leading our party.

"What did you bring with you?" I ask him in a meager attempt at small talk.

"A few supplies," he tells me. "The Professor gave me some medication in case we find wounded on our side who need treatment."

"They have hospitals in the Arc, you know."

"I'm aware. But they're run by the Directorate."

"Not anymore," I reply with a smile. "I suspect that most are on our side now."

We walk for many hours, stopping only when we reach the frigid creek where Rys and I used to fetch water—the creek just beyond Sector Eight that we could only reach via an old drainage pipe that pierced the Directorate's wall.

But as we near the high wall that surrounds the Mire, Rys raises his hand, signaling the rest of us to stop.

"I'm going to send Atticus ahead to check out Sector Eight," he tells us. "To scan for patrols…just in case."

While he cradles his small glass screen in his palm and watches, I stay close to Finn, who has temporarily pulled his uniform's cloaking fabric away from his face. He's looking even more tense than usual, as are Illian and Kurt under their hoods.

"What is it?" I ask Finn, but he just shakes his head.

"I'm not sure," he tells me. "But it seems I'm not the only one who has a bad feeling right now."

"Bad feeling about what?"

After a few seconds Rys tightens, and I'm certain I hear a small cry escape his lips.

"Rys? What's happening? Is Atticus okay?"

When he fails to reply, I step toward him, looking over his shoulder at the small screen in his hand.

At first, what I'm seeing looks like nothing more than a large, uneven hill of dirt and random dark-colored detritus.

It's only when I see the precariously-leaning remnants of a blackened wall that I realize I'm looking at the charred remains of a streetscape.

"What *is* that?" I ask, confused.

"It's...my house. They've burned it. They've burned *everything*."

Without another word or thought, I start sprinting toward the corrugated drainage pipe that so often led Rys and me out of our old neighborhood and into the foothills beyond the wall.

"Ash!" Finn's voice cries from behind me, but my feet are already stomping their way through the pipe, metallic foot-falls echoing around me in a traumatic drumbeat.

As if in greeting, plumes of smoke rise up from the ground as I step into Sector Eight. The asphalt is half-melted, the few trees that lined the street turned to charcoal.

"They destroyed it," I say under my breath as Finn catches up to me and takes hold of my arm. "They torched our homes..." And then, the worst occurs to me.

"The children."

I turn to see Rys stomping toward me out of the pipe. His eyes, like mine, are fixed on the smoke rising mockingly into the air.

"Gone," he says, his voice filled with bitter certainty. "They're gone. Every one of them."

"The other Sectors?"

"You and I both know this wasn't random. Sector Eight is the only one they destroyed."

"It was a punishment. For you, for me. And a warning to others." Sickened, I slip away from Finn, pressing a hand to the round edge of the drainage pipe and doubling over as a surge of nausea hits. I throw up, releasing only a fraction of the rage and pain surging inside me.

Wiping my mouth, I turn back to the others.

"This was her doing," I say, pulling my eyes to Finn's. "Your mother's."

"I know," he tells me. "And when we find her, I may have to kill her myself."

INFILTRATION

THE ONE SILVER lining to the Directorate's bombing of our homes—if there can possibly be such a thing—is that there are no patrols in the area. No one is awaiting our arrival when we step out of the drainage pipe and make our way toward the underground tunnel that will lead us to the Arc.

We cup our hands over our faces as we're greeted by the toxic remnants of a world taken down by one woman's spiteful cruelty and malice. *I will not breathe in the stench of death. I will not give the Duchess that satisfaction.*

When we arrive at the underground platform, there is no train. After sending Atticus to search the tunnel for it, Rys tells us it has halted a couple of miles up the track with no indication that it will ever run again.

"They've disconnected the power," he says. "We'll have to walk. And when we arrive, we'll have to stay out of sight in case any Directorate Guard are still on active patrol around the Hub."

"Walk?" I say wearily. "But it's miles to the Hub."

"I know, but we have no choice."

After two more hours spent hiking along the track in near total darkness, we find ourselves trudging toward a distant spot of light. With the rest of us cloaked, Rys snaps a silver bracelet onto his wrist and tells us his new secret identity is Kevin Miller, and that he's a Directorate Guardsman who's been on duty two years.

I might find it amusing, if I weren't exhausted from the trauma of seeing the neighborhood where I grew up in ruins.

Tense and wary, we follow him silently out of the tunnel as he approaches a guard who has been tasked with protecting the entrance to the nearest Conveyor.

The guard narrows his eyes at Rys, scanning him from head to toe.

"What were you doing in the tunnel to Sector Eight?" the guard asks.

"I was...I...was checking for..."

It's one of the few times I can remember seeing Rys at a loss for words. It seems the destruction of our old homes is weighing on him as heavily as it is on me.

"Wait a minute." The guard, a young man of twenty or so, lifts his chin and says, "I recognize you."

I reach silently for my dagger, prepared to hurl it at the man's throat if he makes a move to notify the Directorate of Rys's presence.

"You're Rystan Decker!" the guard says. But even as I pull the blade from its hilt, steel whispering against leather, he beams like an excited child.

Confused, Rys asks the question we're all thinking.

"Why the hell are you smiling?"

"You're the Crimson Dreg's sidekick! You're the guy with the birds! The *Genius Dreg*!"

Rys turns around and shoots us a look before remembering he can't actually *see* us.

Turning back to the guard, he sputters, "Aren't you going to try and arrest me or something?"

"*Arrest* you?" the young man chuckles. "Hell no." With that, he reaches for the gold rose on his chest and rips it away to reveal a Consortium logo underneath: the familiar circle crossed by two swords—the signature my father used on his paintings.

O for Oliver. T for Tessa.

"I'm one of you," the guard beams.

Stunned, I pull the cloaking fabric from my face, pressing my fingers to my palms to disable my uniform's stealth mode, and step toward the man.

"Holy crap. Ashen freaking Spencer herself," he says, and for a second I'm convinced he's on the verge of bowing before me. "I'm honored to be in your presence."

"Are you for real?" I can feel the rest of my hidden party edging up next to me, no doubt as skeptical as I am.

"I can assure you that I am. My name is Clifton. I'm a former Dreg from Sector Three."

"How long have you been in wearing a Consortium logo?"

"A...while," he grins. "You know, you and I have a friend in common, Ashen."

"A friend...?" As I say the words, my mind clears. "Diva, you mean. You're the Directorate Guardsman who got her to New Mexico?"

Clifton nods excitedly. "I've watched every one of your broadcasts multiple times. I can't wait to introduce you to the others in HQ. Is Diva okay? I saw what happened..."

"The attack," Peric interrupts, speaking for the first time in what seems like ages. "You saw it?"

Clifton's excitement wanes as he studies Peric's expression. "We all did. The Directorate likes to broadcast their kills now. They used to keep them secret, but it's gotten to the point where they're proud of their cruelty."

"I'm glad they're proud," Peric says bitterly. "It'll make it that much easier when the time comes."

When the time comes for what?

I tell myself he must be talking about the future trials—the day we finally bring the Directorate's leaders to justice. A day we all look forward to.

He's right. Their pride will definitely make it easier to throw them all into the Hold.

"Clifton, you said something about HQ," I interject. "Where is it?"

"You don't know?"

I shake my head. "I didn't even know there *was* a Headquarters."

"Come with me, then," Clifton says, scanning the space behind me in an attempt to make out figures in the shadows. "All of you. Come on—Finn Davenport must be hiding back there somewhere, right? The *Rebel Aristocrat* is my hero."

"Rebel Aristocrat, is it?" I say, turning to look for Finn's eyes.

"Could be worse," Finn says as he pulls himself out of stealth.

"There he is," Clifton replies, his smile glowing under the lights. "I am losing my mind right now, just for the record."

"That makes at least three of us," I reply under my breath.

"I'll take you all to HQ," Clifton promises, his voice animated as he leads us onto the Conveyor. "You're going to love it."

Once he's programmed our destination, Kurt aims his

weapon at Clifton's head in warning. "I appreciate that you're wearing our symbol on your chest, but you understand that we're not stupid, yes?"

Sweating, Clifton nods. "Of course I do. Your broadcasts have managed to turn the tides in the Arc. No one thought that was even possible."

"Good. So you understand that if the Conveyor doors open to an army of Directorate Guard with their weapons trained on us, *you* die first."

Clifton nods again.

"It's all right," Rys tells Kurt. "I know exactly where he's taking us."

"Where?" I ask as the Conveyor comes to a stop.

"A place you've seen before, Ash."

When the doors slide open, we step out into a large white room filled with paintings. On the far wall is a portrait encased in glass—one I've seen a thousand times, though never in person.

"The Mona Lisa," I breathe. "We're back in the Louvre?"

Clifton nods. "Also known as Consortium HQ. It's an incredibly secure building—security checkpoints and cameras everywhere. We took it over days ago…with a little help."

He leads us through several rooms filled with impressively forged artwork until we reach a large chamber that's been stripped bare, its walls pure white. Scattered over the marble floor are dozens of chairs, small desks, and one long conference table. Hovering in the air are a number of holo-screens showing a multitude of the Arc's corridors.

"You knew we'd be coming here, Rys," Illian says as we enter the room. "How?"

"I *may* have helped set this place up from a distance."

"You're full of surprises, aren't you?"

"I just wanted us to get ahead of the game. We have a lot of work to do."

"Let's get started, then," Illian replies with a smile.

Clifton continues to lead our party, but when I notice Finn lagging behind, I stop to wait for him. He looks preoccupied, his expression grim.

"You all right?" I ask, searching his eyes for the faraway look I've come to dread. "What is it?"

"They're so confident the Directorate will simply do as they wish, now that we're here," he says. "But we both know there's one person who will never agree to any demands we may have."

"Your mother, you mean."

He nods. "My mother is dangerous at the best of times, but back her into a corner and she becomes a wild, snapping dog."

"Tranquilizer guns exist for a reason," I say with a bitter snicker.

But his grim expression only deepens.

"What is it?" I ask, more serious this time. "Have you had another of your visions?"

He shakes his head. "It's not that I've seen her in my mind's eye. It's that I haven't—but I can *feel* her scheming. She won't stand quietly by while we take the Arc. It's not in her blood to surrender without a brutal fight."

"What is it that you think she'll do?"

Pulling my hand to his lips, he kisses it before looking me in the eye and saying, "For once, I only wish I knew, so I could stop it before it starts."

Over the next several hours, we're treated to a show of the Consortium's newly impressive strength.

The Louvre is swarming with men and women who have thrown off the Directorate's shackles and taken up arms against them. Soldiers. Former Chaperons whose drug-releasing implants have been summarily ripped out. Former Directorate Guard who, like Clifton, are tired of lies.

It seems there aren't more than a handful of Directorate Guardsmen who have remained loyal to their cowardly overlords.

I revel in the thought that the Duchess and her colleagues really have lost, and delight to think how it must eat away at her.

Finn, too, seems to have relaxed a little since our arrival, as if he too can see a light at the end of our grim tunnel.

Rys busies himself introducing Illian and Kurt to members of the new army who have helped him to hack into the Directorate's systems. It seems my old friend has been busier than he ever let on.

After a time, Illian takes Rys and me aside.

"I'd like to make a broadcast," he says to Rys before turning my way. "And if it's all right, Ashen, I'd like to speak to the Arc's population for the first time. Would you be willing to introduce me?"

"I'd be happy to," I tell him with a quiet sigh of relief. The truth is, I want nothing more than to fade into the shadows, to disappear from the memories of those in the Arc who have stared at my face with misplaced reverence.

I never wanted fame or glory—all I ever wanted was freedom for those who, like me, have suffered greatly at the hands of the Directorate.

With Illian's leadership, there is hope now as a new dawn

breaks in the Arc. Those who were lied to have had their blindfolds ripped away, and are free to make their own choices. They're even free to leave, if they so desire. Free to watch as we bring the Directorate to justice…and to celebrate as the lie called the Blight fades into distant memory.

After I've changed into my red dress and spent some time contemplating how best to introduce Illian, I find myself scanning the room for Peric's face. He should be as pleased as anyone to find we're about to bring down the government that ruined his life, though I can't exactly expect him to feel anything close to happiness.

When I don't spot him, I ask Rys if he's seen him.

"He was here earlier," he informs me. "I was showing him some of the feeds to the Directorate's residences. He seemed really interested; he kept asking questions about the tiny drones I use for surveillance. He wanted to know if there was a way to access them himself."

"And is there?"

"Sure. I gave him a tour of the system I use to control them, showed him how to move them from one residence to the next—even how to send new ones in if he chooses. It seemed to take his mind off his pain, so I left him to it."

With a sigh, I reply, "I'm glad he has a distraction. Thanks for looking out for him."

Illian interrupts to ask if I'm ready to address the Arc.

"I am," I tell him with a smile.

Stepping over to the side of the large room, I position myself in front of the camera, nodding when I've inhaled a deep breath. Diva isn't here to polish my appearance, but my excitement has brought a flush to my cheeks. My hair hangs down in ribbons around my shoulder, and the red dress, as always, stands out like fresh blood against the Arc's white walls.

When the camera's familiar light appears, I exhale and begin.

"I come to you today from the Consortium's headquarters within the walls of the Arc. We have taken control—not by force, but by truth. And now, with your help, we will bring the Directorate to justice. But it's time for me to step away from the camera. I will no longer be showing my face to the masses. After all, I am a rebel, a Dreg from Sector Eight. I am no politician or leader. I am one of you."

With a smile, I look over at Illian, who's tense as he waits for me to finish.

"I wish to introduce you to someone who is a *natural* leader—a man I trust with my life. He gave me shelter when I had none. He has saved the lives of countless men, women, and children. He is a man who will protect those of you who live in Arc just as he's protected so many others."

With that, I step away, beaming with pride as Illian positions himself in front of the camera in his Consortium uniform.

His tone is authoritative but gentle when he says, "My name is Illian. For years, I have lived in an underground stronghold with several hundred of my people. We watched as the Directorate killed thousands. We wept for those lost to the Blight, to the government's cruelty. And so, I would be lying if I didn't tell you we have waited for this day for a very long time. Those who ran the Arc—who brought so many of you to this place under false pretenses—have a long history of cruelty for cruelty's sake. But I'm not here to seek vengeance. I'm not here to tell you they need to suffer and die. I'm here to tell you judgment day has come for the Directorate.

"As I speak, those accused of crimes against humanity are incarcerated in their homes on the Arc's highest levels. One by one, we will bring them to the Arenum for trial. We will form a jury of fair-minded individuals, as was the tradition in the days before the lie known as the Blight took hold. And I promise you, we will grant the Directorate what our people never received: a chance to defend themselves. With your support, justice will be served."

As Illian continues to talk, I look around at the Consortium's new members—the men and women who stand at attention, watching their new leader approvingly.

I have no doubt that like me, many of them would love to see the Directorate destroyed.

But Illian is no destroyer. He's a true leader, a man driven by reason rather than emotion—one who will treat them with kindness while simultaneously commanding respect.

When he's finished speaking and the camera feed has been cut, he returns without ceremony to talk to his new military force.

Rys steps over to me, his eyes locked on the small glass screen he uses to monitor his birds and other drones.

"What is it?" I ask, seeing the look of shock in his eyes.

He turns to look at me, his face pale as he says, "It's...for you."

His hands shaking, he hands me the screen.

"I'm sorry, Ash. I was watching her. I...don't know how she managed it..."

When I see the face grinning at me from the screen's surface, it's all I can do not to let it fall to the ground and shatter into a thousand pieces.

I search for Finn, catching his eye as he speaks to Kurt.

When he steps over and takes my hand, I'm grateful for his warmth, his strength. I need it now, more than ever.

"What is it?" he says softly, concern lacing its way through his voice.

"It's…your mother. She's in the Arenum."

4 2

FACE-OFF

My blood freezes, a shiver running over my flesh as I stare into the Duchess's cold eyes.

"Ashen Spencer," she says in that sickly sweet voice of hers, "I have a proposition for you."

"What do you want?" I ask coldly.

"I'll tell you only when I have you all to myself. Come meet me in the Arenum. Alone."

I could ask how she got out of the Davenport residence, how she managed to evade Rys's lockdown. But instead, I force out an attempt at an amused laugh. "Why would I do that, when we could easily send our troops to arrest you?"

"Because of this," she replies. The camera pans slowly to her left, where I see Peric standing between two Directorate Guardsmen, one eye bleeding, his head drooping slightly. "If you wish to see your friend alive again, I'd suggest you do what I ask. As I said...come alone."

When she cuts the feed a moment later, Finn grabs my arm.

"You know her—you know what she's capable of. You can't do this."

"If I don't go, you and I both know she'll kill Peric."

His voice is grim when he says, "Peric is already as good as dead."

I shake my head, my eyes burning with bitter tears. "No, he's not. You saw him—he's alive. It's me she wants. He's a negotiating tool, nothing more."

"She'll kill you, Ash," he pleads. "Please, don't do this."

My voice is gentle when I say, "You have nothing to worry about—I can defend myself."

"But will you?" he asks, his voice stretched by grief. "If she threatens to take Peric's life, will you trade yours for his?"

Ah. So that's what he's afraid of.

I stare into his eyes, pressing a hand to his cheek. So many times, I've watched him push his emotions to the side as he was overtaken by the visions in his mind. Horrors of what was to come.

But now, all I see is pure, raw desperation. I see love. I see need.

"What have you seen in your mind, Finn?" I ask him. "Have you seen my death?"

He pulls back, closing his eyes. "A wall of flame. An explosion. I can almost taste the odor of burning flesh. I…I see your face, contorted with sorrow." His eyes open. "But no. I haven't seen your death."

"Then you have nothing to worry about. You gave me a gift, remember? The Surge. I'm not afraid to use it, not anymore."

"Ash," Rys interjects, "I'm with Finn. This is lunacy. She's not going to meet you alone—she'll bring Cyphers with her, for one thing. By my count, there are still two unaccounted

318

for in the Arc, and I would bet all my drones she has them at her beck and call."

"Then you can give me two Needlebeaks to take them down," I say sharply. "I'm not going to walk in there empty-handed, you two. I have a blade. I have my wits, too."

"I…" Rys bows his head and lets out a rough breath. "Of course I'll give you Needlebeaks, Ash. But I still don't like where this is going."

"You don't have to like it. Just…trust me. Please."

"Fine," Rys says, slipping over to his bag and extracting two small silver eggs. When he hands them to me, I slip them into a pocket on the red dress.

"You should be wearing your uniform," Finn says. "For protection."

"I'm the Crimson Dreg," I reply with a smile. "And I don't need a uniform to make me strong."

"You'll need more than strength." Finn looks desperate when he adds, "Even without Cyphers, my mother is not to be underestimated."

"Yeah?" I ask, raising my chin. "Neither am I."

⊗

A few minutes later, I find myself at the Arenum's center with my blade sheathed at my waist—a strangely empowering accessory to accompany my red dress.

I could have worn the silver uniform as an extra layer of protection, as Finn urged me to do. But I refuse to cower in fear before the Duchess. Whatever she throws my way, I'm prepared for a counterattack.

If I have to kill her today, so much the better.

When the door at the far end of the Arenum's dirt floor

opens, I brace myself, my hand reaching into my pocket to feel for Rys's silver eggs.

The Duchess enters in a tailored pantsuit of pure white. Her features are hard and brittle above her collar, her mouth drawn into a tight line.

But it's what's behind her that makes my muscles tighten.

Two Cyphers. A man and a woman, each with a dagger at their waist.

The man is slight and shorter than average height, with a receding hairline and a dark suit that seems to hang unnaturally off his frame. The woman is taller than he is, and pretty, with long, light brown hair.

I wonder with a wince what the two of them are capable of. Will they try to take over my mind? Shoot lasers at me with their eyes?

I conclude with a grimace that there's only one way to find out.

"What's this proposition of yours, Duchess?" I call out. "Are you hoping to be spared the Consortium's justice?"

Instead of answering my question, the Duchess simply makes a small, quick gesture with her fingers. One of the Cyphers—the man—leaves her side to head down the small corridor toward the cellblock where Dregs are held before they're thrown into the Arenum to meet their fates.

A few seconds later, the Cypher returns, his hand on Peric's shoulder as he strides back in.

"Are you all right?" I call out, my eyes fixed on Peric's face. One of his eyes is nearly swollen shut by now, though the other one looks alert and focused.

"You shouldn't have come, Ash," he growls. "They'll kill us both."

"They won't kill you, Per," I assure him. "You're just a lure."

He shakes his head as if he knows something I don't, but doesn't reply.

"Your friend here was discovered in one of my husband's labs," the Duchess says, her finger under Peric's chin. "Trying to steal a certain biological weapon known as the Ubiquity Formula. He was planning a mass murder of every member of the Directorate—as well as many Aristocrats."

My eyes shoot to Peric, then back to the Duchess. "That's a lie," I spit. "Tell her, Peric. Tell her you would never..."

But when his head bows again, the truth hits me like a freight train.

His talk of making the Directorate pay. His keen interest in Rys's nano-drones.

This has been his plan since the moment his parents died in that valley.

"Did you know," the Duchess asks me, "that the list your friend possesses—the one that would allow him to target each Directorate member with pinpoint accuracy—does not include the DNA of my family members? We were careful to keep that information out of the wrong hands, you see, for fear of something like this happening."

"Congratulations on being a paranoid whack job," I reply. "You caught him. But he hasn't done anything wrong. No one has died."

"Not yet," the Duchess says. "But they will. You see, I *want* you to release the weapon, Ashen."

I stare at her, my jaw slack. I almost want to laugh. "Peric's not going to do that. Not now that you've stopped him."

"I didn't say anything about Peric. I said *you*. I want you, Ashen Spencer, to release the Ubiquity Formula. And then I want you to confess to your loyal sheep what you've done—tell them that their great crimson savior waltzed into the Arc and promptly committed a mass murder."

Now, I *do* laugh.

"You know I won't do that. Not in a million years."

"Ah. And I don't suppose it would change your mind if I told you I'll kill your friend?"

I stare at Peric, who shakes his head almost imperceptibly as if to say, "Just let her take my life."

"Peric is honorable," I scowl. "He would never ask me to sacrifice so many lives for his own."

"No, I don't suppose he would," the Duchess says, tapping her chin with her fingertip. "Which is why I won't offer you that choice. Instead, I'll offer you one that's *much* more interesting."

My eyes on Peric, I brace myself for whatever cruelty she's about to inflict on us both.

But instead of explaining herself, she gestures again. And this time, a series of screens burst to life around us.

At first, I'm confused by what I see. Treetops bending in the wind. Mountains rising in the distance. An idyllic view of the wilderness, to be sure.

But what is her point?

My question is answered when the camera's view shifts and pulls back to reveal more detail. A surge of pain slams into my chest as I begin to recognize the landscape.

A small clearing. A series of pine trees. Among them, a massive oak tree that has no business being there.

The entrance to the Pit.

"I understand your younger brother is hiding out inside Illian's forest stronghold," the Duchess says. "I would be only too happy to bomb it into oblivion if you refuse to comply with my request. Oh, yes—I still have drones in my possession, in case what happened in New Mexico wasn't evidence enough for you."

I shoot a panicked look at Peric, and I can tell we're thinking the same thing.

How did the enemy find the Pit?

"Veer," I breathe.

"You think Veer is the one who betrayed you?" the Duchess laughs. "You never cease to entertain, do you, Ashen? It wasn't Veer, or the shady Professor Lyon. Believe it or not, this was your fault. Yours, and your friend Rystan's."

"Rys and I would never betray the Consortium," I snarl, rage reddening my flesh.

"You really don't get it, do you?"

"No," I say though gritted teeth, "I suppose I don't. Please—enlighten me."

"One of the most valuable commodities in the Arc is something called a Quantum Source. A battery that never runs out, one capable of powering entire cities. You stole four of them, you greedy little thing. And astonishingly enough, it never occurred to you that a thing of such value would come equipped with a tracking device."

Tracking device.

A swell of nausea overtakes my stomach as the truth assaults my mind:

I led the Consortium to the Dwelling.

I led them to the Pit.

People are dead because of what I did. Peric's parents are dead because of me.

Kel…

Narrowing my eyes at the Duchess, I raise my hands, palms toward her and her Cypher protectors. *One blast would kill you all. One explosion of power, and I would never have to hear your hideous voice again, Duchess.*

Sensing what I'm thinking, she steps sideways and clamps a hand onto Peric's shoulder, instantly turning him into a human shield.

"It seems you're in a bit of a quandary," the Duchess says with a mocking laugh. "Now what will it be—a mass killing in the Arc, or the destruction of the Pit and everyone in it? Or, of course, I could have my Cyphers kill both of you."

If Hell exists, this must be what it feels like. Excruciating agony accompanied by sick-making turmoil.

Lowering my hands, I pull the blade from my waist and grasp it between my fingers, ready to hurl it at her.

Seeing the threat in my eyes, she slips behind Peric, concealing her entire body behind his.

Defeated, I weigh my hideous options.

I've dreamed of murdering each and every member of the Directorate. Of seeing them suffer for their crimes, watching them writhe on the ground as agonizing pain eats away at every nerve in their bodies.

But for all of my plentiful hatred and rage, there's a part of me that clings to my humanity, forbidding me from becoming the monster the Duchess craves so desperately.

"I can't."

My voice is nothing more than a faint whisper as I collapse onto my knees, dropping my blade.

My vision is blurry, tears blinding me. The woman who has tortured me so many times, who has found every sadistic means to destroy me—has somehow outdone herself. I'm frozen, lifeless, screaming inside…yet completely numb.

"Ash," Peric says weakly, "I need to ask you for something."

"What?" I ask miserably.

I wipe my eyes to look at him—to stare into his own one last time. Tears stain his cheeks, but in his eyes is a strange, eerie resolve.

I recall with a surge of emotion how he looked when his parents died. The searing pain written on his features, the torment in his heart. I see them now, but this time they're focused and powerful, morphed into pure hatred for the woman who destroyed his family without an ounce of remorse.

"Do you have any eggs?" he asks, his chin lowered, eyes narrowed. "I'm in the mood for eggs."

I nod. "Two," I tell him, pulling the silver orbs from my pocket and clenching them in my hand.

"I'd really appreciate if you'd send them this way."

Understanding his meaning, I slip my fingers over the fine lines on the eggs' surfaces and hurl them into the air. As they split apart, Peric reaches for the blade at the waist of the Cypher next to him and presses it to the Duchess's throat.

Faster than my eye can register, a Needlebeak lunges at each of the Cyphers' necks, injecting them with the Professor's toxic cocktail.

They collapse in unison to the ground, skin pale, eyes staring into a void.

Neither moves again.

I fix my gaze on the Duchess. She looks frightened, her eyes wide as she shakes her head and mutters, "No...please..."

As Peric presses the blade into the her neck, I almost envy him the privilege of what he's about to do. A trickle of blood runs down her skin, deep red against pure ivory.

I wonder for a moment why he doesn't take her life swiftly, but the look in his eyes answers the question for me.

He wants to feel her fear.

His voice is a wild snarl when he says, "You've taken everything from me. Do you hear me? *Everything*. And now, you're mine. Oh, I wanted to kill every one of your Directorate minions. But they don't matter, not when *you're* the one who runs the show. I look forward to staring into your lifeless eyes when you're dead, you absolute monster!"

When he's finished his rant, a sound meets my ears that sends a harrowing chill along my flesh.

High-pitched laughter.

The Duchess finds this *funny*.

Even helpless, even knowing she's about to lose her life, she manages to mock us.

"Kill her," I command, stepping toward Peric. "Do it now!"

He hesitates, choking out a sob as he tightens his grip on the knife.

The Duchess shoots me a cold look, lowering her chin. "He won't," she sneers. "Don't you see? He's too weak. He doesn't have it in him to take a life. He's not like you or me, Ashen."

As she says the words, a grim smile spreads over her lips, all traces of color vanishing from her irises.

I recoil in horror as they turn the ghastly, pale shade of a Cypher's eyes.

Her hands begin to crack and glow with angry red veins as she takes hold of Peric's wrists. Crying out in pain, he drops the blade and leaps backwards. He stares down at his arms, the skin branded red where she just touched him.

"She burned me!" he shouts, horrified.

Spinning around to face him, the Duchess grabs him by the neck and squeezes. The sickening odor of burning flesh meets my nose as I watch, horrified.

Peric falls to the ground, his neck blackened and bloodied, its skin half melted away.

The Duchess turns to face me one last time, her eyes glowing as she raises her hands, palms out, toward me. Her face is crackling with the same searing veins as her hands, her skin threatening to burst into angry flames. I can feel her heat from where I'm standing, my breath trapped in my chest.

"You try and you try," she scoffs. "But you never win. When will you learn, Ashen?"

Thrusting my palms toward her, I mirror her stance, tears streaking down my cheeks.

"Never," I spit. "I will *never* stop trying to take you down."

An awful smile works its way over her lips when she drops her hands and says, "So do it. Kill me here and now."

My eyes cast down to Peric, choking on the ground at her feet as he writhes in agony.

If I kill her, I kill him. The Surge would take them both.

"So weak," the Duchess says. "So...*weak.*"

My rage renewed, I scream as I lunge for the silver dagger on the ground by my feet.

Anticipating the move, the Duchess thrusts her hands toward me, hurling a ball of angry flame through the air.

There is no time to retaliate. No time, even, to duck out of the way.

Finn's words race through my mind as I freeze, a missile of pure fire shooting toward my face.

I see a wall of flame...I see your face, contorted with sorrow.

What comes next, Finn?
Is this how I die?
My chin high, I brace myself for the end.

43

DEATH...AND LIFE

As if by a miracle, the fireball seems to slam into the air itself, flattening and faltering against some unseen barrier before falling to the ground in a fizzle of harmless embers.

In the space between the Duchess and me, a million tiny points of light flicker and fade like a sea of tiny fireflies.

A shimmer-wall.

Gasping, I spin around to see Finn standing behind me, his chest heaving.

"I didn't see it clearly," he says, breathing hard, tears in his eyes. "I didn't understand what she was going to do. I was so afraid for you that I didn't see Peric in my mind's eye. I'm so sorry..."

"It's not your fault," I tell him, my voice thinned by sorrow. "You didn't make your mother into what she is."

A flash of red-orange light fills the Arenum, blinding us both. I pivot back to face the Duchess, but she's gone, vanished into thin air while the Cyphers remain lifeless on the ground.

Peric is still struggling, his chest tight as he fights for breath.

Finn flicks a hand in the air, bringing the shimmer-wall down, and I leap over to kneel by Peric's side. Choking with each attempt to breathe, he stares into my eyes.

"She took everything from me," he rasps.

"I know she did, Per. I know," I say through a veil of tears. "Don't talk. I have to get you help. I have to—"

He shakes his head weakly, his eyes clouding over. "You don't understand. She took everything but *you*, Ash...and you gave my family back to me."

"Peric..." I say, reaching for his hand. "Please..."

He smiles faintly when he breathes, "You were my friend."

His head droops, his eyes locking on something so far away I cannot see it. Crying out, I press a hand to his chest, desperate to will him back to life.

But Peric is gone.

"I should have stopped her sooner," Finn murmurs. He looks down at Peric then falls to his knees, his eyes filled with tears. "I feel like I've failed you both."

I shake my head. "None of us saw this coming. It's not up to you to save the world. None of us knew your mother would implant herself, or that Peric would try to..."

I stop myself.

No one must ever know about his treachery, his plan to murder so many using the Ubiquity Formula.

That's not how he deserves to be remembered.

"We'll send Atticus to scatter his ashes in New Mexico," I say quietly. "In the valley where his parents were killed. They hardly had a chance to be together in life. They should be together in death."

Finn rises to his feet, steps over, and takes me in his arms as I break down into sobs.

"We'll find my mother," he promises me. "We'll make her pay for this. For all of it."

"Finn," I manage through shaky vocal cords. I pull away and look into his eyes. "She knows about the Pit."

⊗

After the Consortium's soldiers have collected Peric's body, Illian assures me he's already sent a fleet of vehicles to collect the entire population of the Pit.

"They'll be safe in the Arc," he tells me with a bitter smirk. "There are many luxurious residences here that will soon find themselves empty. We may as well take advantage of the space. Don't worry, Ashen—I promise your brother will be well looked after."

The thought makes me wince. I don't wish this for Kel. I never wanted him to live inside the Arc, between the confining walls of a building constructed as a glorified prison.

But he isn't safe in the Pit, not as long as the Duchess knows its whereabouts.

When Rys has promised me for the fiftieth time that his birds are watching the skies and the woods around the Pit in case of incursion, Finn takes me to the secure residence Illian has assigned us inside the Louvre and tells me he has news.

"My parents are gone. I suspect they took one of the King's air jets and left the Arc. They've most likely gone east to follow the King and Queen."

My voice is full of misery when I say, "They took Merit, didn't they?"

With a nod, he says, "After all my nightmares—after hurting you as I did...yes, they're the ones who took him."

"Then you should go after him. And I should go with you."

He kisses my forehead. "I intend to follow them. But I can't do it, not as I am now. Not with the nanotech eating away at my mind. It's time."

I hold my breath as I ask, "Are you saying..."

In response to my unfinished question, he reaches into his pocket and extracts a small silver sphere.

A Needlebeak egg.

"I've thought long and hard about Professor Lyon's Xeno-cells," he tells me. "The way they destroy hostile cells—or in my case, hostile technology. And I've wondered if there was a way I could adapt them to leave me the desirable gifts while taking the undesirable ones away." Looking into my eyes, he adds, "I don't want to suffer through the visions anymore, Ash. They were killing me, and I could see how much they hurt you, too. They pulled me out of myself, turned me into something I didn't recognize. So I've adapted the Professor's formula. If it works, it should stop the visions but allow me to keep a little power. I need to be able to protect those I care about."

"The shimmer-walls, you mean."

He nods.

"And if the injection doesn't work?" I ask, my hands shaking.

He shrugs, a sad smile on his lips. "I've died once before. What's another death?"

"Finn...Are you sure you want to do this?"

He pulls himself close, kissing my lips. "There are two people I truly love in this world, Ash. I don't intend to lose either of you. It will work. I promise you that."

"Then I won't stop you."

With a final smile, he runs a finger over the seal surrounding the orb, and watches as it cracks open. A tiny bird flits out, its dagger-like beak aimed perilously close to Finn's neck.

"I'm ready," he says, closing his eyes.

I take his hand as the needle pierces his skin...and wait for him to come back to me at last.

NEXT IN SERIES: FALLEN

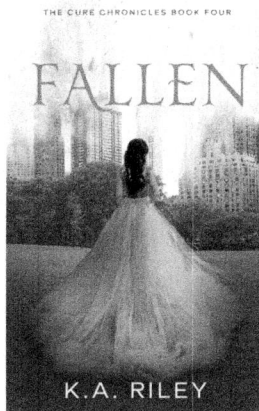

After the storm comes the calm.

When Ashen sets off to find those who have been sent to the Behemoth, a massive arcology at Manhattan's center, she begins to make discoveries that will change the course of the war, her life...and the lives of those she loves.

Grab the next book in the Cure Chronicles here: *Fallen*

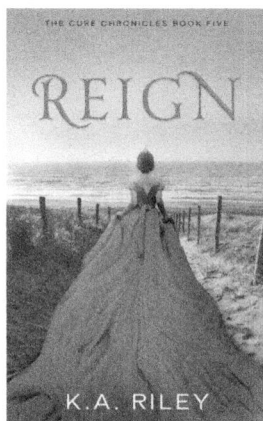

Coming in June, 2022: *Reign,* the fifth book in the Cure Chronicles!

ALSO BY K. A. RILEY

If you're enjoying K. A. Riley's books, please consider leaving a review on Amazon or Goodreads to let your fellow book-lovers know about it.

Dystopian Books:

The Cure Chronicles:

The Cure

Awaken

Ascend

Fallen

Reign

Thrall Series:

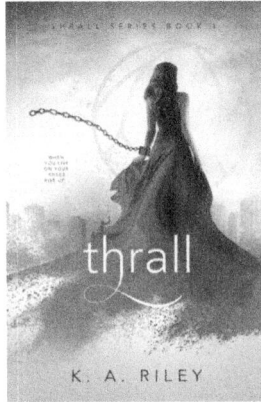

Thrall | Broken | Queen

Resistance Trilogy:

Recruitment

Render

Rebellion

Emergents Trilogy:

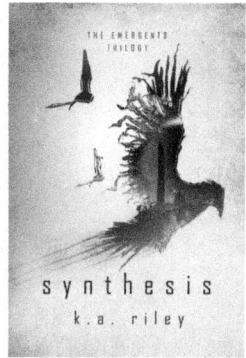

Survival

Sacrifice

Synthesis

Transcendent Trilogy:

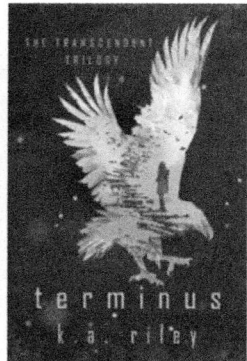

Travelers

Transfigured

Terminus

Academy of the Apocalypse Series:

Emergents Academy

Cult of the Devoted

Army of the Unsettled

The Ravenmaster Chronicles:

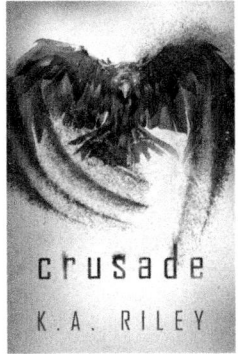

Arise

Banished (Coming in January 2022)

Crusade (Coming in April 2022)

Athena's Law Trilogy:

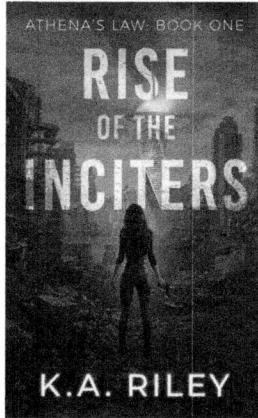

Book One: *Rise of the Inciters*
Book Two: *Into an Unholy Land*
Book Three: *No Man's Land*

<u>Fantasy Books</u>

Seeker's Series:

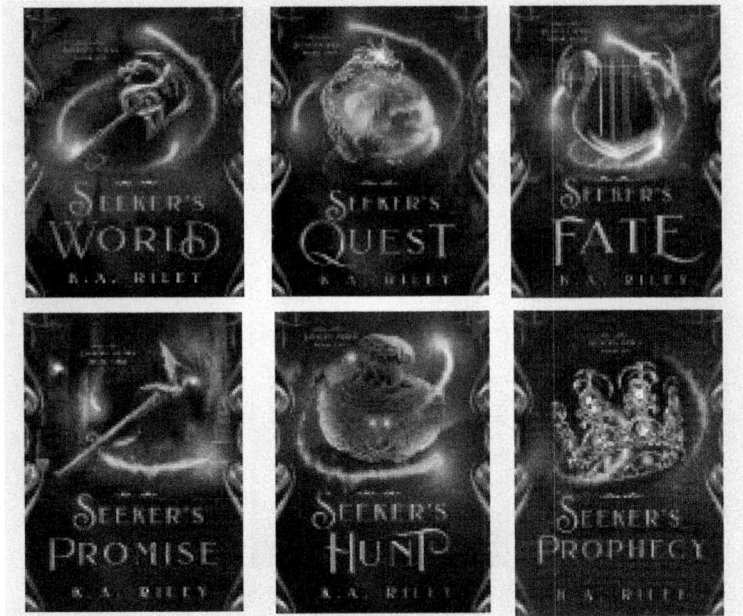

Seeker's World

Seeker's Quest

Seeker's Fate

Seeker's Promise

Seeker's Hunt

Seeker's Prophecy (Coming in 2022)

To be informed of future releases, and for occasional chances to win free swag, books, and other goodies, please sign up here:

https://karileywrites.org/#subscribe

Printed in Great Britain
by Amazon

61886640R00201